Aut...us
the
Pirate Ghost

Lucinda Williams

Pen Press

First published in Great Britain by Pen Press

All paper used in the printing of this book has been made from
wood grown in managed, sustainable forests.

ISBN13: 978-1-78003-175-0

Printed and bound in the UK
Pen Press is an imprint of
Indepenpress Publishing Limited
25 Eastern Place
Brighton
BN2 1GJ

A catalogue record of this book is available from
the British Library

Cover artwork and design by Claire Spinks

Dedication

For my daughters, Charlotte and Philippa and my grandchildren, Amelie, Harry, Reuben and Elodie, and also for Catherine and Polly who knew about Gertie Pink from the beginning.

About the Author

Born in Hong Kong, Lucinda Williams spent her early years in Australia. Educated in England and Scotland, she worked in London and Rome before settling in rural Hertfordshire with her husband. She has always enjoyed writing but this is her first full-length novel. It began as a story told to amuse the children on the daily school run but has gradually developed over the years.

If you've enjoyed it, look out for the sequel, *The Medicine Tree*.

Contents

Chapter 1

Number 14 Willow Close

After everything that had happened, Emily didn't believe things could get any worse. But she was wrong.

"I'm sorry, darling, but you're going to have to stay with the Pinks for a few days," Mum told her. Emily couldn't believe what she was hearing. This was the last straw.

"It'll only be for a short time," her mother went on, "just until I come out of hospital."

Emily was furious... and scared. As far as she could see, all the bad things were Mum's fault and she didn't think she'd ever be able to forgive her, especially for not letting her keep the puppy.

A blustery wind was blowing when they arrived at No. 14 Willow Close, which was where the Pinks lived and it was like a bad dream when the door opened and there stood Laura Pink with her freckles and her red pony tail, looking down at Emily and making her feel small and stupid, like she always did. So she didn't kiss Mum goodbye because she was so angry with her and anyway, Mum was in a hurry. All Emily could do was to follow Laura inside the house.

"Wait there," Laura ordered. "I'll fetch Mum — she's getting the washing in," and she disappeared leaving Emily standing there, clutching her bag. Laura's mum, Gertie Pink, was the school lollipop lady and Emily liked her, but she didn't like bossy Laura and her twin brother, Harry. They were in the class above her at school and made Emily feel uncomfortable because they were much taller than she was and always so noisy and full of themselves. And there'd probably be a Mr Pink too, she suddenly realised with a sinking heart.

Soon she heard voices and Gertie appeared, wearing an apron with big yellow sunflowers on it and her red corkscrew curls in a tangle because of the wind.

"My, look what the March wind's blown in," she laughed, giving Emily one of her big hugs. "Where's Mum?" she asked, looking around in surprise.

"She had to go," mumbled Emily and felt the corners of her mouth turning down.

"Well, I expect she's got things to do before she goes into hospital tomorrow," said Gertie briskly, taking Emily's bag. "Laura," she shouted and Laura reappeared, holding a tiny tortoiseshell kitten. "Take Emily upstairs will you luvvie? You can let her see the kittens later. Help her unpack and show her where everything is and then come on down for supper. Don't be long."

Gertie took the kitten from Laura, handing her the bag, and Emily reluctantly followed Laura up the stairs. Her heart sank even further as it dawned on her that she'd be sharing a bedroom with her.

The walls in Laura's room were covered with pictures she'd obviously painted herself, as each one was signed with her name. She seemed to be brilliant at everything, thought Emily, always coming top and winning prizes at school.

Laura plonked Emily's bag down on the bed nearest the window and sat on the other one, swinging her legs. Emily noticed that it was getting dark outside and had started to rain, which just made her feel even more miserable.

"I've cleared out the bottom two drawers of the chest so you can put your things in there," said Laura, pointing. "Shall I help you unpack?"

"No thanks," Emily said quickly, unzipping the bag.

She took Marigold out and laid her on the pillow and blushed as she realised what a baby she must look. There were no dolls in Laura's room. She arranged her few belongings in the chest, but was dismayed when she turned round and saw Laura bending over her bag, looking inside.

"Oh my goodness, what's that?" she squealed and before Emily could stop her, she'd reached in and pulled out a glass jar. Emily felt the blood rushing to her face.

"Don't," she shouted, snatching the jar from Laura and almost dropping it on the floor. She hid it behind her back. Laura stared at her in surprise.

"OK, OK, I only wanted to have a look at it. Go on, let me see," she commanded, holding out her hand.

Emily didn't want to show it to her, but there seemed no way out of it. She laid the jar on the pillow next to Marigold and Laura peered at it. Inside was a long, pink, wormy-looking thing, floating in liquid.

"Ugh!" said Laura. "What on earth is that? Is it alive?" She poked the jar gingerly with her finger and then jumped back in alarm. "Ooh yes, I saw it move! Oh, whatever is it?"

"Of course you didn't see it move, it's not alive," said Emily, surprised at the way Laura was behaving. "It's my appendix," she added grudgingly. "You've got one just like it inside you, you know. Everyone has, it's quite normal."

"Oh wow!" gasped Laura, clearly impressed. "Your appendix! Can I hold it for a moment? Go on."

"No, I don't think you'd better," said Emily. "It's precious and you might drop it and break the jar and the appendix will go bad if it falls out. It's in some special stuff which stops it going off."

"Yuk!" said Laura, making a face. "When did you have it taken out? Have you got a scar? Oh, go on – let's see your scar!"

Emily was proud of her scar so she lifted up her skirt and pulled down the top of her knickers.

"Oh, it's tiny," said Laura, sounding disappointed. "Did it hurt?"

"Yes, before they took it out and then afterwards I had a tummy ache. But it's fine now." Emily pulled her skirt down and laid the jar carefully in the bottom of the chest of drawers, covering it over with her socks and knickers.

"Please don't tell anyone else about it, they'll only want to look and it'll just get broken."

"I won't tell anyone, I promise," said Laura, grinning. "It'll be our secret but you must let me look at it now and again. It's really awesome." She tossed her ponytail.

"Come on, let's go down now, I want to show you Firefly's kittens." She opened the door and pointed down the passage. "The bathroom's at the end there with the loo next to it and that's Mum and Dad's room on the other side. Harry's opposite us."

As they came into the kitchen a large black and white dog with a thick curly coat came bouncing over to Emily, its whole body wagging joyfully. It sat in front of her and held up its paw. Harry, Laura's twin brother, got up from the table and came over, catching hold of the dog's collar.

"This is Izzie," he announced. "She's very pleased to meet you."

Emily took the dog's paw and couldn't help smiling. "Hello, Izzie," she said.

"She's my dog," said Harry proudly. "And I'm teaching her all sorts of tricks." It was hard to believe that he and

Laura were twins. Apart from being about the same height, Harry's hair was dark and curly whereas Laura's was straight and a carroty red.

"She is not your dog," protested Laura hotly.

"Well, I look after her the most," argued Harry.

"You do not!" Laura glared at him.

"Now, now, you two, let's not have an argument," said Gertie. "Harry, give Dad a shout, will you, supper's ready."

Meal times at the Pink's house are quite different from at home, thought Emily, as they all sat round the table. At home there was just her and Mum and they quite often ate with their plates on their laps, watching TV. Here, everyone talked at once and laughed a lot and Emily couldn't believe how many cups of tea they all drank.

She didn't feel the least bit hungry; there seemed to be a lump of lead in her stomach, so she just sat and listened and watched the six kittens lying with their mother, Firefly, in a basket near the cooker.

Mr Pink, whose name was Bert, talked about his clothes stall at the market and was very smiley and jolly and winked at Emily and said, "Thank God it's Sunday tomorrow". Harry went on and on about a cart he was making and Laura chatted about a girl in her class who wanted to have one of the kittens. And all the time Gertie nodded and chuckled. She was plump and cuddly with dimples in her rosy cheeks, which came and went as she talked and her voice was round and friendly, like the rest of her. Mum had told her that Gertie came from Devon, which was a place by the sea and that she had a Devonshire accent. I wish I could be like Gertie when I grow up, thought Emily. Everyone likes her, but I don't suppose I will be because I'm small and thin and people say I'm quite a serious person.

That night she just couldn't get off to sleep, so many thoughts were going round in her head. She felt terribly homesick and for the first time wondered why Mum was going into hospital. She missed her, but she was still angry with her for everything that had happened. How could she have made them move out of their nice house with the swing in the garden and the ponies in the field, into that horrible, cramped, third-floor flat where there was nowhere to put anything and no pets were allowed?

And how could she have made her take so many of her toys and books to the charity shop? That had been really hard. But the very worst thing in the whole world was having to give Nugget back to the breeder, when she'd had him for such a short time and had waited for him for so long. She didn't think she'd ever get over that. She remembered the feel of his little bare, pink tummy and the lovely puppy smell he had. She thought of Izzie and the kittens downstairs and stifled a sob. It was so unfair to think she'd never be able to have a pet of her own. At that moment she hated Mum.

The rain was beating against the window and then the thunder started. A flickering light lit up the room and she could see Laura in the bed next to her, sound asleep and not a bit bothered by the storm. The thunder crashed and Emily screwed up her eyes, burying her head under the pillow. She hugged Marigold tightly. Marigold was scared of storms.

Chapter 2

Uncle Wilf Arrives

She must have gone to sleep because the next thing Emily knew, the doorbell was ringing and she could hear Izzie barking downstairs. It rang several more times.

"Oh for goodness sake," mumbled Laura at last, switching on the bedside light. She looked at the clock and groaned. "It's only quarter to six, who on earth can that be at the door?"

Emily pulled one of the curtains aside and looked out of the window. It was still dark.

"Mum and Dad'll never hear it," grumbled Laura when the doorbell rang again. "They wouldn't wake up if the house fell down. We'd better go and see who it is. Come on."

She turned on the landing light and, clutching Emily's hand, led her downstairs and opened the kitchen door. Izzie, with all her hackles up, rushed out and tore over to the front door, barking madly. Then Harry appeared on the stairs in his pyjamas, rubbing his eyes, as the doorbell rang yet again. This time, whoever it was kept their finger on the button.

"It can't be the postman, it's far too early," whispered Laura.

"There's only one way to find out," said Harry, marching to the door and opening it, letting in a gust of wind and rain.

The three of them stood in astonishment. On the doorstep stood a small man in pyjamas, whose bushy white hair was blowing about wildly. His feet were bare and he was shivering from head to toe. On the doorstep next to him was a birdcage with a squawking parrot inside it.

"I'll get Mum," said Laura in a panic and ran upstairs.

"Pass the rum," the parrot shrieked, dancing up and down in his cage. He was as wet and bedraggled as his owner. Izzie kept on barking and Harry had to hold tightly to her collar.

"Do you think I could come inside?" the man said at last and they could hear his teeth chattering.

"Hang on, just a moment," said Harry. "Mum'll be down in a second."

"Can't we just let him stand inside?" whispered Emily, looking at the man's feet which were blue with cold.

"OK," said Harry uncertainly. He held the door open and the man came inside, bringing the parrot's cage with him. A pool of water started to form around his feet.

"Pass the rum, boys," screamed the parrot again and again.

"What on earth's going on?" came Gertie's voice from above. "Be quiet, Izzie."

She came down in her dressing gown and slippers, her red curls standing to attention round her head. When she saw the man and his parrot, she stood stock still and seemed unable to move or speak. The parrot swore again and made a noise like water going down the plughole.

"What's the matter, Mum?" said Harry.

"Uncle Wilf?" said Gertie. "It is Uncle Wilf, isn't it? Oh, my word, whatever's happened to you?" She ran forward and took the man by the arm. He looked as if he might fall over at any minute. "Shut the door, Harry, for goodness sake."

She led him through into the kitchen and sat him down on one of the chairs at the table. Harry, Laura and Emily followed, crowding round and staring.

Shall I bring the parrot in here too?" Emily asked. He was still squawking and flapping round in his cage by the front door.

"Yes, yes, bring him in," replied Gertie distractedly, "and for goodness sake take Izzie out of here. I can't hear myself think."

Emily took Izzie by her collar and pulled her back into the sitting room.

"Shhhh, Izzie, lie down!" she said and the dog lay down quietly and looked up at her. "Good dog," she whispered and then bent down and peered into the cage. She'd seen pictures of parrots, but never a real, live one. The ones in the pictures had had brightly-coloured feathers, but this poor thing was drenched through and seemed to be mostly grey, except for its crimson tail. It regarded her unblinkingly with its yellow eye.

"Hello," said Emily softly and the parrot put its head on one side and burped.

Emily giggled.

"Come with me," she said gently, picking up the cage and carrying it into the kitchen. "You stay out there, Izzie." She shut the door behind her.

Gertie was sitting at the table next to the strange man and Emily put the cage down on the floor near him. Then, she went to stand opposite with Laura and Harry so she could see what was going on. Firefly was in her box, feeding her kittens.

For a few moments nobody said anything, then Gertie seemed to pull herself together.

"Laura," she said, "put the kettle on, quick as you can, and let's all have a nice cup of tea." Uncle Wilf was still shivering so she fetched a coat, which was hanging on the back door and put it round his shoulders.

"Can you tell me what's happened, Uncle Wilf?" she said kindly, sitting down again. "Why are you wearing pyjamas and where are your shoes?"

After a long pause the man began to speak and, although his voice was shaking, Emily noticed that he spoke in the same way as Gertie, with a Devonshire accent.

"Gertie, m'dear, a terrible, terrible thing's happened and I don't know what I'm going to do." He paused and Emily was shocked to hear him give a deep sob. "I'm lucky to be alive." His glasses had misted up and he took them off, leaving one side swinging from his ear while he wiped his eyes with the sleeve of his sodden pyjamas.

"Take your time," said Gertie putting a hand on his arm. "Hurry up with that tea, Laura."

Laura brought over a tray with five cups of steaming tea and a bowl of sugar and put it down on the table. The children sat down, dying to know what the strange man was going to say next. After a few sips of his tea, which seemed to revive him a little, he took a deep breath and put on his glasses again. Everyone waited.

"Last night there was a terrible storm and I was nearly killed," he said and paused before saying in a choked voice, "My house was washed into the sea."

"Bless my socks," gasped Gertie.

"Wow!" said Harry, wide eyed. "How did you escape?"

"I only just got out in time, it was terrifying. I managed to grab Autolocus and scramble to the garage, which is up the path at the back of the house. The wind was screaming and blowing so hard, I could hardly keep upright and the rain was lashing down so that I was soaked through before I even got into the car." He paused again and ran his hands through his hair. "As I started up the engine and put on the headlights, there was this awful rumbling sound." He stopped and wiped his eyes again and didn't seem able to go on.

"Drink your tea," said Gertie gently.

Emily found herself biting her thumbnail as she waited to hear what had happened next.

Uncle Wilf took a few more sips of the hot tea, holding the cup between his hands to warm himself. They all waited eagerly for him to go on.

"Suddenly, as I watched, the ground between the house and the garage broke away with a horrible roaring sound and part of the cliff and the whole house were torn away by the waves... and everything just vanished into the sea."

Gertie gasped and put her hand over her mouth.

"A huge column of water rose up in front of me, spraying the car with pebbles and sand and I realised there were only a few feet left between the garage and the edge of the cliff. I edged the car forward slowly, terrified the ground wouldn't hold, and managed to drive down the hill towards the village. But two trees had blown across the road and I couldn't get through." He put down the cup and held his head in his hands. "So I turned round and drove here - it was the only place I could think of. I expect, by now, everyone will think I've been washed into the sea with the house." A tear ran down his cheek and plopped into his tea. Emily was shocked - she'd never seen a grown up man cry before.

"But that's awful. You poor, poor thing," said Gertie. "You must have been driving all night. We're miles from Devon."

"I've been driving for hours."

They all sipped their tea in silence. Nobody seemed to know what to say.

"Gertie, m'dear," said Uncle Wilf at last, "do you think I could stay with you for a bit? I've nowhere else to go."

The parrot screeched and then swore.

"My hat," said Gertie, her mouth dropping open, "wherever did he learn to say those things?"

"Autolocus, behave yourself, you daft old bird," said Uncle Wilf, wearily, looking down at the parrot.

Gertie recovered herself. "Of course you must stay, Uncle Wilf, for as long as you like. Now, you just sit there and finish your tea and I'm going to go and run you a nice hot bath and get a bed ready for you. I'll be back in a jiffy." She looked up at the clock on the wall. "Good job it's Sunday," she muttered.

Uncle Wilf was left with the parrot in the kitchen and the three children followed Gertie upstairs.

"How Dad's managing to sleep through all this I don't know," she said.

"Mum, where's Uncle Wilf going to sleep?" asked Harry when they reached the landing.

"In your bed for the time being," said Gertie, marching into his room. Emily followed them. Mum always said *she* was untidy, but this was something else. Clothes, shoes, books and toys were scattered everywhere and against the wall stood a table on which lay coils of wire, pieces of string and bits of cardboard and wood. A big box lay in the middle of the floor, with a hammer and a box of nails beside it.

"He can't come in here," said Harry flatly, "the room's too untidy. But that's 'cos I'm in the middle of making my cart."

12

"So, I see," said Gertie. "Look, I'm sorry, Harry, but you're going to have to clear this lot up. No, it's no good sitting down on the bed. Get up - I want it done right now."

"But where am I going to sleep?" wailed Harry.

"On the blow-up bed in with the girls," Gertie replied shortly, stepping over the piles of stuff on the floor and stripping the duvet off the bed. "Now, Laura, go and turn the bath on for Uncle Wilf."

"Oh, no I'm not," Harry yelled.

"Oh, no!" shouted Laura. "We're not having Harry in with us, he snores!"

"And how am I going to make my cart?" shouted Harry.

"Now look here," said Gertie, turning round and putting her hands on her hips. Emily had never seen her looking cross before but she was quite red in the face.

"Don't be so selfish!" she shouted. "Just suppose it was your house that had been washed away into the sea in the middle of the night and you had nothing in the world except what you stood up in."

Laura and Harry scowled at each other.

"He's got his parrot," Emily reminded her. "He's got Autolocus."

"Yes, that's true," snorted Gertie, "he's got Autolocus. And a fat lot of good he is to anyone."

Chapter 3

The Silver Box

It stopped raining soon after breakfast and Gertie said it would be a good idea if the children took Izzie for a walk. It was an excuse to get the three of them out of the house, Emily realised. Harry had been made to clear up the worst of the mess in his room, so that at least you could walk across the floor without tripping over. After having something to eat, Uncle Wilf was tucked up safe and sound in Harry's bed. Laura had been told to carry Autolocus upstairs and put him in Harry's room as well.

"He's a horrible parrot," she said. "He pecked my finger really hard when I tried to stroke him."

"I don't want you all making a lot of noise downstairs when Uncle Wilf's sleeping," Gertie said. "He's exhausted. So why don't you go up to the pet shop and buy a kilo of parrot food."

"It's Sunday, Mum," Laura reminded her. "The shops are shut."

"Oh, drat, of course," said Gertie. "Oh well, I've got some sunflower seeds, he'll have to make do with those till tomorrow. But the newsagent's is open, so pop in and get the Sunday paper for Dad, will you? And remember to be quiet when you get back." She gave them some money and they set off.

It was still windy and the daffodils in the little front garden had been flattened by the storm. There were puddles everywhere along the road. Emily was pleased because Harry let her hold the lead, but Izzie was so keen to

14

get to the pet shop she nearly pulled Emily off her feet, and in the end she had to let Harry take her.

"Sorry, Izzie, you're out of luck today – the pet shop's shut," he said. "She always gets a titbit when we go in there," he explained.

To get to the shops you had to turn left out of No. 14, where the Pinks lived, go to the bottom of Willow Close and turn right into the main road. From there you walked up a steep hill to the row of shops at the top. Emily had never been there because she lived in a different part of the town and she and Mum usually went to the supermarket. The pet shop was at one end of the row and a newsagent's and general store called Jo's Shop was at the other end. In between were a butcher's, a greengrocer's and a junk shop with 'B. S. Leach Antiques and Curios' written over the top in black letters. All the shops, except Jo's, were shut so after they'd bought the newspaper they walked along to have a look in the window of the junk shop.

"I'm looking out for an old pram in here," said Harry importantly. "I'm going to take the wheels off it and use them for my cart."

"Oh you and your stupid cart," said Laura and made a face at him. "We'll come back after school one day, Em, when the shop's open. I love looking round 'cos there's all sorts of weird things in there. It's really spooky. There's even a skeleton on a stand at the back and a real skull with a candle inside it!"

The shop window was crammed full of unusual objects. A stuffed lizard in a glass case took up a lot of space, and a golden dagger with a jewelled handle caught Emily's eye plus a lantern made of shells and some dolls with china faces and staring eyes and lots and lots of other things.

"I know," said Laura, "let's play that game Mum taught us - you remember, Harry? We had to look at all the things in the window, Emily, while Mum counted up to twenty, and then when we got back home we had to write down everything we could remember. Whoever remembers the most gets a prize. But Mum's not here today so I'll do the counting."

"Oh, and you're going to give the prize too, are you?" scoffed Harry.

"Well, I expect Mum'll have something," said Laura. "OK, Em? Everyone ready? I'm going to start counting. "One, two, three, four, five, six..."

"Stop!" shouted Harry. "You're going much too fast, silly. You've got to count slowly. Start again, but do it quietly or I can't concentrate."

"All right, all right, bossy boots," said Laura crossly. "You do it then. I'll be able to remember more things if I'm not doing the counting."

Harry cleared his throat. "OK. Ready, steady, go! One... two... three... four... five... six..."

Emily pressed her nose against the glass and tried to remember all the things she could see. She didn't know what some of them were so didn't bother with those. Then, when Harry had got up to about fifteen, she suddenly saw something right at the back that she recognised. It gave her such a surprise that she screamed.

"For goodness sake, Emily, you nearly made me jump out of my skin," said Laura. "What's the matter?"

Emily pointed to the back of the window. "There," she said, "next to that jar with the butterflies on it and just in front of that teapot thing with the long spout."

"You mean that little picture in the frame?" asked Harry.

16

"No, no, not that," Emily said excitedly, "just behind that, a bit to the left. The silver box."

"Yes, OK, I see it," he said. "What's so special about it?"

"It's my mum's box that she used to have on her dressing table before we went to the flat. It got lost in the move. But that's it, I'm sure it is."

"It can't be," said Harry. "What would it be doing in there?"

"I've no idea," Emily said.

"Wow!" said Laura. "Perhaps it was stolen."

"Nah," said Harry. "There's probably loads of boxes just like that one."

"No, I'm sure that's Mum's," Emily insisted, breathing on the glass and polishing it with her sleeve.

"Well, what are we going to do about it?" asked Laura. "The shop's shut. Let's go home and tell Dad."

It was downhill all the way back to the Pinks' house and they ran as fast as they could, splashing in the puddles as they went. Once home, they barged into the kitchen through the back door. Bert was sitting at the table drinking tea and eating toast and marmalade and Gertie was planting little seedlings into small flower pots.

"Shhhh," she said as Harry and Laura both started talking at once. "I asked you not to make a noise. Now take your boots off and wipe Izzie's feet before you let her come in the house."

"Is that my newspaper?" asked Bert. "Give it here then and let's have a look at what's going on in the world." -

"Dad, we want to tell you what we saw," said Harry, taking a towel off a hook inside the cupboard and wiping Izzie's feet.

17

"We were looking in the window of the junk shop..." interrupted Laura.

Emily wanted to tell Gertie about the box. After all, it was her mum's box and she'd been the one to see it, but she couldn't get a word in edgeways.

"Slow down, slow down," said Bert, laughing, "you sound like a couple of express trains and I can't understand a word."

"We were playing Mum's game up at the junk shop," said Harry patiently.

"You know, Mum, the one where you have to count up to twenty and try and see how many things you can remember," said Laura.

"But then Emily let out this great big scream," said Harry, "and we both nearly jumped out of our skins."

"'Cos she saw her mum's box in the window," finished Laura.

Bert stopped eating his toast and looked at Emily. His face was serious.

"What's all this about, Emily, love? What did you see?"

"Well, Mum used to have a box on her dressing table," Emily explained. "She had her necklaces in it and she loved it because it used to belong to Nan. Then, when we moved to the flat, she was very sad because she couldn't find it when we unpacked. And I saw it just now in the window of the junk shop when we were playing the game."

"What's the box like, poppet?" asked Gertie, laying down her trowel. She had her sunflower apron on and her hands were covered in earth.

"It's silver and it's got squirley patterns on the lid," Emily told her. "They look a bit like snakes. The box has got a little dent at the back, but we couldn't see the back, only the front."

"There could be more than one box like that, pet," said Gertie. Emily looked disappointed. "Tell you what. You'll have to wait till tomorrow, but after school we'll go in and have a proper look at it, shall we?"

Emily felt excited. Mum would be so pleased if she'd found her precious box. "I know it's Mum's," she said.

"Look, why don't you all sit down and find something quiet to do," said Gertie, putting the flower pots on the kitchen window sill. "There, that's those on the go. Once I get them out in the allotment they'll go up like little rockets." She washed her hands and dried them on a stripy towel hanging by the back door. "Now I'm just going to pop upstairs and check on Uncle Wilf."

She came down a few minutes later. "I've put Autolocus on the sideboard in the sitting room. "He's making such a racket that Uncle Wilf can't possibly sleep."

The children went through to the sitting room and looked at the parrot, which was squawking and doing a little dance on his perch – two steps to the left, then he lifted up one leg and two steps the other way and he lifted the other leg. Then he let out a loud belch and they all laughed.

"Autolocus is a really weird name," said Harry. "I wonder how you spell it."

"I think it's rather a stylish name," said Laura. "We've got to think of some good names for the kittens, well anyway for the little tortoiseshell one we're going to keep. I thought of Gauguin - you know, that artist we're learning about who used to paint in all those bright colours. That'd be a good name for a cat with lots of colours in her fur."

"Gauguin!" snorted Harry. "That's a daft name for a girl cat. Anyhow, it's my turn to choose and I think Paintbox would be a good name."

They started to squabble and Gertie came and told them to be quiet and come into the kitchen.

"Mum, who exactly is Uncle Wilf?" asked Laura, lifting the tortoiseshell kitten out of the box and cuddling it. "You've never really talked about him before."

"Uncle Wilf is granddad's brother, so he's your great uncle," said Gertie, breaking some eggs into a bowl. "When I was a little girl, about the same age as you are, Emily, I sometimes used to go with my brothers and spend a week or so in his house in the summer holidays. It was a great big house with a lovely garden, which ran right down to the edge of the cliff, with a steep drop to the sea below. At night time when you were lying in bed, you could hear the waves crashing on the rocks – it was wonderful."

Emily tried to imagine what Gertie must have been like when she was the same age as her. She wished she had a sister or a brother.

"And now the house isn't there anymore. So where's he going to live?" asked Laura. The tortoiseshell kitten was struggling to get free and she put it back in the box. Emily knelt down and stroked Firefly who started to purr.

"Well I really don't know," said Gertie, beating the eggs with a fork. "He's going to have to stay with us for the time being. You'll like Uncle Wilf when you get to know him." She chuckled.

"What's he like?" asked Harry.

"Well, he was lots of fun when we were kids," said Gertie. "I remember the races we used to have down the stairs in that big old house. You could either slide down the banisters or come down the stairs on a big tin tray. Imagine me trying to do that now! It was a very wide staircase so you could have two trays going down at the same time. Uncle Wilf could do it quicker than any of us. I never saw him walk down the stairs – he usually slid down the banisters."

"Did he really?" said Laura, giggling.

"Sounds pretty dangerous to me," said Bert. "It's a wonder you didn't all end up with broken legs or worse." He poured himself another cup of tea from the big brown teapot. Emily thought of her uncle – Uncle Brian. He was Mum's brother and was very boring.

"'Course some people in the village used to say the house had a ghost, but we never saw one – it was just because it was an old house and looked a bit spooky standing all by itself on the cliff," said Gertie

"Wow! A ghost! Weren't you frightened?" asked Laura.

"Not in the least, no we loved going there. Like I said, we never saw any sign of a ghost at all. I remember Uncle Wilf set us wonderful treasure hunts along the seashore and in the caves." She smiled, showing the dimples in her cheeks and her blue eyes lit up. "I loved those treasure hunts. Oh and I remember he liked experimenting with food and mixing things together – like the time he mixed chocolate powder into the scrambled eggs and they went a funny khaki colour. Chocolate Scramble he called it."

"Yuk," said Laura, pulling a face, "What did it taste like?"

"Pretty horrid I expect," chuckled Gertie, "but he was always doing weird things like that. There was the time he made toffee apples and gave one to the postman. Only the toffee was so chewy that the postman's teeth got stuck together. He got quite angry, I remember, and made such funny faces trying to get them unstuck. We just couldn't stop laughing. Yes, I suppose you could say Uncle Wilf can be rather mischievous sometimes."

It started raining again later and turned colder, so the children spent the rest of the day trying to be quiet, doing jigsaw puzzles and watching TV and Harry made a cart out of Lego. They had some homework to do too. Emily was feeling very homesick again and Gertie said they'd ring Mum the next evening and see how she was.

After supper they all sat round the fire and Bert read to them. Emily cuddled up to Gertie on the sofa and that made her feel quite a lot better. Bert always read a chapter of a book to them on Sunday evenings and the first time Emily was there he was just finishing a story called 'Black Beauty', which was about horses. It was very sad.

"Next Sunday we're going to start *Treasure Island*," he said.

"Why can't we have *Harry Potter* or something like that?" grumbled Harry. "You always choose old-fashioned books, Dad. What's boring old *Treasure Island* about anyway?

"Pirates," said Bert and chuckled, his blue eyes twinkling.

Chapter 4

The Junk Shop

When Emily came out of school the next afternoon she could see Gertie on the crossing, wearing her yellow coat and hat and holding her lollipop stick with arms stretched wide. Parents and children were milling around, but there was no sign of Harry and Laura. She'd been thinking all day about Mum's silver box and couldn't wait to go to the junk shop. She hoped Harry and Laura hadn't gone ahead without her because she wanted to be the one to find out if the box really was Mum's. If it was, then it must have been stolen when they moved to the flat.

"Hello, luvvie," Gertie greeted her with a smile, "had a good day?"

"It was OK," said Emily. "Can we ring the hospital when we get home and see how Mum is?"

"'Course we can, pet," said Gertie.

Some of the kids from Emily's class came skipping along the pavement and Gertie saw them safely across the road.

"Bye, Emily, bye Gertie," they called, "see you tomorrow."

"Are we going to the junk shop," Emily asked. "To get Mum's box?"

Gertie clapped her hand to her forehead, "Oh Emily luv, I'm sorry. I'd clean forgotten. The thing is, I'm worried about Uncle Wilf. He's taken a turn for the worse and I've got to phone the doctor and get him to come out and see him. He's got a high temperature and I can't leave him for long - just while I do me lollipop and then I've got to go straight back."

Another crowd of kids with their parents came surging up to the crossing and Gertie held the traffic up and saw them safely to the other side of the road. They were little kids from the reception class and they were carrying pictures of Easter bunnies and fluffy yellow chicks. Emily was terribly disappointed when Gertie said, "Sorry, pet, I can't come with you today. We'll go tomorrow if Uncle Wilf's a bit better."

"But suppose someone comes into the shop and buys the box," Emily protested. "Can I go by myself? Please, Gertie."

Just then she saw Harry and Laura and a few others from their class coming out of the school gates. They waved.

"Can I?" Emily persisted. "Please."

"Hang on a minute, sweetheart, wait till Harry and Laura get here."

The twins arrived at last, both of them complaining loudly that they'd been given too much homework.

"Right," said Gertie, looking at her watch, "a quarter to four. That's the end of me lollipop for today, let's go."

It was decided that Emily would go to the shop with Harry and Laura and Gertie would go home and see to Uncle Wilf. She said they must be sure to look at lots of things, not just the box, so that the owner of the shop wouldn't be suspicious. If the box had a dent in the back it would mean that it did belong to Mum and that it had been stolen and passed on to the junk shop to be sold. They mustn't let the man in the shop realise that they knew it had been stolen, because he might get nasty. So they agreed that, if they saw it, they'd just come home and tell Gertie and she'd decide what to do next.

"Pop in and get a kilo of parrot food from Trevor at the pet shop while you're up there," Gertie said, and gave Harry some money. "And then come straight back and get your homework done."

They decided to get the parrot food first. A loud buzzer sounded as they opened the door of the pet shop. It was cramped inside, with shelves from floor to ceiling along both side walls and more running down the middle. They were stacked with bags, cartons and tins of all kinds of pet food for every kind of pet.

Bowls of different sizes were piled on top of each other, and collars and leads hung from hooks alongside toys for animals to play with, and beds for them to sleep in. Emily wished so much that she could have a pet. It just wasn't fair.

At the back of the shop she could see some glass tanks with guinea pigs and rabbits in them, and there was sawdust and straw for them to make their nests in. Mum would never let me have something like that in the flat, she thought; it would make too much mess.

Trevor was tall and skinny with a big nose and even bigger grin. A shank of hair hung over his forehead, which he kept pushing back out of his eyes. He wore a red T shirt with 'Chinchillas are Charming' written on it. Emily wondered what Chinchillas were.

"Hi there," he said cheerfully. "Where's Izzie today?"

"Hi Trevor. We've come straight from school," said Harry, "so we couldn't bring her today. We just want some parrot food please. A kilo."

"A parrot, eh?" said Trevor, picking up a small shovel and digging it into a paper sack. "That's something new, isn't it?"

"Yes," said Laura. "We've got one staying with us for a few days. His name is Autolocus and he can speak."

"Well, well, well," said Trevor, pouring the food onto the weighing scales and then into a paper bag. He grinned at them. "What sort of parrot is he then?"

"Don't know," said Harry. "Just an ordinary one I think. He's grey and he's got a red tail."

"He can make a noise like water going down the plug hole," Emily said proudly, "and he can burp too."

"And he can swear like anything," said Laura. "You should hear him. Mum was shocked."

Trevor laughed and handed the bag of parrot food to Harry. "Sounds like an African Grey," he said. "They're the best talkers. Nothing for Izzie or Firefly today?"

"No, that's all, thanks," replied Harry.

"Kittens coming along well, are they? Make sure Firefly gets plenty of milk to drink, she's got a big family to feed." He flicked the hair out of his eyes. "Righty-ho then, that's just £2.60."

They left and went next door to look in the window of the junk shop. Emily saw immediately that the box had disappeared.

"Look," she cried, pointing to the back of the window. "It was there – next to the little picture in the frame – but it's gone."

In the space where the silver box had been stood an ugly black statue. Her heart sank.

"He must have sold it already," said Laura.

"He might have just moved it," said Harry. "Let's go in and have a look round."

"Ooh yes, and I'll show you the skeleton, Em - it's really scary!" Laura grabbed Emily's hand and marched her through the doorway.

It was gloomy inside and there was a musty, dusty smell mixed with something else, which Emily didn't recognise. It made her nose tickle. Nobody seemed to be around so they started to look for the silver box, but it was difficult because there was so much stuff everywhere. As well as tables and chairs, there were chests, lamps and piles of rugs filling every space between them, while stacks of books and boxes of china and glass were piled in corners. Shelves, laden with knick-knacks, lined the walls, and trays covered with an assortment of ornaments and jewellery spilled out of boxes onto the tables.

Laura clambered onto an old green velvet settee just inside the door and tried to peer into the window to see if she could spot the box.

Suddenly, there was a movement at the back of the shop and a tall, thin man got up from a chair in the corner and came towards them like a spider scuttling across its web. His face was long and pale and his black hair was scraped back from his high forehead. He reminded Emily of Dracula. He did not look pleased to see them.

"Get down off there at once," he shouted at Laura. "You'll ruin it with your shoes!" He looked suspiciously at each of the children in turn. "Now, what brings you in here?"

"Well, we just want to have a look round," said Harry coolly. He cleared his throat. "Um, have you still got your skeleton?"

"Of course I have - it's over there," the man said and pointed towards the back of the shop. "You may look at it, I suppose, but on no account must you touch anything."

He walked with them to where the skeleton hung from a stand, its face grinning down at them.

Emily was fascinated. It was the first time she'd seen a skeleton.

"Did he die a long time ago?" she asked.

"It must have been a long time ago, stupid," said Harry, "or it would still have bits of skin and stuff hanging off it." He turned to the man. "Do you let it sit down sometimes, or does it always have to hang around like that?"

"What a curious idea," said the man. "As far as I know it's always been attached to the stand and it might well fall to pieces if it's moved. No! Don't touch it," he shouted as Harry put out his hand, "it's very delicate."

Emily noticed the skull with the candle inside it on a high shelf. The light shone out of its eye sockets and mouth like the Halloween pumpkin she and Mum had made.

"I'd rather like to have a skeleton," said Harry. "I could dress it up sometimes. How much is it?"

"It's NOT for sale," said the man firmly. "Now, is there anything else?"

Nobody said anything for a moment then Harry cleared his throat again.

"Actually, I'm in the middle of making a cart," he said in an off-hand way, "and I'm looking for an old pram so I can take the wheels off it and use them on my cart. Have you got one?"

The man sighed impatiently. "This is an antiques and curios shop," he said, "not a second-hand junk shop."

"Oh," said Harry sadly. He cast his eye round the shop and suddenly spotted an object in a far corner. His face lit up. "What's that over there then?" he said, pointing to something that did indeed look a bit like an old pram. "That's got wheels - it'd probably do for my cart."

"That is an Edwardian bath chair," said the man stiffly. "It's a very fine piece."

"It looks pretty old – but the wheels might do," said Harry. "Here, Em, hold this a minute." Before Emily had time to think he'd thrust the paper bag of parrot food into her hands and clambered over a pile of rugs and vases to have a better look at the bath chair. She was taken by surprise and tried to clutch the bag, but it split open and the parrot food shot out in every direction.

"You careless children!" shouted the man. "Now look what you've done! It's gone everywhere!" His pale face was flushed with anger.

"I'm sorry," Emily said, kneeling down, trying to sweep some of the food into a pile with her hands. "It would be easier with a brush you know." She looked up at him. "Have you got a brush?"

The food had spilled into one of the boxes packed with china cups and plates and was scattered all over a tray loaded with delicate glass ornaments.

"For goodness sake leave it alone," said the man. "You'll only break something."

"I think we'd better go home," said Laura firmly, walking towards the door. "Come on."

"But we haven't asked about the box," Emily blurted out, wiping her hands on her skirt, "and that was the whole point of coming in here!" A horrible silence followed and she felt herself turning red.

"What box?" asked the man suspiciously.

"Oh, we want to buy our aunt a nice box for her birthday," said Laura, quickly coming to Emily's rescue.

"And we saw one in the window yesterday. It was silver. Only it's not there now."

The man looked hard at Laura for a moment. "You must have been mistaken," he said abruptly. "I haven't had any silver boxes."

Emily was disappointed and then she felt herself getting angry. After all, they'd all seen the box in the window. She wanted to tell him that she knew he was lying, but there was something in his expression that made her decide not to say anything.

When they got home they told Gertie all about it.

"It's not the first time I've heard about Mr Leach dealing in stolen goods," she said.

"We could tell the police, but I don't suppose they'd do anything about it. We've got no proof that it was your mum's box, Emily. Better forget about it."

Emily didn't like giving up, but there didn't seem anything she could do. Later, in the evening Gertie phoned the hospital and was told that Emily's mum had had her operation and was sleeping peacefully.

Again that night Emily couldn't get to sleep. She tossed and turned and kept thinking about the man in the junk shop and about Mum, and she could hear Uncle Wilf in Harry's room across the passage, coughing and coughing. And Harry, who was sleeping on the airbed by the door, was snoring.

The clock downstairs struck one and Emily decided she needed to go to the loo. She fumbled her way over to the door, nearly tripping over the airbed, and managed to open the door softly and creep out of the room and along the passage.

As she was coming back, she stopped for a moment outside Harry's door. She could hear Uncle Wilf coughing and then she heard his voice, although she couldn't make out what he was saying. He must be talking in his sleep, she thought, but was surprised to hear another voice, a deep one, which she didn't recognise. The doctor must be in there, she thought, and went back to bed. Poor Uncle Wilf must be very ill indeed if he needs to have the doctor in the middle of the night.

But when she told Gertie about it in the morning, Gertie ruffled her hair and told her she must have been dreaming.

"The doctor hasn't been yet," she said. "I phoned him yesterday afternoon and he's coming to see Uncle Wilf this morning just as soon as I get back from doing me lollipop."

But Emily knew she hadn't been dreaming.

Chapter 5

Mrs Skeet Meets Autolocus

Emily came back from school with Gertie on her own the next day, because Harry and Laura were staying late to rehearse their parts in the end-of-term play. One of the other parents was going to drop them back later. But Emily could tell that Gertie's mind was on other things when she told Emily that Uncle Wilf had had to go into hospital.

"Poor old fellow's got pneumonia quite badly – hardly surprising when you think of the state he was in, and driving all that way up from Devon in his soaking wet pyjamas. The hospital rang about your mum too," she went on, taking off her yellow lollipop coat and hat and hanging them in the cupboard under the stairs.

There was a lovely smell of cake baking and Emily followed her into the kitchen and watched her take some flapjacks and rock buns out of the oven and put them on a wire tray to cool.

"They said that she's come through the operation well, but that she's going to have to stay in for a bit longer and rest. Now, you're not to worry, sweetheart," she said, putting her arm round Emily's shoulders.

But Emily was worried. "When can I go and see her, Gertie?" she asked.

"I think it's best if we leave it for a day or two. The nurse said she's feeling tired just now and needs to sleep a lot."

Emily bent down and lifted the little tabby kitten out of the box. All the others were asleep and there was no sign of Firefly – she must have gone outside for a bit of a break.

Emily sat down and put the kitten onto her lap and stroked it.

"Have you got homes for all the kittens, Gertie?" she asked.

"Yes, I think so, except the little tortoiseshell one, which we want to keep." Gertie turned and looked at Emily. "Mum told me how much you wanted to have a pet of your own."

"But I can't, because we live in a flat and pets aren't allowed."

"I know," said Gertie. "But I tell you what, Emily, love. Uncle Wilf asked if one of you could look after Autolocus for him while he's in hospital. So, I thought, as Harry looks after Izzie, and Laura seems to want to take care of Firefly and her kittens, you might like to be responsible for Autolocus. What do you think? Would you like to do that?"

Emily was so excited she thought she was going to pop.

"Oh, yes please!" she shouted. "Oh yes, oh yes, I'd love to do that!" She put the little kitten safely back in the box and rushed into the sitting room where Autolocus was sleeping in his cage on the sideboard. He seemed to be calmer lately. Gertie followed her through.

"What do I have to do, Gertie?" she asked. Autolocus opened his eyes and ruffled his feathers.

"Well, you have to make sure he's got food in his tray and clean water in his bottle – I'll show you how to fill it – and at night time you have to remember to cover his cage with a cloth and take it off in the morning. Oh, and you have to clean him out of course – once a week I should think. Do you think you could do all that?"

Emily nodded excitedly. "And I can teach him some new words, can't I?"

"That would be no bad thing," laughed Gertie. "I can't think where he learnt all those dreadful swear words. I'm sure Uncle Wilf didn't teach him to speak like that."

"Did Uncle Wilf have Autolocus at his house when you were a little girl?" Emily asked.

"Well, he certainly had a parrot. Whether it was Autolocus or not I really can't remember. But parrots live to a great age, so I've been told."

Emily peered through the bars of the cage and grinned at Autolous, who stared at her solemnly. He gave a whistle, then took a sunflower seed and cleverly opened it with his beak. She noticed that one of his claws was slightly bent.

Gertie came over. "He must have damaged it at one time," she said. "Doesn't seem to bother him though, does it? Uncle Wilf says he likes to come out occasionally. If you look, you can see he's got a little ring on one of his legs – look there it is. You slot a bit of string through it and then he can have a fly round, but you can get him back when you want to."

"Oh can we try it now – please, Gertie!"

"Well, I suppose we could," Gertie said, a bit doubtfully. "I hope he'll behave himself. Hang on a minute then while I get some string." She disappeared into the kitchen.

"Now, Autolocus," said Emily, "you're going to come out for a little exercise, but you've got to be a good boy and do what you're told and go back when I tell you."

Gertie returned with a piece of string and Emily carefully opened the door of the cage, all the while talking to Autolocus in a quiet voice so he wouldn't be frightened. She was slightly worried that he would peck her, but he seemed to know what she was going to do and held out his leg so that she was able to slip the end of the string easily through the little ring. She slid her other hand in and made a knot.

"My, you're a clever girl, Emily, love," said Gertie, watching all the time. "I wouldn't fancy doing that – Laura said he gave her quite a peck."

Emily felt pleased. "I'm not sure what to do next though," she said. "Let's wait and see if he comes out on his own." She held on firmly to the other end of the string.

Sure enough, Autolocus came waddling out confidently through the door of the cage and, to Emily's great surprise, fluttered up onto her shoulder.

"My hat," cried Gertie in astonishment, "who'd have thought it!"

At that moment the doorbell rang. "Oh, lawks who can that be?" said Gertie.

"Now I'm going to have to open the door, Emily, so make sure you hold on tight to that string."

She opened the front door and there on the doorstep stood an extraordinary-looking woman. She was tall and bony with large hands and feet, but what Emily noticed first about her was the bright red turban she was wearing on her head, fastened with a glittering green brooch.

"Oh, hello, Mrs Skeet," said Gertie cheerfully. "What can I do for you? Come on in for a moment. This is our little visitor, Emily, who's staying here for a few days while her mum's in hospital. Mrs Skeet lives four doors down the close, Emily."

Mrs Skeet stared unblinkingly at Emily and then at Autolocus.

"That a parrit you got there?" she enquired which Emily thought was rather a stupid question.

"Yes, this is Autolocus. He belongs to Uncle Wilf, but I'm looking after him while Uncle Wilf's poorly."

Mrs Skeet came closer. She had a thin face and a sour expression and Emily noticed that her eyebrows, which were very dark, weren't real. They were drawn in with black felt tip pen.

"He's a fine bird," she remarked. "An African Grey. Me brother had one years ago – taught 'im to say all sorts of things, 'e did."

"Oh Autolocus can say all sorts of things too," Emily said proudly. "Some of them are a bit rude though, aren't they, Gertie?" She giggled, wondering if Autolocus was going to behave.

"I should say so," said Gertie, laughing.

Autolocus stared at Mrs Skeet. "You daft old bird," he shouted suddenly. "Pass the rum."

For a moment nobody said anything and Emily held her breath, trying not to giggle. Then, to her astonishment Mrs Skeet let out a shriek of laughter and her expression changed completely, as though someone had turned on a light inside her face.

"Who's a pretty boy, then?" she said, grinning, and held out her hand. Emily felt Autolocus doing a little dance on her shoulder.

"Heave to, shipmates," he shouted and made a noise like someone's tummy rumbling.

Mrs Skeet erupted in laughter and slapped her hand against her thigh. "You've got a good 'un there," she yelled.

All at once Autolocus took off, flew round and round the room, squawking, then swooped and landed on Mrs Skeet's turban. She gave a scream and he flew off again. He did it over and over and Gertie and Emily joined in with Mrs Skeet, who was doubled over and clutching her sides. Every time he landed she let out an even louder whoop of laughter. Gertie's face was the colour of a raspberry milkshake and tears were pouring down her cheeks.

In spite of laughing so much, Emily remembered to hold on tight to the piece of string, and then, at last, Autolocus must have got tired because he came to rest on top of his cage. He lifted one leg up casually and scratched his head.

Gradually they calmed down, although the tears were still streaming down Gertie's face and the muscles in Emily's tummy were aching.

"Oh, dear, oh dear," cried Mrs Skeet, wiping her eyes. "I haven't had so much fun since Uncle Archie died."

"I think he likes the brooch on your hat," Emily spluttered. "It's very shiny and he could see himself in it."

"I told him he was a pretty boy," said Mrs Skeet and let out another shriek.

"We'd better put him back in his cage now, Emily dear," said Gertie breathlessly, mopping her face with a handkerchief. "That's enough excitement for one day."

Autolocus was very good about going back in his cage and Emily took the string out of the ring on his leg and shut the door of the cage firmly.

"Come and have a rock bun, Mrs Skeet," said Gertie when they'd recovered, and they went into the kitchen and had several rock buns and flapjacks. And of course they all had cups of tea.

"Can't remember why I came round now," said Mrs Skeet, brushing some crumbs off her skirt. "'Course I'm on me own in the house most of the time." The sour expression had returned to her face. "Just me and Billy — that's me budgie. And it's me birthday soon and all."

"Well, you'll have to come round and have lunch with us some time, won't you?" said Gertie.

Chapter 6

"Treasure Island"

Harry was allowed back into his own room while Uncle Wilf was away. "But you'll have to move in with the girls again once he comes out of hospital," warned Gertie.

"Can I have another look at your appendix?" whispered Laura one evening while she and Emily were getting ready for bed.

"Why?" Emily asked. "It's just the same as before." She didn't feel so scared of Laura any more.

"I know, I know, but Harry's not here and I'd just like to see it again. Oh go on, Em, I won't touch it, I promise."

"Oh, all right then, I suppose you can." Emily opened the drawer and, pulling socks and knickers to one side, lifted the glass jar carefully out and laid it on her bed.

"Ooh, it's really awesome, isn't it?" said Laura. "It makes me feel all funny just looking at it. A boy at school had his tonsils out, but they didn't put them in a jar for him to keep. You're so lucky."

Emily enjoyed looking after Autolocus and used to buy him special treats from the pet shop. She took him there once and Trevor told her he was a Grey Parrot from Gabon in Africa. She loved him and got used to having him on her shoulder, where he'd sit and gently nibble her ear making a noise like a car's engine starting up.

The weather turned warmer and Gertie started to get excited about the Horticultural Summer Show. Emily used to go to the allotment with her after school when Laura and

Harry were rehearsing for the play. She'd take Autolocus with her and let him have a good fly round.

"It's nice to see him getting his exercise," said Gertie. "Birds shouldn't be kept in cages, it's just not right. But whatever you do make sure you hold on to that bit of string," she warned. "Uncle Wilf would never forgive me if he flew away."

One of the allotments near Gertie's belonged to a man called Colin Rowe, who owned a fish stall at the same market as Bert's, and he was often working on his plot of land when Emily was there. He had a face like a lump of dough and bulging, watery eyes. His mouth hung slightly open most of the time so that he looked like a fish himself. Bert and Gertie used to call him Coddie Rowe, but not to his face of course. Emily never once saw him smile.

From time to time Coddie's son, Kenneth, came to the allotment with his dad, but he never seemed to do anything to help, just sat around looking bored and throwing stones at the pigeons or picking his nose. He was in the same class at school as Harry and Laura. Most of the children in that class had nicknames – Harry's was Saucepot because his initials were HP, like HP Sauce, Laura was called Pinky, and Kenneth Rowe was known as Lip-up Stinky because his top lip jutted out and he smelled of fish, like his father.

Coddie worked hard on his flowers and vegetables and had won lots of prizes at the horticultural shows over the years. He was very conceited and boasted about all the certificates he'd won, and had them on display, pinned up on the door inside his shed.

Gertie had a shed too but, hers was smaller. Sometimes, when Emily let Autolocus fly, he'd land on Coddie's shed and Coddie would shake his fist and shout, "Get that bird off my shed," although Autolocus wasn't doing any harm at all.

Emily didn't like him and she didn't like Lip-Up Stinky either, especially when she heard that he had a dog, but never took it out for walks.

Sunday came round again and it was time for the next chapter of *Treasure Island*. It was a warm evening and all the windows were open in the sitting room. Harry had been persuaded to stop working on his cart and come downstairs. He grumbled because he wanted to get on with it before Uncle Wilf came back and he had to move out of his room again. He said he thought the story was boring.

They all sat round the fireplace – Laura and Emily cuddled up on either side of Gertie on the settee and Harry on the floor stroking Izzie. Autolocus had been put in the kitchen so he wouldn't interrupt.

Emily was enjoying *Treasure Island* – she never thought she would because some of it was hard to understand, but Bert explained the difficult bits. He loved reading out loud, you could tell, and he made all the people in the story talk with different voices. It was really scary in parts, especially the bit about 'Black Dog' coming to the Admiral Benbow Inn and the old blind beggar, Pew, tap-tapping with his stick along the road.

Now they were ready for the next chapter. Bert had just begun when the doorbell rang. Gertie heaved herself up and opened the door. They could see Mrs Skeet standing on the doorstep.

"Oh no," groaned Harry, "what does she want?"

"Evening, Mrs Skeet," said Gertie cheerfully, "Bert's just reading to us. Is there something I can do for you?"

Mrs Skeet peered past Gertie and held up a large book. "I got this out the library – it's about birds and that. Thought you might be interested to read what it says about parrits."

"That's really kind of you, Mrs Skeet," said Gertie, taking the book, "I know Emily will enjoy it - she's got a real way with Autolocus. And there's a parrot in *Treasure Island*, isn't there, Bert?" she called over her shoulder. "That's the story we're having at the moment – Bert reads us a chapter or two every Sunday night before the kids go to bed."

"Oh, *Treasure Island*," said Mrs Skeet fondly. "I read that when I was a girl – a rollicking good yarn that is. Don't suppose you'd mind if I joined you, just for a short while?"

Harry groaned again quietly. "Shhhh..." said Bert prodding him with his foot.

"'Course not," replied Gertie, "you're very welcome. Come on in." She was always nice to everyone.

She held the door open and Mrs Skeet, wearing a black dress and matching turban, stepped inside. She sniffed and looked disapprovingly round the room.

"Bit stuffy in here, isn't it? Where's the parrit?"

"Come and sit down, Mrs Skeet," said Gertie, pulling out the little armchair next to the settee. "Autolocus has been put to bed – we thought the story might give him bad dreams." She laughed.

Mrs Skeet sat down heavily in the little chair and stretched out her legs. She did indeed have very big feet, Emily thought, and Harry and Izzie had to shift to make room for her.

"Well?" she said, looking expectantly at Bert, "Let's get going – I'm listening."

Bert cleared his throat and started to read. Emily stared across at Mrs Skeet. She had a good view of her from where she was sitting and studied her face carefully. It's her eyebrows, she thought; that's why she looks so grumpy. She is rather grumpy anyway, but her eyebrows make her look much worse. She's drawn them in the wrong place; too far down her face, too close together and much too black.

At that moment Mrs Skeet turned her head and caught Emily staring and to her astonishment gave her a brilliant smile, which changed her whole face completely. Emily smiled back nervously and hugged Gertie's arm.

The next part of the story was about Jim and his mother opening Billy Bones's sea chest. As they sat listening, the room suddenly seemed to get colder.

"Brrr," it's chilly in here," said Gertie after a moment. "Sorry, Bert, hang on just a tick while I shut the windows."

She sat down again and Bert went on with the story. The front of Emily and the side of her which was next to Gertie felt nice and warm, but there was a cold draught round her neck. Perhaps someone had left the back door open. She glanced over her shoulder. What she saw there, in the kitchen doorway, made her freeze in terror. For what must have been ten seconds she just stared at it, unsure what she was seeing.

Her heart was hammering and at last she tore her eyes away and pulled Gertie's head down towards her so she could whisper in her ear.

"Gertie, there's someone in the kitchen - look!"

Gertie turned sharply and at that moment Izzie leapt to her feet and started to bark furiously. Mrs Skeet swivelled round to see what they were looking at and let out a piercing scream. Bert got up, dropping the book to the floor and Laura and Harry and everyone stared to where Emily was pointing.

As she watched, the figure that she'd seen standing there slowly melted away.

"Whatever's the matter, Emily, luvvie?" cried Gertie in alarm.

Emily didn't say anything. She couldn't. She was shaking so much that her voice had disappeared. Izzie was still barking like mad with all her hackles up; then suddenly she ran over to the door and dashed through into the kitchen. That started Autolocus off and they could all hear him shrieking and swearing.

"What are you on about, Emily?" demanded Laura crossly.

"What was it?" said Harry. "I can't see anything."

"Are you all right, Emily?" asked Bert. "She's gone dead white, Gertie – is she OK?" He got up, walked over to the door and turned on the light in the kitchen.

"Shut up, Autolocus," he said, "and you too, Izzie," but they both kept on barking and shrieking. He had a good look round, then turned out the light and came back in, shutting the door firmly behind him.

For a few moments everyone waited, and at last Emily managed to speak, although her voice was shaking.

"I saw someone – standing over there in the doorway. I promise you I did."

"What?" said Gertie. "Bert, I think this story's too exciting to read to the kids just before they go to bed." She put her arm round Emily's shoulders. "It's all right now luvvie, calm down. Look, there's no-one there, is there? See? Have a really good look now – there's no-one there."

"But there was!" Everyone turned and looked at Mrs Skeet. Her face, against the black of her turban, was bone white. "There most certainly was," she said. "I saw 'im too!"

The clock on the mantelpiece ticked softly. There was no other sound. Gradually the room felt warmer.

"But what did you see, Mrs Skeet?" Gertie demanded, breaking the silence.

"It was… a-a-a man," stammered Mrs Skeet. "He was standing there… and he was, he was… listening, yes, that's what he was doing. He was listening to the story."

"Yes, that's what I saw," Emily said.

"That's nonsense," said Bert. "How come he's not there now? There's no-one in the kitchen and the back door's been locked all the time."

"What did he look like?" asked Laura, looking scared.

Neither Mrs Skeet, nor Emily answered straight away. Emily knew that what she was going to say would sound ridiculous and she was sure no-one would believe her. She looked at Mrs Skeet who nodded her head.

"Go on," she said.

Emily took a deep breath and the words came rushing out. "He looked like a pirate – just the sort of pirate you see in pictures."

"Yes, that's just what I saw," agreed Mrs Skeet. "Right fearsome he was with a big hat on and a beard and a black patch over one eye. Couldn't see exactly what he was wearing though, could you, because, because…" Her voice trailed away.

"Because you could see right through him!" Emily finished for her. "I could see the fridge through him."

"Yes, she's right," agreed Mrs Skeet. "He wasn't solid at all – kind of watery looking – transparent, yes, that's the word, transparent."

"I've never heard such nonsense!" Bert's voice rose angrily. "Your imagination's running away with you. Stands to reason, doesn't it – you've been listening to *Treasure Island* for the last half an hour or so. It's all about pirates and such like. It's just your imagination working over-time."

"And how come only you and Emily saw him?" asked Gertie. "Come on now – be realistic!"

"But Izzie saw him, I know she did," Emily insisted. "That was why she started barking like that."

"Well, where's he gone to now, I'd like to know?" asked Bert and managed a weak laugh. "Just evaporated like… like steam?"

His words seemed to hang in the air.

"Yes," Emily whispered. "Yes, that's exactly what he did. He was a ghost!"

Chapter 7

A Narrow Escape for Johnny

Bert took Mrs Skeet back to her house – she was too scared to walk down the close by herself and you couldn't blame her. Nobody slept very well that night because Harry, Laura and Emily all got into bed with Bert and Gertie, and it was a terrible squash. Laura and Harry didn't want to sleep in their own beds - and Emily certainly didn't.

When she woke up the sun was streaming through the window and the alarm clock was ringing. For a moment, she wondered where she was and then she remembered everything that had happened the evening before. Had she had a bad dream? No, she thought, I couldn't have dreamt the ghost or why would we all be in Gertie's bed?

Bert must already have left for work – he got up at five every morning – and there was now more room in the bed without him, although Laura's knee was pressing into her back. She stretched a bit and then cuddled up to Gertie. She wanted to go back to sleep, but the alarm kept ringing.

"Come on now, this'll never do," said Gertie at last, giving a big yawn and turning over. She whacked the alarm clock to stop it ringing. "Up sticks everyone, it's Monday morning again." Harry and Laura moaned. "Never mind," said Gertie, "it'll be the holidays soon and we'll all be able to have a nice long lie-in."

The sun was shining when they left the house, but you could tell it had been raining in the night because the roads were glistening and there were puddles everywhere.

They turned left out of the close and into the main road.

"Fifteen men on a dead man's chest, yo ho ho and a bottle of rum," sang Harry and Laura, as they skipped along the road ahead of Gertie and Emily. That was the song the pirates sang in *Treasure Island.* Nobody mentioned the ghost and Emily knew that they still didn't really believe her.

A white van racing along the road behind sent a spray of muddy water over them as it passed.

"Slow down, you hooligan," shouted Gertie, shaking her lollipop at it. "These roads round here get more dangerous every day," she complained. "Now, don't you ever try and cross on your own, do you hear me?" she warned the children.

They reached the crossing and Gertie saw them safely over. "Bye now," she called, as they ran along the pavement to the school gates

When they got home after school that afternoon, Harry and Laura went straight to the fridge to see if there was anything that needed finishing up. Izzie stood nearby in case something nice dropped on the floor.

"Ooh, good, there's some of that treacle tart left," said Harry. "Want some Emily?" They were always starving by the time they got home, and there was a smell of something yummy cooking in the oven, which made them feel even hungrier.

Gertie disappeared outside to her greenhouse and Emily noticed there were more pots of little plants on the kitchen window sill. Autolocus was clambering round in his cage and she went to say hello to him, munching a piece of treacle tart. She poked a bit of pastry through the bars of his cage and he took it from her with his bent claw.

Suddenly, there was a ring at the door and Izzie started to bark as they all ran to see who it was. A spotty-faced young man, holding a briefcase and with a camera slung round his neck, stood on the doorstep.

"Mrs Pink in?" he asked.

"Shhh, Izzie, be quiet," said Harry. "Yes, she's in the garden. Hang on a minute and I'll get her."

After a moment he came back and they heard Gertie at the back door, taking off her boots. She appeared wearing her gardening gloves and red stripy socks. You could see she wasn't pleased at being interrupted.

"Mrs Pink?" enquired the man on the doorstep.

"Yes, that's me," replied Gertie, taking off her gloves and running a hand through her curls which made them stand on end. She had a streak of mud down one cheek. "What can I do for you?"

"I'm from the Gazette," he explained. "I wonder if I might have a word with you about that incident on the crossing this morning?"

"Mum?" said Harry. "What's he on about?"

"Oh that," replied Gertie, "there's not much to say about that."

"Would you mind if I came in for a moment?" said the young man, wiping his feet on the doormat. "I'm sure I won't keep you very long. I can see you're busy."

He came in and Harry shut the door behind him.

"You'd best sit down, I suppose," said Gertie, pointing to one of the chairs. She sat opposite him and the three children crowded on to the settee. "Look, you three, why don't you just go in the kitchen and get on with your homework."

"Oh Mum, let us stay, we'll get it done straight after," whined Laura. They were all curious to know what was going on.

"Well, all right, you can stay, I suppose, if it's not going to take too long. But don't interrupt."

The young man cleared his throat. "Well, I gather you were quite a heroine this morning, Mrs Pink. Now I'd just like to write a small article for the Gazette about what happened. Would you mind if I record the interview?" He took a recording machine out of his briefcase and placed it on the coffee table.

The children stared at Gertie. What on earth had she been up to? It must have happened after they'd gone into school.

"Are you a reporter?" asked Harry.

"Shhhh," said Gertie, looking at the machine suspiciously. "Well, all right. But I don't want you making anything up. You're not to put anything in that I don't say."

"Of course not." The young man looked offended. "Now I'm just going to switch this on – there." He pressed a button. "Right now, Mrs Pink. You're the crossing patrol officer for St Catherine's Primary School, aren't you?"

"Yes, that's right," answered Gertie, pulling her socks up.

"Can you tell me what time you were on duty this morning?"

"The usual time," said Gertie. "I get there at 8.15 and finish just after 9 o'clock."

"Now, I gather from witnesses that the incident occurred after you'd finished your patrol duty. Can you tell me exactly what happened?"

"Well, I always hang around for a few minutes after 9 o'clock, just to be really sure that none of the kids are going to turn up late. Let's see now. I probably waited until about five past nine or so, and then I decided I'd pop into the garden centre on the corner to get a few more packets of seeds and some rooting powder."

"Rooting powder?"

"It's for when you take cuttings," said Gertie, "from plants. You dip the end of the cutting in the rooting powder before you stick it in the compost and it helps the little plant to grow its roots. I always use it for my geraniums. 'Course you need to give them really good compost when you plant them out, and well-rotted manure with plenty of pink worms in it."

"Mum," exclaimed Laura, "he doesn't want to know all that."

"And where exactly is the garden shop, Mrs Pink?"

"Just opposite the school."

"Can you tell me what happened when you came out of the garden centre?"

"Well, I was just coming out the door and I happened to look up the road. And there was little Johnny Watkins tearing along the pavement, with his school bag bumping up and down on his back and his shirt hanging out of his trousers. Splashing in all the puddles he was. The crossing was a few yards from where I was standing and I could tell he was going to run straight across without looking, I just knew he was. Then suddenly, this huge lorry came whizzing round the corner – the corner's just a few yards from the crossing you see – a snarling red monster it was – and the driver was really putting his foot down and zooming up the road behind Johnny. Well, I threw down me lollipop and me shopping and I've never moved so fast in all me life." Gertie's red curls were bobbing up and down as she spoke.

"I raced up the pavement and reached the crossing, just as little Johnny was about half way over, and I threw myself at him and snatched him back in the nick of time, as the lorry came screeching to a stop right on the crossing. We both landed in the road in a shower of water and pebbles and goodness know what else. And then, would you believe it, the driver sounded his horn – afterwards, after he'd stopped – what a maniac!"

"Mum! You never said," cried Laura.

"Shhhh," said the spotty-faced man. "Go on, Mrs Pink."

"Well, that's all really," said Gertie. "We picked ourselves up – Johnny's shirt was torn where I'd scraped him along the ground, and he had a nasty graze on his leg. I was a bit shaken up too, I can tell you." She laughed. "But no real damage was done. People came running out the garden centre and crowded round and someone phoned the police. The lorry driver got out of his cab – his face was white and he looked shocked, 'cos he knew it was his fault, stupid idiot. He was going much too fast and his brakes must have skidded on the wet road.

"Well, I took Johnny into the garden centre and they got out the first-aid kit and I cleaned his leg up. Then someone rang his father (luckily Johnny knew his number) and in a few minutes, he came round in his car and took him home. I had to give a few details to the police and so did the lorry driver, and then I came home. That was it. Somebody picked up me lollipop for me, but I lost me seeds and me rooting powder. I'll have to get some more."

"Well, Mrs Pink," said the young man, switching off the recording machine and putting it away in his case, "you're certainly a very brave lady and little Johnny Watkins had a lucky escape. Now, I'd just like to take a picture of you, if I may, to go with the article. No, no need to get up, just stay sitting there. That's right. Now, maybe a little smile – yes, perfect. Thanks very much."

As soon as he'd gone, the telephone rang and Gertie answered it. "Bless my socks," she said. "Never a dull moment! That was the hospital. Uncle Wilf's coming home tomorrow."

Chapter 8

Uncle Wilf Owns Up

As well as the call from the hospital about Uncle Wilf, there was one about Emily's mum. They said that she was a lot better, but it would be some time before she was properly well again. Emily was disappointed because, although she'd spoken to her on the phone, she hadn't been to visit her in hospital. But Gertie said it would be much nicer to see her again when she was really fit and well.

The next afternoon when they got back from school Uncle Wilf was there. Emily hadn't seen him since that first evening when he'd arrived in the storm, wearing nothing but his pyjamas. He was in the greenhouse, helping Gertie with her plants – there were masses of them everywhere.

Laura and Harry and Izzie and Emily all tried to crowd into the greenhouse, but there wasn't enough room, even though Uncle Wilf was small, not much taller than Harry really. He had lots of bushy white hair and a white beard. If you'd dressed him up, he'd have looked just like Father Christmas, Emily thought, or perhaps one of his elves. He was wearing a navy-blue track suit off Bert's stall and Autolocus was perched on his shoulder. Just then Bert came down the path and tried to get into the greenhouse too.

"Come on, come on," laughed Gertie, pushing them all out. "This isn't a tube train, you know. Let's go inside and have a cup of tea."

She had made chocolate brownies and they sat round the table in the kitchen, munching and drinking tea. At home Emily hardly ever drank tea, but she'd got to like it since living with the Pinks – nice and milky though, with plenty of sugar.

She had a good look at Uncle Wilf. He had large, pointy ears and his eyes were very green and twinkly behind his glasses. He really is rather like an elf, she thought, or maybe a gnome, but gnomes are usually grumpy and Uncle Wilf's face certainly wasn't grumpy. Most of the time he looked as if he was about to burst out laughing.

He was very different from the first time she'd seen him and so was Autolocus who was sitting on his shoulder, enjoying a piece of chocolate brownie. Emily suddenly felt sad when she realised that she probably wouldn't be needed to look after him anymore.

Uncle Wilf caught her eye. "Well, well," he said, "you must be the young lassie who's been taking such good care of my naughty parrot while I've been in hospital."

She nodded and felt herself blushing because everyone was looking at her.

"And have you been teaching him some better manners?"

"Get off of my shed, get off of my shed," squawked Autolocus and then burped.

They all laughed. "That's what Coddie Rowe always shouts at him when we're down at the allotment," Gertie explained. "Emily's been letting him have a fly round, like you said, but for some reason he loves sitting on Coddie Rowe's shed and it makes Coddie mad."

"I'm always very careful to hold tight to the string," Emily said quickly.

"He won't go far," said Uncle Wilf. "He's had his wings clipped. Still, it's just as well to keep hold of the string."

Gertie poured out more tea and handed round the brownies.

"Would you like to see our kittens, Uncle Wilf?" asked Laura. She picked up the little tortoiseshell one and handed it gently to him. "We're keeping this one, but all the others are going soon. They're getting big now and they keep climbing out of their box."

"My, my, she's a little darling, isn't she?" said Uncle Wilf. "What have you called her?"

"We can't make up our minds about a name," said Laura. Her mum's name's Firefly, which is really cool, don't you think?"

"It's a cracking name," said Uncle Wilf. He took off his glasses, leaving one side dangling by its wire frame from his ear, then lifted the little kitten up and studied her closely. He paused. "Her name's Josephina," he exclaimed, tickling the kitten under her chin. "Yes, without a doubt it's Josephina!"

"How do you know?" Emily asked in astonishment. The name seemed to suit the kitten exactly.

"It just fits her nicely, don't you think?" said Uncle Wilf. "I'm thinking of Joseph and his coat of many colours, of course. But you've got a little girl here, so Josephina seems the obvious answer. What do you think, Laura?" He put his glasses on again and handed the kitten back to her.

"Yes," agreed Laura, "Oh yes, I love it. Josephina's a sweet name, don't you think so, Mum?"

"Yes, I really like it," said Gertie.

"Where are you going to live now?" asked Harry abruptly, "now you haven't got a house anymore?"

"Harry!" said Gertie.

Uncle Wilf's face clouded over. "It's nice of you to let me sleep in your room for the time being, Harry, but I know I'm going to have to make other plans soon... and I will do. By the way, that's a splendid-looking cart you're making." Harry beamed at him.

There was a question Emily had been dying to ask him and she decided that this was the right moment.

"Did your house in Devon really have a ghost?" she asked. Uncle Wilf went on stirring his tea and Emily wondered if he'd heard her.

"Why do you ask that?" he said at last, taking off his glasses and polishing them on his handkerchief. "Gertie been talking?"

"She said some people thought your house was haunted but that nobody ever saw a ghost," said Harry.

"I saw a ghost," Emily said. "Last night."

"Now don't go upsetting yourself again, Emily," said Bert. "It was just her imagination," he explained. "Too much *Treasure Island*." He chuckled. "We'll have to think of something less scary for next Sunday evening."

"What did you see, Emily lass?" asked Uncle Wilf. "Tell me."

"I wasn't the only one who saw it," Emily said stoutly. "Mrs Skeet did too... And Izzie. We were all sitting round the fireplace in the sitting room and Bert was reading to us, and suddenly the room felt cold. I thought maybe the back door was open and I looked over towards the kitchen... and... and that's when I saw it."

Uncle Wilf stared hard at her. "What exactly did you see?"

"It was a pirate! He was standing just there – in the doorway." She pointed to the kitchen door. "I could see his

56

head quite well – he had a big hat and a beard and there was a patch over one of his eyes. He was standing quite still, and he seemed to be listening to the story. I couldn't see the rest of him very well because he was sort of... sort of ... transparent - I could see the fridge through him. I'm not making it up, I promise. Mrs Skeet saw him too... and Izzie."

Uncle Wilf looked down at his hands and didn't speak.

"Uncle Wilf?" said Gertie at last. "What's going on?"

He let out a big sigh and blew his nose hard several times. Then he coughed.

"You all right, Uncle Wilf?" asked Bert.

"Yes, yes," he replied. "But I'm afraid I've got something to tell you, which I don't think you're going to be very pleased to hear."

"Go on," said Bert.

Uncle Wilf spoke slowly, stirring his tea round and round in the cup. "For as long as I can remember Cliff House in Devon – where I used to live – had a ghost!"

There was a stunned silence.

"A real live ghost?" asked Harry at last.

"You can't have a live ghost, stupid," said Laura. "What sort of a daft question is that?"

"No!" said Gertie. Her face was shocked. "It can't be true. You mean it was there all the time when I was a little girl and we stayed in your house?"

"Yes," said Uncle Wilf. "He sort of came with the house, I'm afraid, when I first bought it all those years ago. But he's quite harmless, you know. And, yes, it's true – he's a buccaneer from about the eighteenth century I should think, judging by what he wears, but he's quite nice when you get to know him."

"This is ludicrous!" exploded Bert and got up suddenly from the table, spilling his tea. "Are you telling us that this, this... pirate ghost came with you and he's here now... in this house? This... this cut-throat buccaneer?"

"Yes, I'm afraid so," said Uncle Wilf calmly. "Let me explain. We lived quite comfortably side by side at Cliff House, the pirate and I. I call him Jack, although of course, I don't know his real name. There were certain rules that Jack had to stick to – certain parts of the house that were out of bounds to him, so to speak. But it had been his home far longer than it had been mine and he does love to haunt, you know – it's what he does best and you can't restrict him too much. He was never allowed to come near any of you kids when you came to stay. I made that quite clear to him. And of course, as Emily here has discovered, not everyone can see him. I can, and one or two people from the village used to say the house was haunted – someone must have seen him looking out of one of the windows or something, I suppose."

"But why on earth has he come here?" demanded Bert.

"That night of the storm, I nearly lost my life," said Uncle Wilf, putting a hand over his eyes. Emily thought he was going to cry again. "I'd gone to bed as usual at about ten o'clock. I could see that a storm was brewing when I looked out of the bedroom window – the waves were enormous and the wind was blowing a gale, and the rain was lashing down." He looked up. "But Cliff House has stood there for centuries, and we've had many, many storms over the years." He paused, remembering what had happened.

"Carry on," ordered Bert.

"I was fast asleep. Suddenly, I woke up. The room was cold and I could see Jack, standing by the window. I got out of bed and turned on the light. He was pointing out of the window, looking all worked up and trying to say something.

58

He speaks, but I can't hear what he's saying, you see. I opened the window and stuck my head out. The wind nearly blew it off, and I could feel the spray from the sea, even from that distance. The waves were crashing on the rocks only yards from the end of the front garden.

"I bet you were scared," said Laura.

"I was absolutely terrified," said Uncle Wilf. "I looked at Jack and he was waving his arms wildly and I could see he was shouting 'Get out, get out' and I realised there wasn't a moment to lose.

"I grabbed Autolocus who was in his cage by my bed, tore out of the bedroom, slid down the banisters and rushed out into the garden and up to the garage. Luckily, the keys were in the glove pocket of the car. My hands were trembling and I was soaking wet because the rain was coming down in bucketfuls. I couldn't fit the key into the ignition straight away, I remember, because my fingers were so cold. Then the engine wouldn't start." Uncle Wilf blew his nose again and wiped his eyes. He seemed to be living the terrifying experience all over again.

"At last, I managed it and turned on the headlights. But I've already told you what happened."

"Go on," said Bert grimly.

"As I looked out through the windscreen, the ground a couple of yards in front of the garage began to crack and I heard an enormous roaring sound. Then, everything in front of me just disappeared. There was a terrible crash and a tall plume of sea water shot up into the air. I realised the house and everything I owned had plunged into the sea! I was terrified that the ground in front of the garage wouldn't hold, but I eased the car out gently, turned it into the driveway and got out into the road. You know the rest of the story."

"But what about Jack?" persisted Bert. "How did he get here?"

"I realised, after I'd driven a little way towards the town and had to turn round because of the fallen trees that Jack was in the back of the car. It was freezing cold, as you can imagine. It's always cold when Jack's there."

"But why did you have to bring him with you?" asked Gertie.

"He'd saved my life!" cried Uncle Wilf. "I couldn't just leave him behind. Where would be go? His house, which he'd haunted for hundreds of years was gone!"

"He could have stayed and haunted your garage," Harry suggested helpfully.

"You can't have a pirate haunting a garage," giggled Laura. "How daft is that?"

"Anyway, if you're a ghost and you're haunting, you need to have people around so you can scare them, I suppose," agreed Harry. "There wouldn't be anyone to haunt in a garage."

"This is an impossible situation," shouted Bert, striding up and down the kitchen.

"He'll have to go! This house gets more crowded every day. Children, relatives, neighbours and now… now pirates! He looked accusingly at Gertie. "And you tell me you've invited Mrs Skeet over to lunch."

"Oh no, you haven't, Mum!" groaned Laura and Harry together. "She's awful!"

"Calm down, Bert," said Gertie. "I'm sure that we can set some rules for the pirate like Uncle Wilf did at Cliff House. As for Mrs Skeet, she's a poor old lady living on her own and it's her birthday at the weekend, so I've asked her to come to lunch, that's all. She's not coming to stay!"

"Well, thank goodness for that at least," said Bert.

"So stop being so selfish all of you," Gertie went on and started clearing away the tea things. "And Uncle Wilf, now you're better, I'm going to have to insist that you and... er ... Jack, move up into the attic. I really can't have him wandering round the house, especially when I can't see him. It'd give me the jitters. I'll make up a camp bed for you up there – it'll be quite comfortable, and you can have an electric heater." She paused uncertainly, "Does er, does Jack need a bed too?"

Laura squealed with laughter. "Don't be daft, Mum – ghosts don't go to bed."

"How do you know?" Harry said. "Maybe he gets tired sometimes, with all the haunting he has to do."

"I'm really sorry about all this," said Uncle Wilf. "I told Jack strictly before I went into hospital that he wasn't to come out of the bedroom. But I suppose he just couldn't resist hearing you read *Treasure Island*, Bert. He loves stories, you see."

"Well, he's not to come out of the attic," said Gertie firmly. "He might wander into me bedroom when I'm putting on me corsets!"

Chapter 9

The Experiment

Suddenly, it was the end of term and Emily went with Bert and Gertie and Uncle Wilf to see the twins in the end-of-term play. Everyone said how good Laura was, and when she came on stage at the end the audience clapped and clapped.

"I'm going to be an actress when I'm grown up," she said.

Now that the Easter holidays had come, Emily wondered if she'd be going home, but Gertie told her that Mum needed a bit longer to get really well and strong again and so Emily stayed on at Willow Close.

Uncle Wilf soon settled down in the attic and he promised he'd make sure that Jack stayed up there. Sometimes at night, Emily had a feeling he might be walking around the house, but she didn't see him. The others didn't seem bothered about him, but that was because none of them had actually seen him and Emily didn't think they really believed in him anyway. Although she was scared that Jack might turn up again one day, she found herself feeling rather sorry for him too; it must be boring for a pirate to have to stay up in the attic and she wondered what he did all day. After a while, they all forgot about him – there always seemed to be so many other things going on.

A few days after Gertie had saved Johnny Watkins from the lorry the doorbell rang, and there was Johnny with his dad. They'd brought Gertie a huge bunch of flowers – roses and all sorts. She was thrilled to bits and they came in and had a cup of tea and chatted and looked at the kittens. Mr

Watkins, actually his name was Professor Watkins, thanked Gertie 'from the bottom of my heart' for saving Johnny from the lorry. "If ever there's anything at all I can do for you, Mrs Pink, anything at all, don't hesitate to let me know," he said and gave her a card with his name and address on it.

And, sure enough, there was an article about Gertie in the local paper. The headline said, 'Heroic Lollipop Lady Snatches Child of Seven from Jaws of Death' and there was a photograph of her. Gertie's hair was sticking out all over the place because she'd been gardening, there was a hole in one of her socks and she had a smear of mud down one cheek. Still, she was pleased with the photo and stuck it up on the wall in the kitchen.

The Easter holidays raced by, and it seemed no time at all before they were back at school again for the summer term. One by one, the kittens went to their new homes. Emily was terribly sad to see them go, especially the little grey tabby, which was the one she'd have chosen if she'd been allowed to have one. She called him Smokey, but the lady who came and collected him said they were going to call him Pepper. She hated parting with him.

Autolocus stayed downstairs on the sideboard and she was allowed to go on looking after him, although she always knew he really belonged to Uncle Wilf.

Gertie and Uncle Wilf were busy all the time over on the allotment, and she would go there sometimes after school with Autolocus and let him stretch his wings a bit.

She couldn't help noticing that with Uncle Wilf there to help, Gertie's plants had suddenly started growing faster and bigger than before. Gertie was especially pleased with her sweet peas.

"Bless my socks, Uncle Wilf," she said, "they're better this year than they've ever been."

Coddie Rowe was furious, you could tell. His sweet peas weren't anything like as good as Gertie's. And his runner beans, which had won first prize for the last three years, didn't really seem to get going. His lettuces were all right, but Gertie's were better. And her tomatoes. He used to stand there, next to his shed, looking over at Gertie's patch of land with his mouth hanging open and his great coddy eyes staring.

Sometimes they saw Lip-up Stinky at the allotment, but you could tell he was bored and would much rather be doing something else. He used to sit outside Coddie's hut, throwing stones and whistling tunelessly through his teeth.

"What's the secret, Uncle Wilf?" Gertie asked one evening at supper. "There's no doubt about it, my plants have taken off like rockets since you arrived!"

"There's no secret, it's quite simple." His green eyes twinkled behind his glasses. "You have to love your plants. You have to understand them, and you have to talk to them. Take your sweet peas, for example, they're very happy flowers, sweet peas, and they love music, so I sing to them."

"What?" said Harry. "I don't believe you!"

Uncle Wilf looked over the top of his glasses at Harry and his face was sad.

"There are a lot of things people don't believe these days. But I can only tell you what I know. I've tried lots of songs, but the one sweet peas like best of all, without a doubt, is 'Somewhere Over the Rainbow.' 'Cos they're rainbow-coloured, you see. Works every time. They grow lovely long stems just like they want to go up, up and right over the rainbow!" he chuckled. "'Course, I sing it very quietly to them so that Coddie Rowe's sweet peas won't hear me."

Could it really be true?

"What about the lettuces?" Emily asked. "And the beans? Do you sing to them too?"

"No, lettuces and beans are different," said Uncle Wilf. "They're food plants and take themselves very seriously. I just tell them what a responsibility they have, to grow up good and strong and delicious and make people healthy. It's the same with most food plants."

Harry snorted. "That's rubbish!"

Uncle Wilf looked hard at him and Emily noticed again how big and pointed his ears were.

"Taking care of something of your own and watching it grow is one of the most fun things there is to do," he said. "Honestly. Ever tried it?"

"No." Harry frowned. "But I guess I'm going to have to because it's our project for the summer holidays – we've got to grow something and then write about it." He pulled a long face. "How dull is that!"

"Dull? It's thrilling!" said Uncle Wilf. "Any idea what you want to grow?"

"I don't want to grow anything. Don't 'spect I'll get round to it till the day before we go back to school."

"It'll be too late then, silly," said Laura "and then you'll be in trouble with Mrs Owen."

"You've got to grow something too, have you Laura?" asked Uncle Wilf.

"Yes," said Laura, "but I don't know what."

"Have you thought about sunflowers?" asked Uncle Wilf. "I could help you – they're very easy."

"There's a 'Tallest Sunflower' competition for kids every year as part of the Horticultural Summer Show, said Gertie, "but it's too late to start them now. What a pity! You have to put sunflower seeds in at the end of April or the beginning of May and it's the middle of May now. Coddie Rowe always enters his son's name for the competition and he always wins, so I've stopped trying. Mind you, I don't think his son takes any interest in it at all – he just likes to go up and get the winning certificate."

"Does he indeed?" said Uncle Wilf. "We'll see about that!" He smacked his hand down on the table, making them jump. "Now then, me old pals, shall we give it a go? Let's kill two birds with one stone and enter the 'Tallest Sunflower' competition and see if we don't beat old Coddie hands down! And that could be your project too, Harry and Laura. How's that for an idea?" He looked at Gertie. "When do they do the judging?"

"It takes place at the end of the summer holidays, just before the schools go back. But it's too late to plant sunflowers now – there's not enough time."

"Well, we are cutting it a bit fine," said Uncle Wilf, "but not everyone knows sunflowers as well as I do." He rubbed his hands together. "Now we haven't a moment to lose."

The next afternoon, the children went with him to the garden centre opposite the school and bought a packet of sunflower seeds – 'Tallest Variety', it said on the packet - and then they went straight over to the allotment. There was no sign of Coddie Rowe or Lip-Up Stinky.

Uncle Wilf unlocked the shed and came out with a watering can and a trowel and filled the can with water from the tap. Then, he took the packet of seeds out of his pocket. "We don't need to use all of these," he explained, "just two for each of you will be enough for my little

66

experiment, and we'll let Autolocus enjoy the rest. Do you want to have a go as well, young Emily?"

"Yes please," she said and they crowded round him.

"This is a nice patch of ground with plenty of lovely manure in it," he said. Gertie's been keeping it specially to plant out her lettuces, but there's room down each side for the sunflowers. So, we'll put three down one side and three down the other. I'll tell you why in a minute.

"Now, the first thing is to choose names for your sunflowers. Let me explain. The real name – the posh Latin name – for sunflower is Helianthus. And I think it would be a nice idea if you gave each of your sunflowers a name beginning with the letter H. They'd like that. So I want each of you to choose two names beginning with the letter H."

"I know," shouted Laura. "Hermione, like in *Harry Potter*. That's one. And the other one could be, let's see, um, I know... Holly. I like that name."

"I know, I know," Emily shouted, jumping up and down. "I'm going to call mine Hattie and Hayley!"

"Splendid," said Uncle Wilf. "And what about you, Harry? Can you think of a couple of names beginning with H?"

"Well, um. Let's see, um... Oh yes, there's Harry, of course and... Henry, and we've got a boy at school called Hamish."

"Oh, I should have said," said Uncle Wilf with a giggle. "Sunflowers are girls. I think it would upset them very much if you gave them boys' names."

"Oh well then, I dunno," said Harry, pouting. "I can't think of any stupid girls' names beginning with H. I'll call mine Hanky-Panky and Hiccups."

The others laughed. "All right, Hanky-Panky and Hiccups it is," said Uncle Wilf.

"Now, hold out your hands." He opened the packet and gave them each two stripy black and white seeds. "I always think they look like zebra seeds," he said.

"Zebras don't have seeds, do they?" Emily asked in astonishment, and then realised what a silly thing she'd said. She felt herself blushing, but everyone else thought it was funny.

Uncle Wilf showed them how to make a little hole in the ground, about 2 cm deep, and put a seed in it, then cover it up with earth and pat it down gently. They each put one of their seeds on one side of the patch of ground, in a line, and the other seed, well away from it, on the other side of the bed, so they were opposite each other.

Then, he gave them two labels each and a pencil and they wrote the names they'd chosen on the labels and stuck them in the ground next to where the sunflower seeds were buried. So on one side, in a line, were Hermione, Hattie and Hanky Panky and opposite, on the other side of the bed, about a metre and a half away, were Holly, Hayley and Hiccups.

"So, this is where the fun bit starts," said Uncle Wilf. "You said you thought that talking to your plants was rubbish, didn't you, Harry?" Harry nodded. "Well, I'm going to prove you wrong."

"How?" said Harry scornfully.

"First of all, you have to understand that sunflowers are sensitive plants. Yes, I know they grow very tall and they have big coarse leaves and great yellow faces, but in fact they're very sensitive and, really, all they want to do is to please you. If you ask them to grow up and up and turn their faces to the sun, then that's what they'll try their best to do. But you have to talk to them and tell them that's what you want. And of course, they've got a great sense of humour, have sunflowers. Tell them a funny story or a joke every day and it'll put inches on them."

All the time he was talking, Emily noticed that Uncle Wilf's pointy ears were getting pinker and pinker.

"Now, what I'm going to suggest is that we try a little experiment," he said, walking over to where Hermione, Hattie and Hanky Panky were buried. "I'm going to say a few words of encouragement to these three seeds to get them started, but I'm going to whisper so that Holly, Hayley and Hiccups on the other side can't hear what I'm saying. So… here we go." He knelt down and whispered quietly in turn, first to Hermione, then to Hattie and lastly to Hanky Panky.

The children started to giggle. He looked so funny, just like a little garden gnome with his white hair and his beard. Or he could have been one of Snow White's dwarfs – yes, Doc, the one with the glasses, thought Emily.

They watched and listened, but couldn't hear what he was saying. Emily could tell Harry was only pretending he wasn't interested. They all wanted to know what was going to happen.

At last Uncle Wilf got up. "Right, I think that should get them going. You see they're nicely sheltered too from the wind here by the shed. Now, we need to give them all a little drink. He picked up the watering can and poured some water on to the ground near each label. "So you see Holly, Hayley and Hiccups have got the same chance as the other three – nice plot of ground, water and sunshine – but we won't be doing any whispering to them. Now, if I'm right, the three on this side of the bed – Hermione, Hattie and Hanky Panky – are going to shoot up and try and reach the sky, because I've told them that that's what I want them to do."

"How long will it take for the seeds to come up?" asked Laura.

"Only a few days, but you must remember to come every day and give them water. The sun's nice and warm now and we don't want the seedlings to shrivel up and die. And of course, if you want this to work, you've got to think of something nice to whisper to your sunflower to make her want to please you."

Chapter 10

The Birthday Lunch

Mrs Skeet had been invited for lunch on Sunday, much to Harry's disgust, and was expected at half past twelve. They were going to have roast chicken with stuffing, roast potatoes, and peas and carrots that Gertie had grown on the allotment. Then, there was apple crumble and custard for afters – Emily helped make the crumble.

Bert was out with Izzie and there'd been no sign of Uncle Wilf all morning. Laura had laid the table in the sitting room and Harry had been told to tidy the place up. He'd tried to shove everything in one of the drawers of the sideboard, and while he was rummaging around, he'd found a box of crackers that Gertie had hidden away.

"Mum," he shouted, running into the kitchen. "Look what I've found – crackers! We could have them today, couldn't we?"

Gertie looked round. She was washing carrots in the sink. "What have you got there? Oh, yes, some of last year's crackers. Well, I suppose we could. Are there enough? There are seven of us."

Harry counted them. "Yes, there are seven, so we can have one each – perfect!"

The table looked pretty with the crackers and Gertie had put a large vase of sweet peas in the middle.

"Come in here a minute, all of you," she shouted from the kitchen. "I want a word with you. Right," she said, drying her hands as they trooped in. "Now I want you to be friendly to Mrs Skeet – it's her birthday, remember. You're not to go disappearing upstairs when she gets here. And try and think of something nice to say to her. She's a lonely old lady and needs to be cheered up."

"But, Mum, she's such a mad old biddy," said Laura, pulling a face.

"I could tell her some of my jokes to cheer her up," Harry suggested. "Oh I know what I'll do — this'll make her laugh." He disappeared upstairs.

"I've got some good riddles," Emily said.

Just then, Bert came back with Izzie and Gertie looked at the kitchen clock on the mantelpiece.

"Great snakes!" she said, "I knew I shouldn't have spent so long over at the allotment this morning — I'm all behind. Emily, put Autolocus outside the backdoor, will you pet? I don't want him swearing while Mrs Skeet's here."

The doorbell rang. "Drat," said Gertie, "the potatoes are nowhere near done. Bert, I'm going to be stuck in the kitchen for a bit. Go and let her in, will you love? Sit her down and give her a glass of something."

Mrs Skeet was wearing her scarlet turban and a summer dress patterned with bright red flowers. She looked really crotchety because she'd drawn her eyebrows even closer together.

"Hello, Mrs Skeet, happy birthday," said Bert.

Mrs Skeet looked all round the room. "Where's the parrit?" she asked.

"I put him outside," Emily said. "He might swear otherwise."

"Do have a seat, Mrs Skeet," said Bert and Harry took her by the arm and lead her to the little armchair she'd sat in before.

"Do have a seat, Mrs Skeet," he sang, doing a little dance in front of her, "and stretch out your feet, Mrs Skeet, and have something to eat, Mrs Skeet!"

"Harry!" said Bert, looking embarrassed. "Take no notice of him, please. He's just trying to be funny."

Mrs Skeet regarded Harry stonily. Brushing an imaginary speck of dust off the arm of the chair, she sat down heavily. A loud explosion erupted – like someone doing a great fat fart. Mrs Skeet leapt out of the chair. Her face matched the colour of her turban.

Harry was hugging himself and giggling. "Really, Mrs Skeet!" he said in a shocked voice, "would you like to go to the toilet?"

"Harry!" shouted Bert, "mind your manners."

Harry looked hurt. "I was only trying to cheer her up a bit like Mum said."

"It's all right," Emily said kindly to Mrs Skeet. "We know it wasn't you doing the fart."

"Emily! You're making things worse. Just leave it now," said Bert.

"Harry put his whoopee cushion on your chair," explained Laura. "It was supposed to be a joke."

"Hmph," said Mrs Skeet, smoothing down her dress.

"I'm sorry," said Bert and glared at Harry. "My son has a mischievous sense of humour. Please ignore him and come and sit over here." He took a deep breath and clasped his hands together. "Now then, what would you like to drink, Mrs Skeet? A glass of wine perhaps?"

She drew herself up haughtily. "No thank you, I never imbibe. Leastways, not alcohol."

"Oh, that's a pity," said Bert, looking flattened. "Er, what about a soft drink then?"

"No, thank you – don't want to ruin me appetite."

"Oh," said Bert, "oh, well, um… look, er, lunch won't be too long I don't suppose. I'll just go and see if I can give Gertie a hand." He gave the children a warning frown and disappeared into the kitchen, leaving the three of them with Mrs Skeet who gazed straight in front of her, every now and again patting her turban.

"Er, would you like to come and see my cart?" asked Harry after a moment or two of silence.

Mrs Skeet swivelled her head round and looked at him frostily. "Your cart?"

"Yes, it's nearly finished, 'cept for the wheels. Don't suppose you've got an old pram, have you? I need some wheels you see. I could give you a ride when it's finished, if you like."

"No," she replied stiffly, "I haven't a pram. The dump's the place to find an old pram."

Harry's face brightened. "The dump!" he cried. "I never thought of that! That's really cool. I'll give you a ride as soon as I've finished it, I promise."

"Really?" said Mrs Skeet. "And where do you suppose I'd want to go in your cart?" She sniffed and looked down her nose.

"Well, I dunno," said Harry, thinking. "I could take you up the road to the newspaper shop I suppose, or you might like to go to the junk shop, which is quite interesting. I nearly bought an old thing in there the other day. A bath chair – all made of wicker it was so it would float in your bath and you could lie back and enjoy yourself."

"Is that so?" said Mrs Skeet. "Well, if I were you I wouldn't want to go in that shop."

"Why not?" Laura asked.

"Mr B. S. Leach is not a man to be trusted," she said darkly. "Mr Blood Sucker Leach, that's what I call 'im.

The children looked at each other knowingly.

A little while later Bert came back, carrying the roast chicken. "Lunch is ready everyone," he announced with relief. "Gertie's just dishing up, so come on over and sit down."

Uncle Wilf appeared as Gertie came in from the kitchen with the vegetable dishes.

They all sat down and Bert started to carve. Mrs Skeet picked up her fork and examined it closely. The plates were passed down the table until everyone was served with chicken and roast potatoes, and they all helped themselves to the carrots and peas.

"What's this then?" said Mrs Skeet suspiciously, poking at the stuffing.

"Stuffing, Mrs Skeet," said Gertie cheerfully.

"Stuffing Mrs Skeet, that's funny," said Harry with a giggle.

"Harry!" warned Bert.

"Can't eat stuffing," said Mrs Skeet firmly, putting down her knife and fork.

"Oh, well – never mind," said Gertie. "I think you'll enjoy my vegetables. They're from the allotment," she added proudly. "I dug and picked them this morning, so they're really fresh."

"Is that so?" said Mrs Skeet. She looked at them closely. "Hope they've been well cleaned. The little girl down the road got worms from eating the soil in the garden."

"Did she really? We're learning all about worms at school," said Laura. "Some kinds live inside you and eat up all your food, you know."

"Yes, tape worms are best," said Harry. "They're flat and white and as long as anything, and they live in your stomach for years and years. You die if you've got more than one."

"Shut up, Harry," said Bert, glowering at him.

Mrs Skeet cut one of her carrots in half and peered at it. "'Course you can't help thinking about all those people starving in Africa," she said mournfully. "Makes you feel guilty, doesn't it when we've got all this." She waved her fork.

"Let's change the subject," said Uncle Wilf, leaning towards her. "Look, dear lady, if I'm not very much mistaken, you've got the wish bone."

"Well, blow me down, so I have," said Mrs Skeet, and for the first time she smiled.

"And we've got crackers too," said Uncle Wilf. "It's just like Christmas come early, isn't it?"

The apple crumble was delicious and Emily felt proud because she'd helped to make it. Everyone, even Mrs Skeet, made a clean plate.

"As it's your birthday," said Gertie, going over to the sideboard and bringing back a bottle, "why don't we have a little treat?"

"What have we got here then?" asked Uncle Wilf, dangling his glasses from his ear and reaching for the bottle. "Ah – sloe gin – my favourite!"

Mrs Skeet smiled broadly. "Me grandfather used to make slow gin when I was a girl. Always let us kiddies have a drop he did."

"Did he?" asked Bert in surprise. "Would you like some now?"

"Oh yes, very partial I am to it. 'Course I haven't had it since I was a wee mite. Made from blackcurrants and sugar, isn't it and takes a long time to mature – that why it's called Slow. And, of course, the beauty of it is, it's not alcoholic. Grandfather was teetotal, you know."

"What's teetotal?" asked Harry.

"It's someone who doesn't drink anything with alcohol in it," said Uncle Wilf.

Emily was puzzled. They'd got it wrong. She and Mum had helped Auntie Pam to make sloe gin once when they stayed with her in Gloucestershire – it wasn't made with blackcurrants at all. You pick lots of sloe berries, which are black and very bitter, then you prick them all over with a pin and plop them one by one into a bottle of gin with lots of sugar. You shake the bottle every day and wait for weeks till it's ready to drink. She'd never had any though because they went home before it was ready, and anyway, Mum said it wasn't something little girls drink because it's got lots of alcohol in it, which makes people drunk.

Uncle Wilf poured some into a glass for Mrs Skeet, helped himself and then passed the bottle down the table to Bert and Gertie. "Cheers," he said and Emily saw him wink. The tips of his ears had turned pink again.

"Cheers," said Mrs Skeet, taking a large mouthful. "My, but this takes me back."

She smacked her lips and leaned back in her chair. The others watched her in amazement. "Aren't the children allowed a tot?" she asked, "After all, it is a kiddies' drink."

"Well, just this once," said Bert and poured each of them a thimbleful. "Cheers everyone."

"Happy Christmas," said Mrs Skeet, taking a gulp. Her pale face had flushed to a rhubarb pink.

"'Course we should play games now," she announced, smiling happily.

Gertie's jaw dropped and they stared at Mrs Skeet.

"Yes, of course, dear lady," said Uncle Wilf quickly, topping up her glass. "What games do you know?"

"I've got some good riddles," said Emily eagerly. She thought for a moment. "I know, what did the number nought say to the number eight?"

"I don't know," said Bert, crinkling up his eyes, "what did the number nought say to the number eight?"

"I like your belt!" said Emily.

Everyone laughed except Mrs Skeet, who looked down at her plate with a puzzled expression before suddenly letting out a whoop of laughter and slapping her hand on the table, making the plates jump.

"How about this one then?" Emily continued. "Well, it's a joke really, not a riddle," and she told the one about the Irishman who wanted to buy a potato clock. It was one of her best jokes, which nobody had heard before and they all laughed, Mrs Skeet most of all.

"And then there's this one," Mrs Skeet said and hiccupped. She told a very long joke, giggling all the way through it, which she said was called a Shaggy Dog Story.

Again everyone laughed and Mrs Skeet drank some more sloe gin.

"Let's pull the crackers now," said Harry, holding one out to Mrs Skeet.

It went off with a splendid crack and she caught the yellow paper hat and novelty, which fell onto the table next to her.

"Well, it's a pity I can't put on the 'at," she said, looking disappointed.

"Why do you always wear a turban?" Harry asked suddenly. "Maybe you should take it off."

"Harry!" warned Bert.

Mrs Skeet looked Harry full in the eye with not a glimmer of a smile on her face and Emily held her breath.

"Because I'm as bald as a coot," she replied slowly.

"I don't believe you!" challenged Harry.

Mrs Skeet drained her glass, then lifted her hands to her head and whipped off the scarlet turban. A shocked silence followed as they stared at the awful shining baldness – then, with no sense of embarrassment at all, she unfolded the yellow paper crown and put it on.

"There!" she said triumphantly.

"Mrs Skeet, you haven't pulled your wish bone," Uncle Wilf said when they'd all recovered. She'd taken it off her plate and it was lying on the table next to her.

"Oh, you're right," she said. "Well then, I'm going to make a very special wish as it's my birthday and all."

"You mustn't tell us what it is or it won't come true!" Laura reminded her.

"Oh, I know that," said Mrs Skeet and shut her eyes tightly. For nearly half a minute she sat there and everyone waited in silence, watching her.

"That's done then," she whispered.

"Happy birthday, dear lady," said Uncle Wilf, raising his glass. "And may your wish come true."

Chapter 11

Gertie Wins First Prize

A few days after Mrs Skeet's birthday lunch, Uncle Wilf took Harry to the dump, but they couldn't find a pram with the right sort of wheels – modern prams were no good and there were no old-fashioned ones there. Instead, they brought back two old wheelie bins. Uncle Wilf said they could take the wheels off those and fit them to the cart. Harry was excited and wanted to get on with it straight away and was disappointed when Uncle Wilf told him he'd have to wait for a couple of days, as he was busy helping Gertie get her plants ready for the Horticultural Summer Show at the weekend.

The weather had turned very hot and Gertie was fussing around, worried that her flowers would wilt. The morning of the show, she and Uncle Wilf went over to the village hall first thing, to lay out her exhibits ready for the judging. She'd entered three classes: sweet peas, runner beans and lettuces. Laura, Harry and Emily went over in the afternoon with Bert after the judging had taken place, to see how she'd got on.

Crowds of people were milling around and at first they couldn't see Gertie. All the windows were open because it was hot and stuffy in the hall. The exhibits were laid out on trestle tables, and as well as the flowers, fruit and vegetables, there were pots of jam and all sorts of cakes and pies that people had made. The sweet peas were together, down one side of the hall – all the colours of the rainbow, just like Uncle Wilf had said. Dozens of vases crowded the tables and the scent was wonderful. The children searched for the name of the winner and spotted it almost immediately.

Emily let out a squeal of excitement: 'Gertie Pink' – the name was written on a little card with a red star on it and 'First' printed beside it. She was so pleased – Gertie deserved to come first. Then, she looked to see who'd come second – and there it was, a card with a blue star and 'Colin Rowe' written on it, with 'Second' printed next to it.

Emily put her nose down to Gertie's vase and breathed in the beautiful scent. As she straightened up, she became aware of another, unpleasant smell wafting around and wrinkled her nose, wondering what it could be. Turning her head, she jumped to find Coddie Rowe standing right behind, scowling, and realised at once what the smell was – fish. Not really surprising, she thought – he's a fishmonger and Coddie's a really good name for him. He looked like a cod and he smelt like one too and he was angry because he hadn't come first like he usually did.

She pushed her way past him and caught sight of Gertie, standing on the other side of the hall in the vegetable section, looking flushed and excited. People kept congratulating her because she'd done so well, coming first in all three classes she'd entered. Uncle Wilf stood nearby, smiling and nodding and twinkling.

After they'd looked at everything Harry, Laura and Emily decided to go home and started to make their way through the crowd towards the door. They could see Lip-Up Stinky, standing on his own near the cake table, looking bored as usual. Glancing round to make sure no-one was watching, he stuck his fingers into one of the cakes, scooped up some icing and shoved it into his mouth. Emily was shocked. It had happened so quickly that she'd been the only one to see it.

"Let's call in at the allotment on the way back and see if our seeds have come up," said Laura.

"We'll probably find lots of little zebras running round all over the place, won't we Emily?" teased Harry, giving her a friendly shove.

Laura and Emily had been good at remembering to water their seeds every day and they'd whispered nice things to Hermione and Hattie. Harry had watered Hanky Panky, but he refused to whisper to her because he said it made him feel daft.

The girls did high skips all the way along the road till they came to the allotment and then the three of them dashed over to Gertie's patch of land, which was on the far side, near the gate into the lane, which ran along the bottom of the Pinks' garden.

"Look!" Laura shouted, pointing excitedly. "All six of them have come up – even Holly, Hayley and Hiccups."

"There, you see," said Harry triumphantly. "They've all come up. Which proves that Uncle Wilf was wrong, doesn't it? I told him all that whispering was a stupid idea."

Emily went and knelt down beside Hattie. She was tiny, with only two little leaves. Was she really going to grow into a great tall sunflower? It was hard to believe it, but Emily was going to give her all the encouragement she could.

"Well done, Hattie!" she whispered. "You're looking great. I just know you're going to be the biggest and most beautiful sunflower in the whole world!"

At the end of the afternoon Uncle Wilf, Gertie and Bert returned from the show. Emily had never seen Gertie looking so happy. She kept laughing and blushing and they were all so pleased for her. She pinned her certificates up on the notice board in the kitchen so that they could all see them.

"Thanks, Uncle Wilf," she said, giving him a huge hug, which nearly squashed him.

"I could never have done it without you."

"I don't think Coddie was too pleased," chuckled Bert. "It must be the first time in years that he hasn't carried off first prize for his sweet peas."

"Well, yes, to tell you the truth, he did look pretty mad, didn't he, Uncle Wilf?" said Gertie. Her eyes were sparkling. "He even tried to argue with the judge, but she wasn't having any of it and told him not to be a bad sport. He didn't like that at all! Anyway, he got second prize so he didn't do too badly. He can't expect to win every time."

"Oh I think he does," said Uncle Wilf.

That night, Emily dropped off to sleep straight away and she dreamed about Hattie. She'd grown so tall that she'd disappeared right up into the clouds and the judge didn't have a long enough tape measure to reach her.

Suddenly, she woke. The house was quiet, but she could hear an owl hooting nearby. She lay still, listening to Laura's gentle breathing and tried to go back to sleep, but she knew she needed the loo. She hated walking down the corridor in the middle of the night in case she met the pirate. Uncle Wilf had promised that he'd make him stay up in the attic, but what was to stop him wandering around when Uncle Wilf was asleep? She tried to persuade herself that she didn't really want the loo, but finally she had no choice but to get out of bed and opened the door quietly, so as not to disturb anyone.

It was dark in the corridor, so she switched on the light and tiptoed along to the door at the end. The opening to the attic was above the toilet door and there was a ladder hanging from it.

She went to the loo but didn't flush it, not wanting to make a noise and wake everyone up. As she opened the door and crept back out into the corridor, she was startled to hear Uncle Wilf's voice coming from above. At first, she thought he must be talking in his sleep, although she couldn't hear what he was saying. Then, to her surprise, she heard another voice – one she didn't recognise, a deeper one. It sounded angry. It wasn't Bert's voice, she was sure of that. So whose could it be?

It suddenly dawned on her, with a feeling of horror, that it must be the pirate! But Uncle Wilf had said that he couldn't hear him, although he could see him. Well, she could certainly hear him – if that really was the pirate he was talking to. Who else could it be?

The talking stopped. She stood there for several seconds, too frightened to move, and then ran back down the corridor as fast as she could and jumped into bed with Laura.

"Laura, Laura," she cried, pinching her. "Oh, Laura, please wake up!!"

"Mmmmm."

She pinched her again, harder. "Oh, Laura, do please wake up – I've just heard the pirate up in the attic!"

"Ouch, stop it!" Laura said, turning away.

"Laura, wake up please, I'm so scared!" She switched on the bedside lamp and Laura turned towards her, screwing her eyes up against the light.

"What's the matter?" she said. "Shut up and stop pinching me!"

"I went along to the loo and I heard someone up in the attic talking to Uncle Wilf! It must have been the pirate!"

Laura rubbed her eyes. "Well, we know he's up in the attic and that's where he's going to stay. Don't worry, Emily – and go back to sleep." She yawned and shut her eyes again.

"Yes, I know," Emily said, "but Uncle Wilf said he could only see Jack, he couldn't hear him. But I could hear him."

"Could you? What did he say?"

"I couldn't hear what they were saying because it was all muffled."

Laura yawned again. "Emily, are you sure you weren't having a bad dream?"

"No, it wasn't a dream."

"Look, stop worrying," she said again. "It'll be all right, you'll see. Uncle Wilf's not going to let him out of the attic – he promised!" It was obvious she wasn't going to talk about it anymore.

"Can I stay in bed with you?" Emily asked.

"Oh, I suppose so. But lie still – you're not to wriggle around. Just go to sleep, Em."

It took Emily a long time to get back to sleep, especially as she had to try and lie flat and straight, like an Egyptian mummy all night.

The next morning she was still feeling frightened about the pirate. It seemed so strange that she could hear him as well as see him. She lay in bed, thinking about it and wondering what to do. It wasn't very comfortable in the same bed as Laura and she was too hot. She'd been awake since the room started to get light and she could hear the birds in the garden. She decided to get up.

She got dressed quietly and crept downstairs – it was Sunday, so everyone else would be having a good old lie-in. The sitting room was filled with the scent of the sweet peas

Gertie had brought back from the show. She'd filled every vase with them.

The first thing Emily always did when she came downstairs was to take the cover off Autolocus's cage and say good morning to him, but because it was so early and she didn't want him to make a noise, she decided to put him in the garden and let him listen to the dawn chorus. He looked at her with his head on one side, as if wondering if she was going to let him have a fly around. She carried the cage down to the bottom of the garden and put it under a bush near the greenhouse, so that he'd be in the shade when the sun came out.

"I'll let you out later," she told him, opening the door of his cage and putting some more food in his dish. "I'm going to write a letter to Mum now."

She walked back to the house and took some writing paper out of the drawer in the sideboard and sat down at the table. She hadn't wanted to worry Mum when she'd spoken to her on the phone because she knew she wasn't well, but she needed to tell her things. This is what she wrote:

Dear Mum,

I hope you are feeling better. There is a parrot here and I look after him. There is also a pirate who is a ghost. He lives in the attic with Uncle Wilf and I can see him and hear him as well. I have two sunflowers. They are called Hattie and Hayley. Hattie is the one I whisper to. I saw your box in a shop and it was stolen. The man in the shop is called Blood Sucker Leach and he is like Dracula.

Love from Emily.

After breakfast, Harry and Laura took Izzie for her walk, but Emily wanted to stay and tell Gertie what had happened in the night. Uncle Wilf and Bert must have been having a lie-in because they hadn't come down for breakfast, so she had Gertie all to herself. Nobody had mentioned the pirate since Uncle Wilf had been told to keep him up in the attic. I suppose they've just decided to forget all about him, Emily thought. She had the feeling that they didn't really believe in him anyway, in spite of what Uncle Wilf had said.

When Emily told Gertie that she'd heard two voices in the attic Gertie just said, "I think you've been dreaming, Emily love," and put the cereal bowls away in the cupboard. "Now let's have that letter you've written to Mum and I'll put it in an envelope and find the address." She bustled about the kitchen, tidying things away.

"I've got some pineapple pieces left over from last night. Would you like to give one to Autolocus? Where is he, by the way?"

Emily was disappointed that Gertie wouldn't take her seriously. "I put him outside when I came down," she said. "It was nice and cool in the garden and all the birds were singing. I wish he didn't have to be in his cage all the time."

"I know," said Gertie. "But anyway, I think you'd better bring him in again now. The sun's starting to get hot and there's not much shade out there."

As Emily opened the back door and looked outside, a blackbird gave its warning call and flew up into a tree. She walked down towards the greenhouse and stopped, her heart thudding. Something awful had happened – she couldn't believe it – the door of the cage was open! Oh no! It couldn't be! She raced towards it and peered inside. The cage was empty.

Autolocus had gone.

Chapter 12

Autolocus Disappears

Emily's stomach was in a tight knot and she felt sick. Where could he be? She looked all around, hoping she'd hear a burp and see Autolocus hopping about on the grass, but there was no sign of him anywhere in the small garden. Perhaps he's flown over the fence into the lane, she thought. She ran through the gate, calling as she went, but he wasn't there, so she tore along to where the lane passed by the allotments. Several people she'd often seen before were tending their plots of land, digging, weeding and watering their plants. She ran from one to another, asking if they'd seen Autolocus, but nobody had.

She stood there, not knowing what to do. She remembered Uncle Wilf telling her that Autolocus's wings needed clipping from time to time to stop him flying very far, and she knew that they hadn't been done since she came to live with the Pinks. That meant Autolocus could have flown anywhere by now!

She tried to stay calm, but her heart was hammering and she was sweating. She thought back to what had happened earlier that morning: she'd taken the cage into the garden so Autolocus wouldn't wake everyone up, and he could enjoy being outside before the day got too hot. She remembered filling up his dish with more parrot food, and she was sure she'd closed the door of the cage – she was always careful about that. But it must have been my fault that he got out, she thought. Nobody else had been near the cage. I should never have put him outside in the garden and then just left him there, all on his own. Oh, this was too awful! What was she going to say to Uncle Wilf? He'd be heartbroken, she knew.

She ran back from the allotments, into the lane and on past the gate into the Pinks' garden, calling as she went, but there was no trace of Autolocus. When she got to the end of the lane where it met the road, she was out of breath and turned round and walked slowly back to the house.

As she came through the gate, she saw that the back door was open and could hear Harry and Laura in the kitchen, talking to Gertie. The next minute Izzie came rushing down the garden to meet her and nearly knocked her over. She sat down heavily on the grass and burst into tears. She wanted to be sick.

They must have seen her from the kitchen window because when she looked up, Gertie, Harry and Laura were standing round her, all talking at once.

"What's happened?"

"Whatever's the matter, Em? Are you OK?"

"I think Izzie must have knocked her down."

They're all being so kind, but they don't know what I've done yet, she thought.

She was sobbing so hard she couldn't speak.

Gertie knelt down and put her arms round her. "There, there, Emily, don't cry – you're all right, aren't you? What's happened, love?"

She buried her face against Gertie, knowing she was going to have to own up. At last she turned and pointed to the empty cage by the greenhouse.

"He's escaped," she whispered, tears streaming down her face. "Autolocus has got out!"

"Oh no!" said Gertie and they all stared at the cage. Then Harry and Laura ran round the garden, looking under the hedge, behind the greenhouse and even out in the lane, calling his name, but it was no use.

"I'm sure he won't have gone far," said Gertie. "Have you looked out at the front, Emily?" She told them that she'd been along the back lane and into the allotments.

"Right then," said Gertie, taking charge. "Harry and Laura, you go round the front and look up and down the close, but don't go into the main road, and then come straight back here. Emily and I'll have another look down the lane. We'll meet here again in 10 minutes."

This is the most awful time of my life, Emily thought. How could she have been so stupid? Uncle Wilf had trusted her with Autolocus and she'd let him escape. What was she going to say to him?

Gertie took her hand and they went through the gate.

"You say you're sure the cage door was properly shut when you put him outside?" asked Gertie, walking so briskly that she had to run to keep up. "You're always so careful."

Emily wiped her eyes and nose on the bottom of her T-shirt and tried to stop the sobs which kept jumping out of her chest. "I'm positive I did," she managed to say.

"Do you think he could have opened it himself?"

"He's never done it before – I'm sure he didn't know how to. Oh, Gertie, what are we going to do? I'm so sorry!"

They walked to the allotments and then along the lane past the house in the other direction, just as she'd done earlier, but with no luck. By now the sun was very hot.

When they got back to the house, the twins were standing by the greenhouse, looking glum. It was obvious they'd had no luck either.

"We looked in all the gardens and called and called, but we didn't see him anywhere," said Harry. "He could be miles away by now; we're never going to find him."

"That's not very helpful, Harry," said Gertie. "Now, we need to think about this calmly. There's no point rushing about like mad things. Let's go inside for a moment or two and have a cold drink."

Emily felt sure there was something they should be doing, but she didn't know what.

They followed Gertie inside and she poured out some orange squash and put ice in it. It made a nice cracking sound.

"Where's Uncle Wilf?" Emily asked fearfully, looking through into the sitting room. She was dreading having to tell him. "Is he still upstairs?"

"No, he came down just before we had breakfast and I asked him if he'd take some sweet peas round to Mrs Skeet. There were so many of them after the show and I'd run out of vases to put them in. He seemed in a funny sort of mood and didn't want any breakfast. Not like him at all."

"Could he have taken Autolocus with him?" suggested Laura. He knows Mrs Skeet likes him a lot."

"No, I'd have remembered if he had," said Gertie. "No, he just picked the sweet peas up and went straight out of the front door with them."

They sat down and Emily took a gulp of orange squash and tried to feel calmer, but the knot in her tummy was still there.

"Have you any idea what time it was that you put Autolocus out into the garden?" asked Gertie. "We need to get some idea how long he's been missing."

"I don't know," Emily said, "but you were all still asleep when I came downstairs. That was why I put him outside – I didn't want him to wake everyone up."

"He's probably been gone quite a while then," said Gertie gloomily. They sat round the table in silence. Suddenly, Firefly and Josephina came running through the back door and Firefly jumped up on Laura's lap. She stroked her absent-mindedly.

"He could have been killed by a cat, you know," said Harry, "he doesn't fly very well."

"Oh, don't," Emily squealed, putting her hands over her ears.

"Shut up, Harry," said Gertie. "What I think is that he's probably gone for a bit of an explore and he'll come back when he's hungry."

"But how did he get out?" said Laura, twirling her pony tail furiously round and round. "Emily said she's sure she shut the cage door. So… do you know what I think? I think someone's stolen him!" They stared at her in horror. "Well they could have, you know," she went on. "Suppose someone was walking along the lane, just passing by our gate, and they heard Autolocus squawking like he does, and asking for rum or something. They might just have opened the gate to have a look and then seen him and decided to take him."

"That's an awful thought, Laura!" said Gertie.

"Well, parrots who can talk cost a lot of money," said Harry. "Wow! That could have been what happened you know – I bet someone's stolen him."

The clock on the wall ticked gently and the ice in the glasses clinked, and Firefly purred as Laura stroked her under her chin. But Emily felt as if she was sitting on an ants' nest. She couldn't sit still, she was so worried.

Thoughts were racing round in her head – was Autolocus still alive? Was he hurt? How long had he been missing? Had he flown away because he wanted to be free? Or… or had someone taken him?

Then, all of a sudden a face swam into her mind. Swam was a good way of putting it because… because it was a fishy face! Coddie Rowe's face! Suppose… Just suppose it had been Codie Rowe who'd been walking along the lane on his way to the allotment, and he'd heard Autolocus as he passed the gate. He'd have recognised his voice, that's for sure, and maybe he'd taken him, to punish Gertie for beating him at the show. It was certainly a possibility. But just as she was about to speak, Gertie pushed back her chair and got to her feet.

"We can't just sit here any longer - I'm going to ring and report it to the police," she announced and went out of the room.

Nobody said anything for a moment. Harry was crunching a lump of ice between his teeth.

"Do you know what I think?" Emily said at last.

"What?" said Harry and Laura together.

"I think," she said slowly, "that Coddie Rowe could have taken him!"

Laura gasped and Harry's mouth fell open.

"Well, Gertie said he was really angry when she won all the prizes at the show," Emily went on, "so maybe he took Autolocus… to get his own back!"

The two of them stared at her. "But why would he want Autolocus – he didn't like him," said Laura.

"Maybe he's just done it to give Gertie a scare," Emily said. "And he'll bring him back."

"Wow!" said Harry, banging his hand down on the table. "I bet that's what's happened. But he won't bring him back, you know - he's stolen him and he'll sell him and get a lot of money for himself."

"Somebody would have seen him though, wouldn't they?" Laura argued. "If he was walking down the lane with him."

"Well, it was very early in the morning – we were all still in bed, weren't we?" said Harry excitedly. "Maybe he was on his way to the allotment and he took Autolocus out of his cage and put him in a sack and hid him in his shed. Then, when it's dark tonight, he'll take him home and then he'll sell him."

Emily sat there, horrified. Poor Autolocus – he'd be so frightened. They could hear Gertie on the phone in the next room. She sounded as if she was having an argument.

"Let's go down to the allotments and see if Coddie's there," Laura said, shooing Firefly off her lap and jumping to her feet.

"Wait a minute, stupid," shouted Harry. "Suppose he is there – are you going to go up to him and ask him if he's taken Autolocus? What do you think he's going to say, stupid?"

"Don't keep calling me stupid," Laura shouted back. "If he's there, we'll look and see what he's doing and then we'll go back later. But if he's not there, we can look through the window of his shed and see if we can see Autolocus."

"We'd hear him, wouldn't we?" Emily pointed out.

"Not if he's all tied up in a sack," said Harry. "Come on, let's go."

They raced out of the back door, almost knocking over Uncle Wilf and Mrs Skeet, who were coming round the corner. "Somebody's in a hurry," Mrs Skeet shouted after them as they raced down to the gate at the bottom of the garden.

It was the third time that morning that Emily had been along the lane. Harry reached the allotments first. Laura and Emily were hard on his heels and both of them crashed into him because he suddenly stopped dead and pointed. Ahead, with his back towards them was Coddie Rowe. He was digging a trench. On the ground by his side was a sack. The door of his shed was closed. Apart from one other person right over on the far side of the allotments, nobody else was about.

Emily suddenly had the most horrible thought and she could feel her legs go all wobbly.

"He's killed Autolocus," she whispered, "He's in the sack and he's going to bury him in the ground!"

She could feel the tears starting to run down her face again.

Chapter 13

Uncle Wilf Explains

Harry and Laura raced along the lane ahead of Emily, but she was in no hurry to get back - besides, her legs were so wobbly she wouldn't have been able to run. Poor Autolocus! She couldn't bear to think about what had happened to him. How could Coddie do such a dreadful thing? She should never have put Autolocus out in the garden on his own. There was no one else to blame - it was all her own stupid fault!

What was she going to say to Uncle Wilf?

She dragged herself along, dreading what he would say when she told him. But then she realised that of course he'd know by now – the others would have told him – and they'd all be waiting for her – in the kitchen! And Bert would be there as well, and Mrs Skeet. She felt trapped.

Just before she reached the gate, she felt sure she was going to be sick and crouched down in the grass that grew tall at the edge of the path. She retched, but nothing happened. After a few moments she got up again and wiped her face on her T-shirt. Then, with a start, she realised someone was standing right behind her. She turned quickly. It was Uncle Wilf!

"Emily, little love" he said gently, it's all right, you know, it's all right."

She looked up at him – and he was smiling! She burst into tears again and felt her whole body shaking with heavy sobs.

"It's all right," he kept saying, "it's all right. Come on into the house now, Emily, and I'll explain. There's an awful lot you don't know." He handed her a big white handkerchief and she took it gratefully and wiped her face and blew her nose loudly.

Putting his arm round her shoulders, they walked up the path to the house. Gertie was standing on the kitchen doorstep, and she ran forward and gave Emily a hug as they came through the door.

As she'd dreaded, everyone was in the kitchen, including Izzie, Firefly and Josephina – everyone except Autolocus. She looked round nervously. She could feel them all looking at her and wanted to run out of the door.

"Can we sit down for a minute?" said Uncle Wilf. "This little lady's in a bit of a state and I've got something I want to tell you."

He stood there, facing them, like a teacher at school. Everyone obediently found somewhere to sit and looked at him expectantly. He took off his glasses, polished them on the bottom of his shirt, and put them on again. Then, he cleared his throat and began to speak.

"It's several weeks now since I was blown in here on the night of that terrible storm – eight weeks to be exact. And for quite a lot of that time, as you know, I've been sleeping up in the attic. That's suited me very well and I'm very grateful to you, Bert and Gertie for letting me stay." He looked round at them and his eyes were clear and green like the sea. "The trouble is," he went on "my friend, the pirate, has been making life very difficult for me recently."

"Oh not that again, Uncle Wilf," said Gertie, in exasperation. "Do you honestly think we believe in all that nonsense? You and your pirate ghost! It makes a good tale, but that's all it is – a fairy tale! And what's it got to do with

97

the parrot for goodness sake? We ought not to be wasting time with rubbish when we could be out looking for him."

Emily knew then that they'd told Uncle Wilf about Autolocus disappearing. But had they told him how it had happened?

"Hang on a minute, Gertie, let me finish," said Uncle Wilf patiently, holding up his hand. "This is all to do with Autolocus's disappearance." He looked down at the floor and ran his hand through his bushy hair, as if struggling to find the right words.

"I know you find it difficult to believe me because, as you know, I can be a bit of a leg-puller at times." He looked up and grinned. Then, his face became serious again as he said, "But what I'm going to tell you now is the straight up and down truth."

He took a deep breath.

"As I've already said, the pirate was living at Cliff House when I first went there. No, no, not living," he corrected himself, "because he's been dead for a few hundred years – I suppose I mean haunting. His ghost was there when I first moved in."

"Get on with you, Uncle Wilf," Gertie interrupted impatiently, "pull the other one!"

"Shhhh, Gert," said Bert. "Let him finish. I want to hear what he's got to say."

"Now a lot of this is guesswork," Uncle Wilf continued, "because, as I've already told you, I can't hear what Jack says. He talks a lot and I know he'd like me to understand, but I just can't hear him. I can see him perfectly well - he looks like the sort of regular cut-throat buccaneer you see pictures of in story books."

"Like in *Treasure Island*," interrupted Harry.

"Exactly," said Uncle Wilf. "And Emily here and Mrs Skeet and Izzie too all saw him that night when I was in hospital. Isn't that right?" He looked questioningly at Mrs Skeet and Emily and they nodded in agreement.

"Proper hooligan he was," said Mrs Skeet, "with his torn shirt and a patch over his eye."

"And he had a big hat on his head, didn't he?" Emily reminded her.

"Yes, that's him all right," nodded Uncle Wilf. "He's a pretty terrifying sight, but believe me, he's quite harmless. Well now, back in the 17th century the seas were full of pirate ships, and buccaneers like my pirate sailed around robbing and plundering. I've no idea what happened to him – how he died, or why his ghost haunted Cliff House. There was obviously some connection; perhaps he was born there or lived there at one time, I don't know. Anyway, after Cliff House was washed into the sea, he escaped with me and he's been living up in the attic with me now for several weeks. He's been pretty good, as far as I know, and hasn't strayed into other parts of the house. But he's been getting very restless, as you might imagine. A pirate, who's been used to a life of adventure on the high seas, must find it a trifle boring being cooped up in an attic all day and night."

Emily sat listening to Uncle Wilf and then glanced over at Gertie and Bert and wondered how much of his story they believed. After all, they hadn't seen the pirate ghost, and nor had Harry and Laura.

"Anyway, last night we had an argument," continued Uncle Wilf. "It's been building up for some time, this restlessness of his."

"How can you have an argument with someone if you can't hear them?" demanded Bert and Emily could see he had a good point.

"It was late last night," continued Uncle Wilf, "and he was pacing up and down, up and down, gesturing wildly, waving his cutlass and shouting too, but of course, I couldn't hear him. But I knew he was trying to tell me that he needed to get out, and I kept insisting that he'd got to stay in the attic. I could see that he was furious!"

Emily realised this must have been what she'd heard the night before when she went to the loo. She'd heard a loud, booming voice, which must have been the pirate's, although she couldn't make out what he was saying. She wondered if she would be able to understand him if he and she were face to face. The thought terrified her.

"So, how did this 'argument' end?" Gertie demanded.

"Well, he's had these fits of restlessness before," said Uncle Wilf, "and when he does, he just ups and offs – goes off on a sort of holiday, a walk-about, rather like the Aborigines in Australia. I think he time travels – goes back to the good-old days when he was pirating on the high seas, visits some of his old haunts, but he always comes back."

"This story gets more and more outrageous," spluttered Bert, getting to his feet and opening the door of the fridge. He took out a can of beer and sat down again. "You still haven't told us how your argument ended."

"I told him to shut up," said Uncle Wilf, "but when I woke up this morning he'd gone! And I discovered he'd done what he did last time – he'd taken Autolocus with him!"

Emily gasped. Did this mean that it wasn't her fault that Autolocus had disappeared? The pirate must have taken Autuolocus out of his cage while she was in the house, writing to Mum. So he wasn't dead! Oh, she was so relieved.

"B-b-b-but," she found herself stammering, "how can you be sure? Where's he gone? Will he be all right and will he come back again?"

"Well, if it's anything like the last couple of times, he'll be having a ball," said Uncle Wilf, chuckling. "It's like a vacation for him, I suppose. The two of them'll be back in a week or so, exhausted but happy. Didn't you wonder where Autolocus picked up all those expressions of his – about passing the rum and so on? He got them from the pirate, which of course means that Autolocus can hear him, even if I can't."

"I can hear him too," Emily said quietly.

They looked at her and Laura said excitedly, "That's what you told me in the night, didn't you Em? I remember now, and I thought you'd been dreaming."

"Yes," she said, "when I went along the passage to the loo last night, I could hear two voices coming from the attic. One was yours, Uncle Wilf, and the other one must have been the pirate's."

"Oh blithering heck fire, that's amazing!" shouted Uncle Wilf, punching the air.

"It means that when they come back you'll be able to ask him all sorts of things that I've always wanted to know. This is wonderful, wonderful!"

"But, Uncle Wilf," said Laura. "Someone else could have come through the gate and taken him. How do you know for sure it was the pirate?"

"Because he's done it before," replied Uncle Wilf. "And because he always leaves me a message."

"A message?" said Gertie. "But if you can't hear…"

"No – it wasn't a spoken message," said Uncle Wilf "He left one of Autolocus's feathers on my pillow, that's how I know."

Chapter 14

Summer Holidays

The next couple of weeks seemed to fly past. Every night before she got into bed Emily wrote down what had happened that day, using an old notepad Gertie had given her. She wondered when she'd be going home – back to that dreary third-floor flat. Mum had written every week and they often spoke on the phone, but it was ages since she'd seen her and now she'd gone to stay with Auntie Pam in Gloucestershire till she was really better. Emily missed her, but felt a bit guilty too because she loved living with Gertie and her family – it was really great.

Uncle Wilf didn't seem to be in any hurry to find somewhere else to live and sold his car to help pay for his keep. Everyone liked having him around, although Gertie was always saying the house wasn't big enough – too many people and too much clutter. The twins' friends from school used to come round to play and the sitting room was often strewn with "samples" that Bert brought back from the market. Plus, Laura was in the habit of leaving her painting stuff all over the place and Gertie was forever telling her to clear it away so she could lay the table. Poor Gertie used to get fed up and started entering competitions to win a bigger house.

"I'd just like a bit more space," she'd cry, throwing her arms in the air.

Every day Emily wondered what the pirate and Autolocus were up to and if they'd ever come back. If he could time travel back to the 17th century, did that mean he turned back into the pirate he'd been when he was alive? Or would he still be a ghost?

She couldn't begin to understand it and nor could anyone else. But Uncle Wilf seemed sure that he'd come back because he always had before.

"The old rogue misses me if he stays away too long," he said. "He looks on me as family."

Emily missed Autolocus and hoped he was all right. He'd always been his happiest sitting on her shoulder, nibbling her ear or chewing on a piece of fruit. She tried to imagine him living with a bunch of cut-throat pirates who drank rum and went round firing their pistols and cutting people's throats.

She gave his cage a good clean out and put fresh sawdust on the floor, and she and Laura went to the pet shop and bought him a new toy. She always made sure she left the cage door open, so he'd be able to get inside when he came back.

Soon after Autolocus and Jack disappeared Uncle Wilf helped Harry finish his cart. It was made of a long wooden box that Bert had brought back from the market. Harry had built the sides up with pieces of wood and nailed a couple of planks across, one for the driver to sit on and the other for a passenger behind. He'd done all that part by himself, but Uncle Wilf helped him to take the wheels and axles off the two old wheelie bins they'd got from the dump and fit them to the front and back of the cart, with ropes tied to the front axle so you could steer it.

To start with, Harry wouldn't let anyone else sit in his cart, only Uncle Wilf, but after a while, he let first Laura and then Emily take it in turns to be passengers behind him.

Willow Close was on a slope, which ran down to the main road, and if you took the cart up to the top end of the close and someone gave you a push to get you going, you went flying down – it was brilliant. Emily would sit on the back plank, with knees bent up and feet on either side of Harry on the front seat and her arms tight around his waist. She'd shut her eyes and squeal with delight as the cart went hurtling all the way down to the bottom of the close. Izzie wasn't allowed out of the house when they were playing on the cart because she'd run alongside barking and once, when she ran in front of it, Harry had to swerve and ended up turning the whole thing over. He got quite a bad graze on his elbow and a cut on his face, but Gertie was more worried about him running into someone walking up the hill.

"We'll fit a brake on it," said Uncle Wilf and he nailed on a piece of wood, which rubbed against the front wheel when you pushed it down. "What we need now is a bell or a hooter to warn people you're coming. That's just the sort of thing our friend Leach might have in the junk shop."

"This isn't a junk shop," said Harry, imitating Blood-Sucker Leach's voice, "I sell antiques and curios." They all giggled, Uncle Wilf most of all.

They got a marvellous old hooter from Blood Sucker's shop, which Uncle Wilf mended because it wasn't working very well. It made a fantastic honking noise when you squeezed the rubber bit. Gertie told them they could only do it to warn someone walking up the close.

"If you make too much noise, the neighbours will complain," she said.

Once Mrs Skeet came out of her garden gate when they were playing on the cart and Harry asked her if she'd like a ride, but she just sniffed and looked down her nose at him. "That parrit come back yet, has he?" she asked whenever they saw her.

As the days went by, Emily wondered if he ever would. He was probably having a wonderful time being a pirate's parrot on the high seas. Why would he want to come back? Trevor, at the pet shop, always asked about him too whenever they went in there to buy something for Izzie or the cats.

But for now, Emily had something else to look after. She couldn't believe her eyes, but what Uncle Wilf had said about their sunflowers was absolutely true. She and Laura used to go down to the allotment every day after tea to water all the sunflowers, including Harry's, because he seemed to have lost interest and they didn't want Hiccups and Hankie-Panky to shrivel up and die. Sometimes, they gave them all some liquid fertiliser too, but they only ever whispered nice things to Hermione and Hattie and that was when they were sure no-one else was listening. They felt a bit sorry for the other sunflowers, but they were determined to carry out the experiment and only talk to their two special ones.

Uncle Wilf showed them how to nip out the side shoots to make them grow stronger, and they did the same for all six sunflowers, and he stuck a strong stick into the ground by each of them and tied them to it, so they wouldn't blow down if there was a wind, although they were well protected by the shed.

By the end of the fourth week Hermione and Hattie were about half a metre taller than the others, and both had grown a lovely yellow bud. Hattie had grown as high as Emily's neck. One afternoon she told her a really funny joke she'd heard on TV and two days later she was taller than Hermione! So it did work!

There were sunflowers on quite a few of the other allotments and Emily supposed they were all going to be entered for the Tallest Sunflower Competition. All of them had been planted before theirs, so they'd had a few weeks' head start, but theirs were beginning to catch up. Coddie had about a dozen sunflowers on his patch of ground, growing next to his vegetables. Once or twice they saw him, but he usually went there early in the morning or after he'd finished work at the market.

"How long is it till the Tallest Sunflower Competition?" Emily and Laura asked Gertie one afternoon, when they got back from the allotment. She was sitting at the kitchen table filling in a coupon in a magazine – it was another competition to win a bigger house. She glanced up. "It's on the kitchen calendar – have a look," she said absent-mindedly. "Sometime in September, I think."

They turned the pages of the calendar till they got to September. There it was – Gertie had put a circle round the date – 3rd September.

"This year they're calling it 'The Tallest and Most Beautiful Sunflower Competition'," she said, "so your sunflowers have got to be beautiful as well as tall to win."

The Pinks didn't go away in the summer holidays like a lot of other families do, but sometimes on his day off Bert would take them out for the day. Gertie would pack up a picnic and they'd go off in his van to the country or to the lido where you could swim or go out in a pedalo.

From time to time, they went and helped Bert at the market. Emily loved it there, although she didn't have any money to spend. She just liked wandering around looking at all the people, and Bert sometimes bought them a hotdog in a paper bag or a doughnut from the American doughnut stall.

Coddie Rowe's fish stall wasn't far from Bert's pitch, and one day Emily went over to look at the fish they were selling. She was wearing a new T-shirt Bert had let her choose from his stall. It had star fish on it and shells and a mermaid and she was thrilled with it.

On Coddie's stand there were all sorts of fish packed in ice to keep them fresh and a large crate with live crabs all piled on top of each other. Poor things, Emily thought.

Coddie was busy serving a customer and weighing out some fish on the scales. Suddenly, Lip-Up Stinky appeared from behind the stall. He was eating chips out of a paper bag, and when he saw Emily, his funny top lip stretched sideways in a grin.

"Heard you lost that parrot of yours," he jeered. "Did he die from drinking too much rum?" He laughed at his own joke.

Emily glared and didn't answer. She'd never liked him since she heard that he didn't look after his dog properly. She hated to think of a dog that was never taken for a walk. She decided to find out why.

"What sort of dog have you got?" she asked.

Lip-Up Stinky looked surprised. "He's a golden retriever – but he's a fat lump." He paused and looked at her suspiciously. "What's that got to do with anything?"

"Oh, I just thought maybe you'd like to bring him along one day when we take Izzie to the woods – we go every morning after breakfast."

"He'd just run off if you took him to the woods," replied Lip-Up, eating the last of his chips and tossing the screwed up bag over his shoulder. "He got lost once, so we don't take him anymore."

"You could put him on a lead," Emily argued.

"He pulls too hard," replied Stinky. "Nah, he's all right – Dad takes him up to the paper shop on the lead at the weekends." He picked up a stick and starting to prod the crabs with it and giggled as they moved around trying to escape.

"I've told you before," shouted Coddie, "leave them crabs alone!"

Lip-Up pulled a face and threw down the stick, which landed at Emily's feet. Just then Harry came wandering over with his hands in his pockets.

"Bet you can't run fast in those," Lip-Up sneered, pointing at Emily's old blue flip-flops.

"Or those either," he said, pointing at Harry's sandals. He laughed. "You want to get some of these – see? They've got fantastic grips on the bottom." He was wearing an expensive-looking pair of trainers and lifted up one of his feet and showed the sole to Emily and Harry. It had an elaborate pattern of zigzag lines and circles on it. "And they've got reflectors on the heels too, so you're safe in the dark 'cos cars can see you in their headlights," he boasted. "I never wear flip-flops or sandals – they're so uncool you know."

Emily looked down at her flip-flops – an old pair of Laura's that Gertie had given her because the strap on her sandals had broken. It was true, they'd seen better days, but it hadn't bothered her before. Now she blushed, feeling uncomfortable and silly.

Lip-Up saw that she was embarrassed and laughed.

"You should get yourself a better T-shirt too. You need to grow up a bit."

Harry scowled at Lip-Up and he and Emily wandered back to Bert's stall. Emily felt angry. He was so rude! And now she felt babyish in her T-shirt. But she was more angry about his dog. How could anyone have a dog and not take it out for proper walks? Going to the paper shop on a lead –

that wasn't any fun. And it was a retriever too – just like little Nugget who she'd only had for a few days.

On one of Bert's days off he decided to take them to the seaside, which was a very long way in the van. Harry kept asking if they were nearly there after they'd gone only a few miles. It was a hot day and the traffic was awful, so they were all hungry and thirsty by the time they arrived. Bert had a job finding somewhere to park the van, and then they had to carry all the stuff down to the beach and find somewhere to sit. They couldn't get their clothes off quickly enough and rush into the sea.

Uncle Wilf was a brilliant swimmer and went out a long way until he was just a speck in the distance, but the others didn't go far out of their depths. Gertie liked to sit in the warm, shallow water at the edge and let the little waves come tumbling in over her; Bert liked floating on his back, and the children liked to duck and dive under the waves and chase each other.

There was a wonderful picnic and Gertie had put a big bottle of Coca Cola in the picnic basket too. After they'd finished eating and the picnic things had been put away, Gertie and Bert went for a walk along the beach and the rest of them built a huge sandcastle with a tower and a moat. Uncle Wilf wandered off to find some shells to decorate it, but he came back quite soon, looking very excited. That was when he played his joke about the famous Russian film star – and the three children were completely taken in.

He told them that he'd seen her sitting under an umbrella just along the beach. He said her name was Olga Vitzvunisvitch and that she was in England making a film. The lady he pointed to was sitting in a deckchair, reading a book. She was very suntanned and was wearing a black bikini and dark glasses. Nearby, lay a man on a beach towel.

"Probably her bodyguard," said Uncle Wilf. He said they ought to get her autograph and that it was a once-in-a-lifetime opportunity. He gave them an old envelope and a stub of pencil that he found in his pocket and they went racing over to her.

Laura was the bravest and did the actual asking, but Harry and Emily stood close behind.

"Excuse me," Laura said, holding out the piece of paper, "can we have your autograph please?"

The lady glanced up at Laura and took her sunglasses off.

"Now why on earth would you want my autograph?" she said, looking amused.

She had a perfectly ordinary voice – it didn't sound Russian at all. She wrote her name on the piece of paper and handed it back. It said 'Jenny Morgan'.

"Oh, no," mumbled Laura, turning bright red and backing away in embarrassment.

That was when they realised that Uncle Wilf had played one of his jokes on them, but when they turned round he was nowhere to be seen. When they did at last find him, he was doubled up with laughter behind the breakwater. By the time they'd finished jumping all over him and covering him with sand, Gertie and Bert had come back and it was time to go home. He was still giggling when they'd left the sea far behind, and Bert stopped to fill the van up with petrol. And it was funny... But not that funny! Emily would have loved to have had a famous Russian film star's autograph. What would the other kids at school have said?

When at last they arrived home they were all tired, but Gertie insisted that they rinsed their swimming things out and hung them on the line to dry. After that, they had something to eat round the kitchen table. It was only later, when they'd flopped down in front of the telly and Bert and

Gertie were dozing off in their chairs that Emily glanced over at the sideboard. She gave a loud scream, making everyone jump and Bert, who was clutching a glass of beer, spilt a lot of it down the front of his shirt.

"What on earth's the matter now, Emily?" said Gertie.

Emily jumped to her feet and ran over to the sideboard. Autolocus was in his cage with his head under his wing.

"He's come back," she yelled at the top of her voice and shut the cage door firmly.

Chapter 15

A Visit to the Vet

Autolocus had indeed come back, but he was very different and for a few awful moments they wondered if it really was Autolocus. Perhaps the pirate had swapped him for another parrot! Emily checked by looking at his funny bent claw and she knew it was him. He looked thinner and seemed to have lost a few feathers, but it wasn't that which was so different – it was the way he behaved. Before, he'd always been so cocky, puffing out his chest and joking around, swearing and screeching.

Now, he no longer strutted up and down, pecking at his reflection in the mirror and preening himself. He wasn't interested in the new toy they'd bought for him and hardly touched the nice pieces of fruit Emily offered him. He just sat on the floor of his cage, looking miserable. And he didn't speak at all!

"What do you think's the matter with him?" Emily asked. Autolocus had been back a few days now and she was starting to get worried. Uncle Wilf took off his glasses and peered into the cage. Then, he lifted Autolocus out and stroked his feathers, scratching him gently on the back of his head which he usually loved.

"Come on now, old fellow," he said, "what's going on?" Autolocus closed his eyes and Uncle Wilf sighed and wrinkled his forehead, before placing him carefully back at the bottom of the cage, which was where he preferred to be these days.

"I think he's probably tired. He's had so many adventures, too much excitement – he's exhausted. We mustn't pester him. We'll just let him rest for a bit, give him plenty of food and lots of peace and quiet. I'm sure he'll soon get over it."

"But was he like this last time he came back?" Emily wanted to know.

Uncle Wilf thought for a moment, scratching his head. His glasses were dangling from his ear as usual and he put them back on.

"Well, no, he wasn't," he admitted. "Just the same cheeky old so-and-so, as far as I can remember." He looked at Emily. "That's true, lass, I've never seen him like this before."

Having Autolocus home again meant that the pirate must also be back in residence – in the attic. Emily was still scared at the thought of seeing him again, but she longed to know where he and Autolocus had been for the last few weeks. Maybe, if I spoke to him, she thought, he'd be able to tell me what's the matter. After all, she was the only one who seemed to be able to hear him – so perhaps it was up to her to do something about it, but the idea of facing him and having a conversation with him absolutely terrified her. She pushed the thought away and hoped that Autolocus would just get better.

But he was the same the next day – if anything he looked worse.

"Know what I think?" Laura said. She was sitting at the table, painting a picture of the parrot and Emily was opposite, writing up her diary. She hadn't done it for a few days and found she couldn't concentrate because she was worried. She got up and peered over Laura's shoulder. The picture was very good and she was taking a lot of trouble over it, painting in the little scrolls of his feathers which looked like sea-shells.

114

"Think about what?" she asked. "Oh, Laura, you are lucky! I wish I could paint like you."

Laura licked her paintbrush and scratched her head with the end of it.

"I'm going to be an artist when I grow up," she said, dipping the paintbrush in the red paint and colouring in the parrot's tail feathers. "But I'll tell you what I think, shall I?"

"Go on then."

"I think we ought to get Uncle Wilf to take Autolocus to the vet, that's what I think. He's not getting any better and he might even die!" Emily was horrified. Gertie agreed that it was probably the best thing to do and so she rang the vet, whose name was Mr Barker.

"Good name for a vet," chuckled Uncle Wilf, "but maybe he only deals with dogs."

The appointment was for five o'clock the next afternoon. Laura and Harry and Emily all wanted to go, but Gertie said there'd be too many in the waiting room. "But you can come, Emily, as you've been looking after Autolocus."

Bert came home early from work so he could take them in the van. It was some distance to the vet and the parrot sat quietly on the bottom of his cage all the way. Emily kept telling him everything was going to be all right.

The waiting room was noisy and smelt of disinfectant. The telephone rang constantly and people came in and out with different sorts of animals, mainly dogs on leads and cats in baskets. One of the dogs – it was a red setter, Gertie said - wouldn't keep still and kept barking and pulling on its lead to get out of the door. Emily couldn't help thinking it was a good thing that Autolocus wasn't making his usual racket – but then if he was, they wouldn't have been there. Gertie picked up one of the leaflets at the reception desk and read it to pass the time.

"Mr Barker will see you now, Mrs Pink," the woman behind the desk said at last and pointed to a door along the corridor. Uncle Wilf carried Autolocus through and Gertie and Emily followed. Bert stayed behind. They went into a little room and Mr Barker was there, in a very white coat, which made his teeth look yellow when he smiled. He wore white clogs and glasses with no rims. He took the cage from Uncle Wilf and put it on a table. There was only one chair to sit on so they all stood round the table.

"Well, well," he said, peering through the bars of the cage, "an African Grey – makes a change from my usual patients." He flashed his yellow teeth at them. "Now what seems to be his trouble?" He raised his eyebrows expectantly.

Emily was surprised - she thought they'd come to the vet so that he could tell them what the trouble was, but Gertie said, "He's not his usual self at all, very mopey and off his food."

"And he doesn't talk anymore," Emily added. "He's been away on holiday with a pirate and Uncle Wilf says he's probably had too many adventures."

"A pirate, eh?" said Mr Barker, showing off his yellow teeth again. "Well, I'll just take him out and have a look at him, shall I?" He opened the cage door and put his hand inside. "Ouch!" he yelled, as Autolocus nipped him smartly on the thumb.

Uncle Wilf nodded at Emily and she spoke soothingly to the parrot.

"It's all right, the vet just wants to have a look at you so he can make you better. Nobody's going to hurt you."

Autolocus looked at her with his beady eye as she put her hand into the cage and picked him up. Normally, he would have climbed quite happily onto her fingers – glad to

116

be out of his cage. She handed him to Mr Barker, who knew just how to hold him, and she leaned over, stroking his feathers gently to calm him down.

The vet looked him over thoroughly, examined his eyes, his feet, inside his beak and ran his hands over all parts of his body. He opened up his wings and looked at his tail, then handed him to Emily and told her to put him back in his cage.

They waited in silence, looking at each other, while Mr Barker sat down in front of his laptop and began typing. It felt stuffy in the little room and Emily was thirsty.

At last he turned his head and asked, "The parrot's name?"

"Autolocus," Emily replied.

"Autolocus." He typed it in. "That's a fine name - hope I've got the spelling right. Age?"

Gertie and Emily looked at Uncle Wilf. "Must be well over 30," he said. "I really don't know. Could be nearer 40 I suppose, I've had him a long time."

Emily gasped. She had no idea Autolocus was as old as that. Forty was really old. Mum had told her that, with an animal, you had to multiply the age by seven, so that meant Autolocus was forty times seven. She wondered what that came to.

Mr Barker typed again, then swivelled his chair around to face them. He paused, cleared his throat and pressed his fingertips together.

"I'm glad to be able to tell you that there's nothing at all wrong with your parrot," he said cheerfully, lacing his fingers together.

They looked at each other and blinked disbelievingly. "But he's…" Gertie began.

Mr Barker cut her short. "Your parrot, Mrs Pink... it is Mrs Pink, isn't it?"

Gertie nodded. "Well, he really belongs to Uncle Wilf," she said.

"Well," Mr Barker continued, "this fine African Grey parrot is perfectly normal... *she's* just feeling a little under the weather, that's all, because... she's about to lay an egg!"

"What?!" shouted Gertie, and promptly sat down on the one and only chair.

Uncle Wilf and Emily stared, first at each other, then at Mr Barker and then at Autolocus. Uncle Wilf's ears had gone bright red and he was grinning, and Emily felt so excited she wanted to shout. Gertie kept saying, "Oh my! Oh my!" over and over and fanning herself with the leaflet she'd picked up in the waiting room.

"Now, your parrot is perfectly healthy, so there's nothing at all to worry about. I would say the happy event could take place any day now, so I suggest you take her home, give her something nice to make a nest with and let her get on with it. Not too much excitement – she needs a bit of peace and quiet.

Chapter 16

Autolocus Needs Some Peace

When they got back, Harry and a friend called Tom, were watching sport on TV and Laura was stretched out on the floor, playing with Firefly and Josephina. Bert began sorting through boxes of clothes, piling T-shirts on the table, draping fleeces over the backs of chairs and hanging blouses, skirts and trousers over the rest of the furniture. The twins wanted to hear what had gone on at the vet and were just as astounded as the others to learn that Autolocus was going to lay an egg!

"That's really weird," said Harry. "How did the vet know?"

They had to admit they had no idea.

Laura and Emily set about making Autolocus a new home in a large, shallow cardboard box that Bert gave them. They scattered sawdust at the bottom and then made a nest out of one of Gertie's old furry sweaters, which she said they could cut up, plus some shredded tissues. They put the food dish in and a piece of mango and fixed the drinking bottle to the side of the box. There was much more room in it than the cage.

Emily couldn't get used to the idea that Autolocus was a girl and nor could Uncle Wilf who kept calling her 'him'.

"It might be better if you changed her name," Emily suggested, helpfully.

Uncle Wilf got all flustered at the idea. "But he's always been Autolocus," he protested. "I can't suddenly start calling him something else after all this time."

Emily thought for a moment. "How about 'Tolly'? It's a pretty name and it sounds better for a girl, don't you think? And it's still a bit like Autolocus."

"Tolly's better than Polly," agreed Harry. "Everyone calls their parrot Polly. Don't know why though."

Autolocus (Tolly) was prodding the pieces of woolly jumper around with her beak and tossing the tissues into the air before arranging everything into a sort of nest to settle on. She swished the sawdust around with her feet and a lot of it shot out onto the floor.

"My, this is going to make a mess of the place," said Gertie, bustling about with a dustpan and brush. "Haven't you got a deeper box, Bert?" But he hadn't and insisted that it would have to do.

Harry and Tom had gone back to watching TV and had turned the volume up. Suddenly the phone rang – it was a friend of Laura's.

"Turn the TV down, I can't hear," she shouted at Harry - he and Tom were cheering because someone had just scored a goal.

Then the doorbell rang and Izzie started to bark. Emily ran and opened the door. It was Tom's mum, come to collect him, and at the same moment Mrs Skeet arrived on the doorstep. They both came in and stared at Tolly; then, Firefly suddenly appeared, jumped up on the sideboard and tried to get into the box too. Gertie shooed her off and stood back with her hand on her hip, looking round the room.

"Be quiet all of you!" she exploded, her red curls quivering like wire springs "Bert, this house just isn't big enough for all this. We haven't got enough space." Emily had never seen Gertie so upset.

But Bert was busily sorting out his boxes of clothes. "Oh not that again," he said, without looking up. "Give it a rest, Gert."

"Well, I'm sorry," said Gertie, throwing the dustpan and brush down on the floor with a clatter, "but that Mr Barker said Autolocus should be left in peace and quiet. Goodness me, if I was laying an egg I wouldn't want all this pandemonium going on round me." She waved her arms in the air. "People coming and going, nosing around to see how I was getting on, staring in at me. Not to mention the cats. It's just not safe. Autolocus hasn't got any protection in this box. No, we're going to have to put her somewhere quieter, otherwise her egg might turn out all wonky."

"Wonky?" said Harry, giggling. "What do you mean, wonky, Mum? You think it might come out oblong, or with pink spots on it or something?" He and Tom collapsed with laughter.

"Shhhh!" Gertie sounded like a rocket going off. "What I mean is that the chick might be born a bit odd or something." She marched over to the television and turned it off. Uncle Wilf had been standing by quietly all this time. Now he spoke.

"Can I make a suggestion, Gertie?" They all looked at him. "I think a very good place for Autolocus... er, Tolly, would be down in the shed on the allotment. It'd be nice and peaceful for her there. One of us always goes down there every day, so we can look in on her, feed her and so on."

Gertie thought about this for a minute and agreed that it was probably the answer.

"I'll go up to the pet shop tomorrow and see if Trevor's got a book on how to rear the chicks when they hatch," said Uncle Wilf.

"Chicks?" cried Gertie, red in the face. "Do you mean to say there might be more than one?"

"Well, it depends how many eggs she lays, doesn't it?" said Uncle Wilf.

"Oh my, oh my!" said Gertie for the umpteenth time, running her hands through her hair so that her curls stood on end. "In that case she must definitely go in the shed. I can't have a dozen little parrots skipping about all over the place, as well as everything else. The kittens were bad enough. Yes, the shed it is."

So the shed became Tolly's new home – for the time being. Uncle Wilf put her back in her cage to take her down there and Bert carried the box, complete with sawdust and nest. Poor Tolly, she must have wondered what was going on. Emily went too, to make sure she was settled comfortably, and then they left her in peace.

"I'll come back and see you tomorrow, Tolly," she promised and gently stroked her feathers.

Bert locked the shed and put the key in his pocket. "I'll hang the key up in the house on the hook with all the others, so we all know where it is," he said and started walking home. "Don't be long – it's supper time," he called back over his shoulder.

Uncle Wilf and Emily had a look at the sunflowers and gave them all some water and a bit of a feed. They'd shot up in the last few days, but Hattie (Emily's sunflower) was the tallest by far. She'd caught up with the sunflowers on the other allotments, which had all been planted before her – she was even taller than Emily now! Emily looked up at her and Hattie looked down at Emily with her big yellow face and swayed gently in the breeze. Emily told her about Autolocus being a girl and about the egg, and could almost believe that Hattie was laughing. She wondered how long it was till the competition.

As they walked back to the house, she could tell Uncle Wilf was thinking about Autolocus and she was too. Why did she seem so different? Apart from being a girl, of course. Maybe it was just because she was going to lay an egg. Emily missed the old Autolocus and wished she knew where she'd been all this time and what adventures she'd had.

Uncle Wilf was having the same thoughts because when they got to the gate he stopped and said, "Emily lassie, would you do something for me?"

Emily's heart started to thud because she knew what he was going to ask and she was dreading it. She quickly tried to change the subject.

"We'd better hurry up, Uncle Wilf, or we'll be late for supper."

"Emily? I think you know what I'm going to say, don't you?"

She shrank back against the gate and wished she could disappear. Uncle Wilf put his hand on her shoulder. "Do you think you could do it for me, lass? It's so strange that you can hear Jack – you seem to be the only one who can. Emily, I really want to know what's been going on – where he goes to. I've been living with him all these years and yet I don't really know anything about him. Could you speak to him for me and ask him where he's been?"

"I can't," she whispered. The thought terrified her.

Uncle Wilf didn't say anything for a moment, then he let his hand fall with a sigh.

"Don't worry, little lassie. It'll just have to remain a mystery – something we'll never know."

But Emily knew she wouldn't be able to leave it like that. Although she was scared to death of coming to face to face with the pirate, she too wanted to know where he and Autolocus had been for the last few weeks. And it was clear that the only way she was going to find out was by asking him. She knew she was the only one who could do it – but was she brave enough?

That night she lay in bed, thinking of Tolly alone in the shed and hoping she was all right. How long would it be before she laid her egg? What if she laid more than one! Would it hurt her when it came out? Hens always made a lot of noise when they laid an egg – was it because they were pleased and proud or did it simply hurt? She decided she'd go over to the allotment first thing in the morning, as soon as she woke up.

As well as thinking about Tolly, she thought about the pirate up in the attic. She knew she was going to have to meet him. But it was so scary! She didn't know what she was most frightened of – that he was a pirate, or that he was a ghost! Still, Uncle Wilf would be there too and he'd make sure she was all right.

She fell asleep at last and dreamt that Tolly laid a huge basket of eggs, and they all hatched out into pirates who marched up and down singing, "Fifteen Men on a Dead Man's Chest, Yo Ho Ho and a Bottle of Rum".

Chapter 17

Uncle Wilf up to his Tricks

Next morning, before breakfast, Emily cut up some pieces of carrot and apple and put them in a bag, then took the shed key off the hook and ran down to the allotment to see Tolly. She unlocked the door and opened it slowly – she didn't want to risk her flying out, as she remembered Tolly was in a box, not in her cage. She went inside, shutting the door carefully behind her. Uncle Wilf had put the box on a shelf near the window.

"Hello, Tolly," she said. The parrot was sitting on the nest she'd made out of Gertie's old pullover and looked very comfortable with her feathers all fluffed out around her. "How do you like your new home – it's quieter in here, isn't it? I hope you won't be lonely, but the vet said you were going to lay an egg and needed some peace and quiet."

Tolly stared at her in silence. Emily took the bag out of her pocket. "Look, I've brought you some carrot and pieces of apple – I expect you're hungry."

She put them in the dish, but Tolly didn't seem interested, so she unhooked the water bottle and went outside to fill it at the tap. When she came back Tolly was standing, holding one of the apple pieces in her bent claw. Emily looked inside the nest and just managed to stop herself letting out a shriek of excitement. There, in amongst the torn-up pieces of tissue, was an egg! It was about the size of a chicken's egg – in fact it didn't look any different from a chicken's egg.

"Oh, Tolly, you clever, clever girl!" she whispered. Tolly finished her piece of apple, looking at Emily all the time with her yellow eye. Then, she shook out her feathers and settled herself comfortably back on the nest. "I'll come back and see you soon," Emily promised.

In the kitchen everyone was sitting round the table, having breakfast, and when they heard her news they all wanted to go and see the egg, but Gertie said it would upset Tolly. It was decided that only one person at a time would be allowed to go down to the shed with Emily when she went to feed her. Uncle Wilf said he wanted her to be in sole charge. She felt very important.

After breakfast, Bert and Gertie went off in the van to visit some friends. They said they wouldn't be back till lunch time.

"Uncle Wilf, how long will it take for the egg to hatch?" Emily asked as they washed up the breakfast things.

"I've got no idea at all, but I think we ought to find out so we'll all go up to the pet shop and see if Trevor's got a book that will help us. We need to know how to look after the chick when it's born."

It started to rain as they left the house. "Oh rats!" said Harry. "Tom was going to come round and have a go on the cart." But it didn't look like the sort of day for doing things outside.

They took Izzie with them – she loved going to the pet shop because Trevor always gave her a treat. When they got there the shop was empty, so they started to look through the books on pets. There were loads of them on one of those stands that spins around.

"Here we are," said Harry. 'How to Care for Your African Grey' – that ought to tell us what to do."

Uncle Wilf took the book from him and looked through it quickly, his glasses on the end of his nose. Just then Trevor appeared through a door at the back of the shop.

"Morning folks," he said cheerfully, "What are you after then? Hello, Izzie, you old rascal." He came round from behind the counter and patted Izzie on the head and threw a biscuit in the air for her. She jumped up and caught it, wagging her tail.

"Morning, Trevor," said Uncle Wilf. "Seems ridiculous that I need a book to tell me how to look after my parrot after all these years, but the truth is, he's just laid an egg and we want to find out what to do."

"Uncle Wilf – *she's* just laid an egg," Laura corrected him. "Not he."

Trevor laughed. "Is that a fact?" he said. "Yes, parrots do sometimes lay eggs – doesn't always mean there's a chick though. 'Don't count your parrots before they've hatched' they say, don't they?" He laughed and nodded. "Yes, that book's excellent – it'll tell you everything you need to know."

Emily felt terribly disappointed as they left the shop. She'd taken it for granted that there'd be a parrot chick in the egg, but now Trevor said there might not be.

It was still raining and they decided they'd take Izzie for a proper walk later on when it had stopped. When they got home Uncle Wilf sat down and had a quick look at the book. "I'll read it properly later," he said, putting it to one side. "Rearing a parrot chick sounds a bit complicated – and who knows, the egg might not even hatch anyway."

"Oh I do hope it will," Emily said.

"Well, we'll just have to wait and see, won't we?" said Uncle Wilf. He looked at the children mischievously. "Now, as Gertie and Bert are out and it's pouring with rain, why don't we have a bit of fun in the kitchen?"

They looked at each other, wondering what he was going to suggest. You never knew with Uncle Wilf.

"I thought we might have a go at making some Cor Blimeys. Gertie ever tell you I worked for a time in a factory that made seaside rock? Not just seaside rock, but all sorts of other sweets as well?"

They looked at him blankly.

"No? Well, there are still a few things you don't know about Uncle Wilf. Learned a few interesting tricks there, I did, and invented a few things too. Like the Cor Blimeys. But in the end, they were never sold in the shops." He sighed. "Pity really, could have made me a fortune. Made a few mistakes too, I have to confess, like the time when I was put in charge of making seaside rock for Torquay. Wasn't very experienced in those days and the writing through the middle of the rock came out backwards – said Yauqrot instead of Torquay!" He giggled. "There were some important people who weren't too pleased, I can tell you! But that was a long, long time ago. Now, let's go and see if we've got everything we need for the Cor Blimeys."

They followed him through into the kitchen in silence and he opened the larder door.

"Now, let's see – first of all, of course, we need lots of sugar. Gertie said she was going to make some jam so, yes, here we are – there's plenty of sugar." He took three packets and put them on the table. "Good! And now we need food colouring – lots of different colours – yes, red, yellow, green, blue – splendid, splendid."

Emily glanced at Laura and Harry.

"The thing about these sweets," said Uncle Wilf, taking a bowl out of the cupboard, "is that they're a bit different.

The annoying thing about most sweets, I'm sure you'll agree, is that the more you suck them, the smaller they get, isn't that the case? But with these ones, the more you suck them the bigger they grow!" He giggled again.

"And they change colour too. They're about the size of a marble to start with and they end up so big that you have to spit them out because there's not enough room in your mouth for them to grow any bigger!"

He opened one of the bags of sugar and took a wooden spoon out of the drawer. Just then the doorbell rang.

"Oh no," said Laura and ran to see who was there. She came back a moment later, making a face, followed by Mrs Skeet.

"Oh, not her!" said Harry under his breath when he saw who it was.

"Morning, dear lady, come in, come in," beamed Uncle Wilf, waving the wooden spoon and pointing to a chair. "Sit down a moment and join in the fun."

"How's that parrit of yours then?" asked Mrs Skeet. "Laid 'is egg yet, has 'e?"

She was looking even more grumpy than usual, if that was possible.

"Yes," Emily said excitedly. "She laid one last night."

"Strike me pink!" said Mrs Skeet. "Just one after all, was there?"

"Yes," Emily said. "Only one. So far. And we don't know yet if there's a chick inside – there isn't always."

"Hmph" said Mrs Skeet. She threw a magazine down on the kitchen table.

"Thought Gertie might like to have a look at this," she said turning the pages. "There you are, she said, slapping her hand down on the page – another of these competitions." She pointed to a picture of a large house. "'Your wish come true'," she read out. "'Win this large family house in Devon, blah, blah...' Gertie's always going on about wanting more space, isn't she? And she'd love this one 'cos she's from Devon, isn't she?"

They all clustered round and looked at the magazine. Uncle Wilf removed his glasses, and looked closely at Mrs Skeet.

"But what about you, dear lady? Has your wish come true yet? You remember? The one you wished on your birthday - with the wishbone?"

Mrs Skeet looked down at her feet. "No," she said glumly, "and I don't suppose for a moment that it will."

"Never give up," said Uncle Wilf, punching his fist in the air. "Never, never give up!" He turned to the three children. "I think the Cor Blimeys are going to have to wait for another time. Right now, we're going to see if we can make this dear lady's wish come true."

"Can't we make the Cor Blimeys first?" asked Harry, looking disappointed.

"How do you know what she wished?" said Laura. "She's not supposed to tell anyone or it won't come true!"

Uncle Wilf's green eyes twinkled. "I'm quite a good guesser, little lassie," he said solemnly, then turned to Mrs Skeet. "Now, I have to admit that this could be rather a messy procedure, but if you're prepared to go ahead with it, I'm ready to bet that by the end of a fortnight your wish will have come true!"

Mrs Skeet snorted. "What are you — some kind of magician?"

Emily looked at Uncle Wilf and saw that his ears were beginning to turn pink.

"I wouldn't go quite as far as that," he said, "but I am able to make up an ointment that has several very powerful ingredients, which, when combined with my own specialised tincture, is pretty well guaranteed to do the trick." He grinned encouragingly at Mrs Skeet and Emily wondered what on earth he was going to do. What was it that Mrs Skeet had wished for with the wish bone?

"What have you to lose?" Uncle Wilf went on. "Dear lady, have a little faith and trust me. No harm will come to you, I promise. We might make a bit of a mess, but that's easily cleared up."

Mrs Skeet sat down heavily on one of the kitchen chairs and looked uncertainly at Uncle Wilf. "Well, I'm not sure…" Her voice trailed away.

"Just think," he said persuasively, "you'll be able to throw away all those terrible turbans – never have to wear one again." Mrs Skeet hesitated. "Come along now, dear lady, be brave, take the plunge."

"Well, I'm not sure, how do I know this is going to work?"

"Trust me," said Uncle Wilf in a solemn, quiet voice. There was a long pause and the clock on the wall seemed to be ticking very loudly.

"Well, all right then," said Mrs Skeet weakly, "I'll give it a go."

"Bravo!" shouted Uncle Wilf. He turned to the children and did a little skip.

"Now I'm going to need your assistance, you three. Are you ready?"

Chapter 18

Mrs Skeet Takes the Plunge

Mrs Skeet sat perfectly still on the kitchen chair with her eyes tightly shut, while Uncle Wilf took some old newspapers that lay in a pile by the back door and gave them to Harry.

"Harry, spread these on the floor by the chair – we don't want to make a mess. Laura, find an old towel please and put it round Mrs Skeet's shoulders and Emily, will you look in the cupboard under the sink and find the rooting powder."

Mrs Skeet's eyes sprang open. "Rooting powder?" she squeaked.

"Don't be alarmed – all's well," replied Uncle Wilf. "We want some good, strong roots to grow, don't we?"

By now Emily had guessed what Mrs Skeet's secret wish had been and she could tell Laura and Harry had too. Mrs Skeet's eyes snapped shut again and she gripped the arms of the chair.

They bustled about doing the jobs they'd been given. Emily found the rooting powder in a carton under the sink and gave it to Uncle Wilf.

"Excellent," he said, pouring the entire contents into a big saucepan. "Next, bicarbonate of soda. Can you find me some of that please, Laura, and we'll need some flour too."

Laura looked in the cupboard where Gertie kept the things she used for making cakes. "Here they are," she said excitedly.

"That's it – makes things rise nicely, does bicarb," he said, emptying the packet into the saucepan, followed by a good shake of flour. He mixed them together with the wooden spoon. "Now, let me see – ah, yes I have it, I have it," he said rummaging around in the cupboard and bringing out a tin of golden syrup and a tin of black treacle.

"Now, here's an important decision for you to make, dear lady," he announced. "You must decide whether you'd like your hair to be a rich, dark colour, or is it to be golden? And then, of course, I need to know if you'd like curls, or will you go for the straight look?"

Mrs Skeet didn't answer. Her eyes were still shut and her face was pale. Emily wondered if Uncle Wilf was playing a terrible joke on her, or was this really going to work? She thought of the Torquay rock and how the writing had come out back to front. Suppose it all went wrong?

"Would you like a cup of tea, Mrs Skeet?" Laura asked gently. No reply. "Mrs Skeet?"

The poor woman opened her eyes, took a deep breath and looked fearfully at Uncle Wilf.

"You're not having me on, are you?" she whispered and Emily suddenly felt sorry for her.

"Dear lady," said Uncle Wilf in a shocked voice. "I would never do such a dreadful thing. I assure you that in next to no time your wish will have come true. Just try to relax and yes, Laura, please make us all a nice cup of tea. While you're doing that and Mrs Skeet is making her decision, I shall just go upstairs quickly and get my bottle of special tincture.

He disappeared and Emily helped Laura make the tea. Harry was sitting on the floor stroking Izzie. Uncle Wilf took longer than they expected and by the time he came back

Mrs Skeet was sipping her tea and looking slightly less nervous.

"Well?" he said expectantly. "What have you decided?" He put a tall thin bottle of green liquid on the table next to the treacle and golden syrup and took the cork out with a loud pop. The liquid was a very dark green, the colour of spinach, and there were golden bubbles in it, which floated to the top and burst with a little fizzing sound.

"Me 'air used to be a mousy colour before it all fell out," said Mrs Skeet, "and it was as straight as a die. So, if I've got a choice, I'd like it nice and dark... and curly."

"No problem!" said Uncle Wilf. "The black treacle it is then."

"Black treacle?" Mrs Skeet asked in shocked voice. "Surely not!"

Uncle Wilf put four enormous spoonfuls of it into the saucepan, then took a mouthful of tea and smacked his lips.

"Curls you want? No problem. Harry, here – take these scissors and carefully cut off some of Izzie's curls – I'm sure she can spare a few! It's just for the DNA, you see – Izzie's DNA is full of curly hair genes!"

Harry's mouth fell open in amazement, but he obediently cut off a good handful of Izzie's thick coat.

"Into the saucepan with it," said Uncle Wilf, taking another sip of his tea.

"Ooooh," wailed Mrs Skeet, screwing her eyes up again.

The four of them stood round the table, looking into the saucepan. "Now for the tincture – the most important ingredient," whispered Uncle Wilf, reverently. He poured about half of the dark green liquid into the mixture. Glug, glug, glug it went as it came out of the bottle.

"Oh dearie me, oh dearie me," Mrs Skeet cried in a quavery voice. "I think I ought to go home now!" She started to get unsteadily to her feet.

"Dear lady, dear lady," said Uncle Wilf soothingly "fear not, all will be well, you'll see!" He pushed her firmly back into the chair. "Now, we just need a little heat to get it all to mix together nicely." He put the saucepan on the cooker and the three children moved over to get a better view. He lit the gas and stirred the mixture round thoroughly with the wooden spoon. It was now a dark, greenish black, and as it started to heat up, gave off a strong peppery smell that tickled the nostrils. For a moment or two nothing happened then, as they watched, it started to fizz and rise up inside the pan.

"Ooooh," Laura squealed, jumping back.

"Oh wow," shouted Harry and sneezed loudly.

Emily held her breath, wondering what would happen next.

"What's goin' on?" shouted Mrs Skeet, clutching the towel and getting to her feet again.

"Do please sit down," Uncle Wilf ordered. "Everything is happening exactly as it should. Now, we'll just wait for this to cool down for a moment or two and then we're ready to apply it. Please take your turban off."

He sounded quite strict and Mrs Skeet sat down obediently and sneezed three times very fast. Then she adjusted the towel round her shoulders and seemed to be holding her breath. The children watched fascinated, as she lifted the green turban off her head and put it on her lap. Emily found it hard not to gasp, although they'd all seen Mrs Skeet's bald head before. It was just that it was *SO* bald – not a hair anywhere – and very shiny. Izzie stared at her and started to howl.

"Harry, please put Izzie in another room or she's going to upset everything," said Uncle Wilf, "and find me a big paint brush." Harry took Izzie and put her in the garden.

Emily looked at the clock – it was a quarter to one and she had the feeling that Bert and Gertie would be back at any minute.

At last, everything seemed to be ready and Uncle Wilf carried the big saucepan over and put it on a chair next to Mrs Skeet. They watched as he dipped the paintbrush into the dark mixture, which had stopped fizzing and shrunk down to half its size in the pan. Quickly, he began to paint it all over Mrs Skeet's head. It was very thick and sticky, a bit like tar, and Izzie's hairs made it all cling together, so that it became a sort of hairy black helmet on her head. She looked awful.

"Now – those eyebrows," said Uncle Wilf, standing back and gazing at his handiwork. "Emily, get a cloth please and wipe off those crayon eyebrows. We're going to put some real ones in their place."

Mrs Skeet looked quite different without any eyebrows – not half so grumpy.

Uncle Wilf dipped one of Laura's small paintbrushes into the black goo and painted a slim arch over each of Mrs Skeet's eyes – nice and well apart!

"There! All done!" he exclaimed in triumph, looking at the clock. "Can I ask you now, dear lady, to put your turban on again – very gently, very gently indeed so as not to smudge the ointment. Yes, that's the way. And you must keep it on for a week – no peeping now! It may itch, but don't be tempted to wash it off. It will take several days for the ointment to sink deep into the scalp. After that, you can take that wretched turban off and hurl it in the dustbin! That's very important – you'll never have to wear it or any

136

of the others again! Then, have a good wash and report back to me."

Just then, they heard Bert's van outside the front gate, and a moment or two later, Gertie's voice in the garden, talking to Izzie, as she and Bert came round to the back of the house.

"Quick, dear lady," said Uncle Wilf, jerking Mrs Skeet to her feet and pulling her out of the room. "Off you go!"

They heard the front door open and shut as Mrs Skeet left and Uncle Wilf came bustling back into the kitchen. Harry folded the newspaper up and put it back on the pile by the back door, and Uncle Wilf cleaned the saucepan and brushes quickly under the hot tap. Laura put the treacle and everything else away and Emily threw the empty cartons of rooting powder and bicarbonate of soda into the bin.

Somehow or other, by the time Gertie and Bert came through the back door everything was in its place and they were sitting round the table, finishing their cups of tea. Although nobody had said anything, there seemed to be a silent agreement between the four of them that it would be best if they didn't mention any of what had just happened to Bert and Gertie.

"Funny smell in here," said Gertie as she came through the door. "What's been going on?" She wrinkled up her nose. Bert put a bag of shopping down on the table and gave an enormous sneeze.

"Make us a cup of tea, will you, Laura love – I'm parched."

Uncle Wilf calmly picked up the magazine that Mrs Skeet had left on the table and pointed to the picture of the house. "Another competition for you to try, Gertie," he said. "Mrs Skeet brought it round a few minutes ago – might be worth a go."

Gertie raised an eyebrow at him and looked at each one of them in turn. "Uncle Wilf, you're an old rascal," she said and her eyes crinkled up in a smile. She looked searchingly round the room, expecting to see something that would give a clue to what had been going on, but everything looked normal.

"I don't know what you've all been up to, but it's bound to come out in the wash sooner or later."

She looked surprised when they all started to laugh. Uncle Wilf winked at them, then did a little skip and went over to the back door.

"Look, it's stopped raining," he said. "I think Izzie would appreciate a good walk after lunch."

When they got back from the walk Emily ran down to the allotment with Laura, so she could show her the egg. They opened the shed door carefully and closed it behind them. Gertie had given them some corn on the cob, Tolly's favourite, and they managed to tempt her off the nest.

"Wow!" said Laura. "It's a bit bigger than a chicken's egg, isn't it? More the size of a duck's egg." They watched Tolly enjoying the corn cob. "You oughtn't to let her stay off the nest too long, you know, she needs to keep the egg warm or it won't hatch. Put her food dish nearer so she can reach it without having to get up."

Emily put some more parrot food in the dish and placed it nearer to the nest.

"There you are, Tolly," she said, putting the corn cob down by the side of the dish as well so the parrot could peck at it without getting up.

Tolly settled herself on the nest, covering the egg well with her fluffed out feathers. They stayed with her for a while and Emily scratched the top of her head and talked to her, but she seemed to want to be left in peace. They locked the door carefully behind them and Emily put the key in her pocket.

The ground was very wet after all the rain so they didn't have to do any watering, but Emily talked to Hattie for a few minutes and Laura had a word with Hermione. They each whispered to them about Tolly's egg and told them about Mrs Skeet and putting the ointment on her head. It all sounded so funny that they staggered about laughing.

"Rooting powder?" Emily squealed, imitating Mrs Skeet's voice.

"Black treacle, surely not!" laughed Laura. "Oh dearie me, oh dearie me, I think I ought to go home now!"

They couldn't stop laughing and the more they laughed, the funnier it all seemed.

"Do you think it'll work, Laura?" Emily asked when she'd managed to get her breath back.

"I've no idea," said Laura.

"I think it might," Emily said. "Look at our sunflowers."

"Do you think Uncle Wilf's a bit magical?" whispered Laura.

"Maybe," said Emily.

Hattie and Hermione were both bigger than Harry's Hanky Panky, and the three on the other side of the bed were nowhere near as tall. They looked over at the other allotments where a few other people had planted sunflowers and they were definitely smaller too.

"Let's bring a tape measure next time we come down here," said Laura. "It's not long now till judging day."

Chapter 19

Meeting the Ghost

Everyone wanted to see Tolly's egg, so Emily decided they should take it in turns. Harry was first on the list because Laura had already seen it. But when Gertie and then Bert came down to the shed, Tolly refused to get off the nest, so they didn't see the egg after all. It was disappointing, but they said they didn't mind.

When it was Uncle Wilf's turn several days later, he and Emily couldn't persuade Tolly to move so Uncle Wilf lifted her gently to one side. They both gasped at what they saw. The egg was much bigger – the size of a goose's egg and it had changed colour. It had been a dirty white, now it was a pale greenish-blue.

"Blithering heck fire," said Uncle Wilf. "I thought you said it was a normal egg, Emily – like a chicken's egg, you said."

"Well, it was," she insisted. "It really was. But it's grown! It's about twice the size now."

Uncle Wilf looked puzzled and scratched his head. "It can't have grown. Eggs don't grow!" He looked around the shed. "Something funny's going on here." He felt the egg with the back of his hand. "It's warm," he said and put Tolly gently back. She rearranged the nest, pushing and prodding the pieces of wool then, turning the egg over gently with her beak, she settled herself down again.

They came out of the shed, locking the door, and Uncle Wilf looked at the other people on the allotment who were doing all the usual things, digging, weeding, watering. Coddie Rowe was picking runner beans and they could see

Lip-Up Stinky nearby, lying on his back, reading a comic. He looked up when he saw them coming out of the shed and scowled. Emily decided to ignore him.

"Look at Hattie!" she cried, pointing at her sunflower. There was no way she could reach up to Hattie's head now – she was enormous!

"What did I tell you?" Uncle Wilf was beaming. "Let's bring a camera down and take a photograph of you standing next to her, shall we?"

"Oh, yes," Emily laughed. "It really does work, doesn't it? She's grown even taller since I told her about Mrs Skeet's bald head."

Uncle Wilf chuckled, then looked serious again as he glanced over towards Coddie Rowe. "I can't understand about the egg," he said quietly. "It almost seems as if someone's taken it and put another in its place."

"Oh no!" Emily was horrified. "Why would anyone want to do a thing like that? Anyway the shed's always locked."

"Yes, I know, it's all very strange. We'll just have to wait and see what happens, won't we?"

"Uncle Wilf?" Emily said, as they walked back towards the house.

"Yes, lassie – what is it?"

She paused for a moment, plucking up her courage, and the words came out in a rush.

"If you like, I'm ready to come and see the pirate. It'll be time to go back to school in a week or so and then I'll be going home, so I'd better do it soon."

They stopped, and Uncle Wilf looked at Emily with a huge smile on his face. Taking hold of her arms, he swung her round.

"Oh my! Will you really do that for me, Emily? Oh, lassie, that would be wonderful. I'll tell you what questions to ask him... oh, there's so much I want to find out! Come on, let's do it right away – there's no time like the present!"

"What... n-now?" Emily stammered. "Oh, I didn't think we'd do it now. Maybe we should wait till tomorrow."

"No, there's no point putting it off – not now you've decided. Don't be afraid, it'll be all right."

Emily could feel her knees starting to shake as they got nearer the house and the palms of her hands were sweaty. When they reached the garden, Gertie came out of the greenhouse, carrying a seed tray. She was on her way down to the allotment to plant out more lettuces and radishes and said she'd be back in time for lunch. Laura and Harry were out at the front, playing with the cart.

"Come on," said Uncle Wilf, "we won't be disturbed."

He climbed the ladder to the loft and Emily followed close behind, her heart thumping so hard she could feel it in her ears. She was terrified at the thought of coming face to face with Jack. When she was almost at the top, she very nearly changed her mind, but Uncle Wilf turned round and pulled her up the last couple of steps.

The attic was bigger than she'd expected and there were two windows in the roof. She looked around quickly, not knowing what to expect. Although it was a hot day and the sunshine was pouring in through the windows, it felt chilly; then she remembered Uncle Wilf saying it was always cold when the pirate was around. She felt a shiver going up her spine.

Next to one wall was a camp bed with a cheerful red patchwork quilt on it. The only other furniture was a rocking chair, a chest of drawers and a small stool – everything looked very neat. But where was the pirate?

"Put this on," said Uncle Wilf, taking a thick pullover out of one of the drawers, "and sit here, Emily lass." He pointed at the little stool. "We may have to wait a moment or two."

She was glad of the pullover – she had started to tremble and her teeth were chattering, but more from fright than the cold.

"Where is he?" she whispered.

"Shhhh – just wait." Uncle Wilf sat down on the bed.

It was silent except for the ticking of a clock on the wall. Then something else – not a sound, but a smell, came wafting through the air. She tried to think what it was and breathed in again. Suddenly, she remembered! She'd smelt it on that day out. It was the smell of the sea! She sat perfectly still, her eyes fixed on Uncle Wilf; then she became aware of a movement. Turning her head sharply, she noticed that the rocking chair behind her had started to rock! Gently, back and forth, back and forth.

She put her hand over her mouth to stop herself screaming. If she'd been able to move, she would have been down that ladder faster than a fireman sliding down his pole, but her legs had turned to jelly. As she looked at the rocking chair, a grey mist began to form around it. Gradually, the mist gathered together and became the shape of a man sitting in the chair. It was the pirate!

"Oh my goodness," she whispered through dry lips as she stared and stared at him.

He was becoming clearer by the minute, not so watery, but she could still see the chair through him. He was a big man, with a dark beard and a scar down one side of his face. Over one eye was a black patch and he had a large, three cornered hat on his head. His long hair was plaited and hung down his back, his ragged shirt tucked inside leather breeches. A belt with a sword hanging from it was

143

slung on the back of the chair. A cutlass, Emily thought – that's what it is, a cutlass.

She dragged her eyes away from him and turned to Uncle Wilf. He smiled at her encouragingly. "Yes, lassie, this is Jack, my pirate – a ghost, yes, but also a good friend. Remember that he saved my life."

The pirate went on rocking, back and forth... waiting.

Uncle Wilf cleared his throat and clasped his hands together. He was looking very excited and his eyes were sparkling again.

"It's difficult to know where to start, isn't it?" he said. "There are so many questions. Er, maybe we ought to have an introduction first – yes, that's it."

He got up from the bed and came over to Emily, putting a hand on her shoulder. "Jack, this is my very good friend, Emily. Now, Emily is very special indeed – probably one in a hundred – because, not only can she see you, but she can hear you as well, which of course I can't. She has kindly agreed to meet you to tell me what you say. After all this time, I shall be able to learn your history. Isn't that wonderful?"

The pirate turned his head and looked at Emily, his face dark and shadowy under his hat. She couldn't see his eyes properly, but he seemed to be studying her carefully. She began to worry that he wasn't going to speak, and if he did, she wouldn't be able to hear him after all. The only sound was the ticking clock and the hammering of her heart – and then his lips began to move. It was a bit like listening to the radio when it's not tuned in properly – the words were all fuzzy round the edges.

"My name is Tobias... Tobias Wood." The chair stopped rocking. He leaned forward and stretched out his right hand. He wanted to shake her hand! No way, she thought, shrinking back, no way am I going to shake hands with a ghost!

"What did he say, what did he say?" Uncle Wilf's hand squeezed her shoulder. "Did he tell you his name?"

Emily swallowed. But her voice had turned into a tiny squeak. "His name is Tobias Wood."

"What? What did you say? Speak up, lassie, I can't hear you."

She licked her dry lips and tried again. "Tobias Wood."

"Tobias Wood – oh my goodness, that's his name, is it?" said Uncle Wilf, getting up. "How are you, Tobias my old friend?" He went over to the rocking chair and held out his hand. Emily wondered what it must feel like, rather like shaking hands with damp air, she thought. She certainly didn't want to try it!

"Oh, there's so much I want to know – where do we start? Er… let's see. Jack, er, Tobias, my old friend – why did you haunt Cliff House for all those years? What happened to you?"

The ghost started to rock again, to and fro, to and fro and he seemed to be looking into the distance, as if he was trying to remember – remember something that had happened long, long ago. And then at last he began to tell his story.

"I was born at Cliff House in 1629," he said, and then he looked at Emily so she could repeat this to Uncle Wilf, but her heart was thumping so much she thought it was going to jump right out of her chest and land on the floor. Again she opened her mouth to speak, but no sound came.

Uncle Wilf came to stand beside her again. His warm hand on her shoulder was comforting and stopped her shaking so much. She noticed that the pirate spoke with a Devonshire accent, in the same way as Gertie and Uncle

Wilf, and that made her feel better too. Taking a deep breath, she licked her lips again.

"He said he was born at Cliff House in 1629," she heard herself saying shakily.

"Oh my!" said Uncle Wilf, giving her shoulder another encouraging squeeze.

"Well done, little lass, well done! Please go on, Jack… er I mean Tobias."

The ghost continued, but sometimes Emily couldn't understand him because he used words she'd never heard before, and he said thee and thou instead of you. It was a long story.

One day, she thought, I'll try and write it all down properly, but this is more or less what he told her.

Chapter 20
Tobias Wood

Tobias Wood was born in 1629 at Cliff House and that was where he lived till he was 17. He loved the sea and when he was growing up he used to spend hours down on the beach with the fishermen. Sometimes they let him go with them when they went fishing.

His father, James Wood, was a rich man who had two big ships – one called The Troubadour and the other The Sea Dragon. He had made lots of money buying and selling spices, which grew on the islands near Africa. When Tobias was 17, his father said he must join the family business and work in the office in Plymouth, which was a big port nearby. Tobias didn't want to do that - he just wanted to be a fisherman and marry his sweetheart, Martha, a girl from the village, whose father was one of the crew on The Sea Dragon. But his father wouldn't hear of it and made him start in the office straight away.

Tobias hated the work and was very unhappy. He had to sit in a stuffy room and add up lots of numbers and make lists and write letters to people with a quill pen. He had terrible arguments with his father. One evening after he'd finished in the office, he was drinking a glass of ale at an inn in the town before going back to Cliff House for the night. Suddenly, some men burst in through the door and forced him and two other young men who were there to go with them and join the crew of a ship, which was setting sail the next day. In those days that is what often happened when they needed more sailors – it was called being press ganged. There was no time to tell his father – he just had to go with them. It was a navy ship called HMS Reliance and their job was to patrol the seas and look after the merchant ships (like the ones his father owned) and protect them from pirates.

It was an exciting time, seeing wonderful new places and after a few months, Tobias began to enjoy life at sea. But it could be very dangerous and they often had battles with pirate ships. He was a sailor on HMS Reliance for three years and then, on one of their voyages back to Plymouth, the ship was caught up in a terrible storm and sank in the Indian Ocean. He managed to survive, but only just, by clinging to a piece of the mast but, as far as he knew, everyone else on board was drowned.

After two days drifting on the seas, he believed he was going to die. Just as he'd given up all hope of being rescued, he was picked up by a pirate ship and made to become one of their gang. That was when his whole life changed.

He was forced to join them in raiding and looting other ships: pillaging, plundering and killing became second nature to him and after a time, he found the danger and excitement thrilling – there was nothing like it. And yet sometimes, he found himself dreaming of his old life back at Cliff House and was determined that one day, if he got the chance, he'd escape and go back there. He still loved Martha and wanted to see her again.

Then, one day his father's ship, The Sea Dragon, sailed into view, on its way home to Plymouth and the pirates decided that they would attack it because they knew it was full of expensive spices. Tobias didn't want to plunder his father's ship, but knew the pirates would kill him if he refused. Then it dawned on him that this might be his chance to escape. He planned that as soon as he was on board, he would join the crew of The Sea Dragon and fight against the pirates.

Once aboard, the pirates began to fight, swinging their cutlasses and firing their pistols. Tobias looked around desperately to see if there was anyone on The Sea Dragon that he recognised, but the years had passed and he realised that most of the crew had changed. Suddenly, he saw someone he remembered – it was Martha's father. He ran over to him, to tell him that he was Tobias Wood and that his father was the owner of the ship, but the man didn't recognise him and shot him through the heart.

Emily was shocked when the story came to a sudden end, but of course that was when Tobias's life had stopped so there was no more to tell. It had taken a long time because she'd had to repeat everything to Uncle Wilf, who kept on interrupting and asking questions and getting very excited. At last the pirate was silent – there didn't seem to be any more he wanted to say.

Uncle Wilf and Emily sat for a while without speaking. Then, at last, Emily plucked up courage and asked timidly, "What happened to Martha?"

Tobias stretched out his long legs in front of him. "I never discovered what became of her," he said sadly in his deep, echoing voice.

"What did he say? What did he say?" said Uncle Wilf and Emily repeated to him what Tobias had told her. There was a long pause.

"Was that why your ghost came back to Cliff House?" asked Uncle Wilf. "Was it because you hoped to see Martha again?"

But Tobias didn't answer – just went on rocking to and fro.

"Don't you want to ask him where he goes off to with Autolocus… er, Tolly?" Emily said.

"Oh, yes, of course, of course... that was one of the things we wanted to know, wasn't it?" said Uncle Wilf. "Er, do you mind telling us that, Tobias my old friend?"

To Emily's surprise, the pirate chuckled. It was a hollow, throaty sound and it echoed round the little attic room.

"To the sea, of course," he answered. "It's my second home and I'll never be parted from it. I go back in time – sometimes, I board HMS Reliance and I'm one of His Majesty's sailors again. Other times, I go back to the pirate ship, when I rode the high seas as a buccaneer, leading a life of excitement and adventure, although it was the death of me in the end."

Emily shrank back as Tobias got up suddenly. He took the big belt with the cutlass hanging on it from the back of the chair and buckled it round his waist. Then, he started to pace restlessly up and down and the smell of the sea became very strong.

"I have to be free," he said, waving his arms excitedly. "I have to have the wind in my hair and the sting of the salt spray on my skin. I have to feel the ocean rearing and plunging under my feet, and look up into the endless blue of the sky." He stopped pacing and looked out of the small attic window. "And sometimes I come to rest on my island – it's beautiful there. So, now and again I have to go back. I time travel and Autolocus comes with me." He turned towards them. Emily still couldn't see his face properly because of the shadow from his big hat.

"Autolocus needs his freedom too," he went on, "It's no life for a bird in a cage. And so we go together - back to the places I used to sail to in the Indian Ocean, to the tropical spice islands and the ports along the coast of Africa. Unless a person has been there he can't imagine the colours! The sights and sounds and smells are unforgettable – the ocean, with its shoals of brilliantly coloured fish, weaving in and out of the coral reefs, the exquisite sandy beaches and shells; the exotic flowers and butterflies and extraordinary trees, one of which they say can cure all manner of diseases, which are home to all kinds of wonderful birds and monkeys. The parrots and parakeets there are free to fly as they please and Autolocus flies off with them until I decide the time has come to leave."

Uncle Wilf didn't interrupt while the pirate was pacing back and forth, but after he'd stopped talking Emily was able to tell him what the pirate had said.

For a moment she tried to imagine the things he'd described to her. It was another world and she longed to be able to see it. Then suddenly, just as she was plucking up courage to ask him another question, they heard Gertie's voice, calling from the bottom of the stairs, "Lunch is ready, come on down." Her voice jerked them both back to reality.

For a moment neither of them moved, then Uncle Wilf got up from the bed.

"Maybe one day you'll take us with you," he said. "Would you be able to do that?"

Emily managed to stand, although her legs still felt wobbly. She had no idea how long they'd been up in the attic.

The pirate didn't answer Uncle Wilf. He was standing near the window and, as they watched, his shape began to get fuzzy around the edges and different bits of him started to blur together and turn back into the grey mist.

"Where are you going?" Emily called out, but there was no reply and after a moment or two there was no longer any trace of him, just a faint smell of the sea.

* * * * * * * *

151

While they were having lunch, Uncle Wilf and Emily told the others about Tobias and all that he'd said.

"Uncle Wilf," said Gertie, looking pale. "This isn't one of your pranks, is it?"

"Strike me pink if it's not the absolute truth," said Uncle Wilf. "Emily here listened to every word he said and then she repeated it all to me. I can't hear him speaking – remember?"

"And you're not making it up, Emily? You absolutely promise?"

"I promise, Gertie. I was absolutely terrified I can tell you, but I said I'd do it."

"Why didn't you let us come up to the attic while he was there?" asked Harry, disappointed at being left out.

"You wouldn't catch me going up there," said Laura.

"Well I would have gone," said Harry. "It's not fair. Even if we couldn't see him, I can think of all sorts of things I'd like to have asked him."

"I don't think he'd have come if we'd all been there," said Uncle Wilf. "Anyway, it would have taken too long. He didn't answer everything we asked him anyway."

Just then the doorbell rang and Gertie got unsteadily to her feet, almost tripping over Izzie who'd been lying under the table and who now rushed ahead of her to the front door, barking excitedly.

"Whoever can that be?" she said, holding on to the back of the chair for support. She looked shaken by what they'd told her. "Look, whoever it is, I think we need to keep this to ourselves. We'll never be able to sell this house if people know there's a ghost here. Oh, and that reminds me, I've entered that competition for the big house in Devon that Mrs Skeet told me about." She took an envelope off the

152

shelf. "I'd like you to stick it in the letterbox for me when you take Izzie for her walk."

The doorbell rang again. "All right, all right, I'm coming," Gertie shouted.

They heard the front door opening and then Gertie giving a loud shriek. It made them all jump and they ran to see what the matter was.

There on the doorstep stood someone nobody recognised at first. Gone was the turban and in its place was a fuzz of short bristles, very straight and very black, a bit like a porcupine. Gertie had collapsed in a heap by the door and was fanning herself with the envelope.

They knew it was Mrs Skeet because of her large feet, but her face was quite different. Instead of the usual grumpy expression, she was grinning from ear to ear, and Emily saw that she had two very nicely arched black eyebrows over her twinkling eyes.

Uncle Wilf looked at her and burst out laughing. "Well, well, well," he said. "That wishbone certainly did the trick, didn't it?"

"It will grow some more, won't it?" asked Mrs Skeet self-consciously. "You said I'd have curls, didn't you?"

"I certainly did," said Uncle Wilf. "A few more days are all you need – just be patient!"

"What have you been up to this time?" said Gertie weakly, as Uncle Wilf helped her to her feet.

Chapter 21

Do Eggs Grow?

When Laura and Emily went down to the allotment that evening to water their sunflowers, Uncle Wilf went with them and took a photograph of each of them with Bert's camera. Hattie was way taller than Emily now and she had to tilt her head back to look up at the sunflower's beautiful yellow face. Laura had to admit that Hermione wasn't quite as tall, and Emily could tell she was a bit annoyed. Anyway, they were sure that theirs were bigger and more beautiful than all the other sunflowers on the allotment and they were well chuffed. They told Hattie and Hermione about Mrs Skeet's hair growing and that she looked like a porcupine. The two sunflowers looked down at them and it seemed for all the world as if they were laughing.

Saturday was to be the day of the "Tallest and Most Beautiful Sunflower" competition and the judge was coming over to measure the exhibits at about midday. There were only three more days to go. Gertie told them there were nine other entries besides theirs.

It was a hot and sticky evening and there'd been no rain for a while, so people were on their allotments watering their vegetables, preparing for the Autumn Show which was to take place in the middle of September. Emily and Laura inspected Gertie's row of Runner Beans, which she was going to enter in the show. They looked very good indeed. Coddie Rowe was over by his shed, leaning on his fork, gawping at them. Emily had brought a special treat for Tolly – a slice of mango. She thought how dull it must be for her to be cooped up in the shed all the time, but it couldn't be long now, surely, before the egg hatched.

It felt hot and stuffy inside the shed, and Emily opened the window as usual to let in some fresh air. Tolly was shifting about restlessly. She'd pushed a lot of the torn-up newspaper and sawdust out of the box where it lay scattered around untidily on the floor.

"I wouldn't like to be shut in here all the time," said Laura, flapping her hands in front of her face. "It's so hot, can't we leave the window open? I'm sure she's much too fond of her egg to want to fly out and leave it."

Emily tickled the back of Tolly's head gently, smoothing down the feathers on her neck. "Is it too hot in here for you, Tolly? Aren't you comfortable?" She lifted her off the nest and then almost dropped her when she saw the egg. It was three times bigger than before and the colour had changed to a deep amber. She gave a squeal and Uncle Wilf appeared in the doorway.

The three of them stared at the egg. Not only was it much bigger than before and a different colour, but it seemed to be glowing! Uncle Wilf put out his hand and touched it, ever so gently, and it began to make a soft humming sound.

"Blithering heck fire!" he exclaimed in alarm, jumping back, almost as if he'd had an electric shock. Tolly was starting to struggle, desperate to get back on her nest, so Emily put her down carefully and she settled herself over the egg, fluffing out her feathers. It was obvious she was having trouble covering it completely.

"What on earth's going on here?" cried Uncle Wilf.

"I thought you said eggs don't grow," Emily said.

"They don't grow and they don't glow either," said Laura.

"This is absolutely extraordinary!" said Uncle Wilf, pushing his glasses on top of his head and wrinkling his forehead. "Could someone be playing some kind of a trick on us I wonder?"

"Do you mean someone might be swapping the egg and putting another one in its place?" said Laura, twiddling her pony tail round and round in her fingers "Or maybe it's not a real egg. Real eggs don't hum like that!"

"Why would anyone want to do that?" Emily said. "And who could do it? We always keep the door locked. And the window's always been shut too."

Uncle Wilf went over to the door, examined the lock, then looked all around the shed, up at the roof and at the window. He shut it, then opened it again.

Emily took the piece of mango out of the plastic bag and held it out to Tolly, who pecked at it hungrily. She wished Tolly could tell them what was going on, but she hadn't said a word for ages. When she'd finished, Emily filled up her dish with parrot food and Laura went outside and put more water in the bottle, which was almost empty.

They all agreed that Tolly needed a bit of fresh air and Uncle Wilf said it would be all right to leave the window open a crack. They stayed with her a bit longer, but she wasn't interested in them at all and just closed her eyes.

"She's concentrating very hard on getting that egg to hatch," said Uncle Wilf. "I think we'd better leave her to it."

"Bye, Tolly, see you tomorrow," Emily called, as they shut the shed door behind them. Uncle Wilf locked it and put the key in his pocket. "Bye, Hattie," she called again over her shoulder as they left the allotment and walked home up the path.

The Porcupine was still there when they got back. (They always called her that now.) She and Gertie were having a cup of tea in the kitchen and Firefly was curled up on her lap, purring contentedly. Emily picked Josephina up and gave her a cuddle – she was getting quite big, but was still very kittenish and loved you to play with her. They told Gertie and the Porcupine about the egg.

"Well I never! Sounds like someone's playing a silly joke on you," said Gertie.

"But why would they want to do such a thing?" Uncle Wilf asked. "And how could they have got into the shed?" He turned to Emily. "You're sure you've always locked the door?"

After what had happened before and the awful panic she'd had thinking she'd left the cage open, she'd always been especially careful to lock the shed after going to see Tolly. She was hurt that Uncle Wilf had even asked her that.

"Sorry," he said, seeing her face, "of course you have." He ruffled her hair. "No, there must be some other explanation. It really is very curious."

Gertie suddenly had an idea. She'd give Johnny Watkins' dad a ring and ask him to come over and have a look at the egg. He was a zoology professor – that was somebody who had studied of all sorts of animals. He'd be sure to know if it was a real egg or not.

"It's a mystery," said the Porcupine, lifting Firefly off her lap and putting her down gently on the floor. "I'd have liked one of your kittens," she said, getting to her feet.

"Turtleshells is always the prettiest. Maybe next time!"

"Tortoiseshells," corrected Laura, "she's a tortoiseshell cat nor a turtleshell. And anyway, I don't suppose Mum'll let us have any more kittens."

"Sounds like I've missed the bus then, doesn't it," laughed the Porcupine. "Anyways, let me know what the Professor says, won't you?"

Soon after she'd gone Bert came home and they told him all about the egg. He was as mystified as the rest of them.

And so was the professor when he called round a couple of days later. He examined the egg, much to Tolly's displeasure, and declared that it was indeed a real egg and would hatch any day now. He also added that he'd never come across one like it in all his years of study.

But the night before the judging of the sunflowers – it was a Friday – the most awful thing happened. In fact two awful things happened.

Chapter 22

The Storm

People kept talking about the drought. There had been no rain for days and the ground was dry and hard. Fierce, black clouds were building up in the sky and on Friday evening, the man on the telly said there was going to be a storm.

"Hope it won't be as bad as the last one." Uncle Wilf was looking anxiously out of the window. "At least we're not by the sea."

"Don't worry, Uncle Wilf," said Gertie comfortingly. "You're quite safe here."

The storm didn't start till they'd all gone to bed. Emily was woken up by a clap of thunder, which was like a bomb exploding on the roof. She lay, hugging Marigold and listened to the storm as it raged around the house. The wind was howling like a wild animal and beating against the window next to her bed, as if it was frantic to get inside. Emily shut her eyes, but she could still see the lightning through her eyelids.

The rain started a few moments later. It sounded as if someone was throwing bucketfuls of water against the window. She remembered how there'd been a storm the first night she'd come to live with the Pinks and she thought about poor Uncle Wilf's house being washed away by the sea. She started to shiver and hugged Marigold harder, telling her not to be afraid, because she knew Marigold wasn't very brave.

As quickly as it had started, the storm died away, and after a while Emily felt able to open her eyes. She looked over at Laura's bedside clock, which had a luminous dial and saw that it was nearly 4 o'clock. She wasn't sure if she'd be able to get back to sleep again before it was time to get up. She wondered where the storm had gone and that made her think of Tobias. Where did he go to when he melted away? Did he stay in the attic or did he just vanish like smoke?

In the morning the sun was shining and there were just a few clouds in the sky. They looked like swans' feathers. It was a beautiful day and not as hot as before. Straight after breakfast, the three children went down to the allotment. They couldn't wait to know if the egg had hatched and they wanted to check on their sunflowers too, because the judging was going to happen that afternoon at half past four.

Leaves had been torn from the trees by the wind and there were puddles all along the lane. As soon as they started out, they realised they should have put on their boots. Gertie wasn't going to be pleased when she saw the state of their sandals!

They came to the end of the fence and turned the corner to go down to the allotment, but stopped abruptly and stared in horror. Their three best sunflowers – Hattie, Hermione and Hanky Panky - were lying face down in the mud.

"Oh no!" Emily shrieked. "The wind's flattened them – they're ruined!" With tears in her eyes, she ran down the slope to get a better look. She couldn't believe what she was seeing.

Harry came up behind her. "They were just too tall, the wind must have snapped them off."

"But they were tied on to sticks," protested Laura, as she caught up with them, "and look, the other sunflowers are all right."

It was true. Hiccups, Holly and Hayley on the other side of the bed were still standing, although they too had been battered by the storm. They noticed as well that most of the other sunflowers on the allotment seemed to be all right, if a bit drunken-looking.

Emily bent down and lifted up Hattie's head. It had been squashed down in the mud and hung limply from the stalk. Her beautiful face was muddy and her leaves were broken.

"Oh, poor Hattie," she wailed, "oh you poor thing! What are we going to do?" The other two sunflowers were in the same state.

"Let's go home and tell Uncle Wilf," said Harry at once. He seemed as upset as she was.

"Hang on a minute," said Laura. She was bending down, examining Hermione carefully.

"What are you doing?" asked Harry impatiently.

"Just looking," said Laura coolly. "It's strange, isn't it," she went on after a moment, "because the sticks are still in the ground and so are the roots." Harry looked at her blankly. "If the wind had blown the sunflowers down, then the sticks would have snapped or come out of the ground and the roots would have been torn up." She pointed at Hermione' stalk. "It looks to me as if it's been cut."

Harry and Emily looked at Hermione's stalk and then at Hattie's and Hanky-Panky's. It was the same with all three. It was as if someone had come along and cut them off with a knife or a pair of scissors. Emily was shocked. Who would do such a wicked thing?

"Come on," yelled Harry. "We'll tell Uncle Wilf. He'll know what to do."

They raced back along the lane, taking no notice of the puddles this time. Their legs and feet were spattered with mud by the time they reached the house. Bert and Gertie had gone shopping, but Uncle Wilf was in the garden, reading the paper. When they told him what had happened he came straight down to the allotment with them, looking grim.

He picked up each sunflower in turn and examined it carefully. "I think you're absolutely right," he said quietly. "Someone's been here and deliberately done this. Which of you spotted it?"

"I did," said Laura. "I'm going to be a detective when I grow up," she added, tossing her ponytail.

Emily started to cry – she couldn't help it. What a horrible, cruel thing to do! She loved Hattie, really loved her – she'd been so beautiful and tall, and now she was lying in the mud, absolutely ruined. She felt she'd really known her, like a friend, and now she was as good as dead. She buried her face in Uncle Wilf's chest and howled.

Some of the other people with allotments came over and looked sympathetically at the sunflowers lying forlornly in the mud. "Quite a storm, wasn't it?" one of them said. "Did a lot of damage to my dahlias too."

"Come on now," said Uncle Wilf briskly, giving them all a peppermint. "Let's go home and get you cleaned up."

"What about Tolly?" said Laura. "Hadn't we better make sure she's OK while we're down here?"

In the shock and upset, they'd all forgotten about poor Tolly. Emily pulled herself together and took a deep breath to try and stop the sobs jumping out of her chest. Taking the shed key out of her pocket, she walked over and unlocked the door.

The first thing she noticed was that the window was wide open. The second thing was that there was no sign of Tolly, or the egg! She started to search frantically amongst the pieces of paper and woolly jumper in the box, but there was nothing there. It was like a nasty dream. Then the others came crowding into the shed behind her.

For a moment nobody said anything; then they all started talking at once. Where was Tolly? She must have flown out of the window. But where was the egg? She'd never have gone off and left her precious egg. So, if she hadn't flown off, had someone taken her? And the egg too?

Emily sat down suddenly on the floor. Her legs didn't seem able to hold her up and her head was throbbing. It was then, through her tears, that she spotted Tolly's red tail feathers. A work bench ran all along one side of the shed, piled with flowerpots, seed trays, gardening tools and so on, and underneath were larger pots and sacks of compost and fertiliser. And there was Tolly, hiding behind one of the sacks. Emily could just see her red tail feathers sticking out.

"There she is!" she screamed, pointing. Tolly was very frightened and at first she wouldn't let Emily pick her up. Uncle Wilf knelt down and spoke to her soothingly, but she pecked his hand when he tried to touch her.

"The poor thing," said Harry, "she's scared to death."

"I suppose it was the storm," said Laura. "You should have brought her back to the house, Em."

"It might have been the storm," said Uncle Wilf, getting to his feet. "But I think it was something else. Where's the egg?"

"Maybe she's hidden it," said Harry, "to protect it from the storm when the wind blew the window open." He began to search the shed, looking inside the flowerpots and behind the stacks of seed trays.

"Don't be silly," said Laura. "How could she hide the egg – she couldn't have picked it up, could she? It's got to be in the box." She searched among the jumble of newspapers and tissues that had been Tolly's nest, but there was no sign of the egg.

Emily put out her hand to Tolly and after a moment she let Emily stroke her. She tickled her behind her head and spoke to her gently, which seemed to calm her. She was looking very unhappy, but after a while, she cautiously came out from behind the sack and let Emily lift her up.

Uncle Wilf opened and shut the window several times and examined the metal arm. Harry and Laura sat down on a sack of grass seed and Emily sat on a large upturned flowerpot. None of them said anything. They were all shocked by the things that had happened that morning. Emily became aware of sounds outside the shed, the birds singing and the voices of people talking to each other as they worked on their plots of land. She could hear them quite clearly.

Suddenly, Uncle Wilf turned from the window. "Come on all of you, we're going home – the egg's not here. Emily, hold on tightly to Tolly and bring her with you. We're going to take her back to the house."

Tolly's cage was ready for her and Emily quickly put some food in the dish and filled the water bottle. The parrot seemed glad to go inside it and Emily put the cover over it so she could go to sleep. She was probably exhausted. Emily felt tired too.

"You'd all better go upstairs and clean that mud off your legs and feet before Gertie gets back," said Uncle Wilf, taking off his muddy trainers and putting on his slippers.

"As for me, I've got a little job to do." He lifted the telephone receiver and punched in a number. "Is that the police? I'd like to report a theft and some criminal damage."

Chapter 23

Laura Plays Detective

"I could have told you you'd be wasting your time ringing the police," said Bert when they told him and Gertie what had happened. "They've got more important things to do than worry about a stolen parrot's egg and some vandalised sunflowers. At least Tolly's safe and we certainly won't be putting her in the shed again."

And that seemed to be that. There didn't seem to be anything else they could do. There was no way they could win the competition now – there wouldn't be any point even going. It was so disappointing.

Emily wondered if the same person who'd ruined their sunflowers had also stolen Tolly's egg. That was really worse than the sunflowers. Poor Tolly! Since they'd brought her back into the house she'd been looking really miserable and had gone off her food. Emily noticed that her feathers had lost their sheen and some of them were falling out again, but nobody seemed to think they could do anything about that either. She'd get over it in time, they said.

The three children sat around glumly on the grass outside the back door. The ground was still wet and Emily soon got up because her shorts were getting damp. Laura was sitting with her knees bent up, staring down at the ground. Emily could tell she was thinking. Then Izzie started whining and they knew she was asking to be taken for a walk.

Laura suddenly sprang to her feet. "I know what, let's go down to the allotment again – we'll take Izzie with us. There's something I want to look at."

She wouldn't tell them what it was, however much they pestered her. Gertie made them put on their wellies and off they went, with Izzie rushing ahead of them along the path. The sun had dried up the puddles quite a bit, but there was still plenty of mud around.

"I just want to have another look at the scene of the crime," announced Laura importantly when they got to the allotment.

"What are you on about this time?" said Harry wearily. "Can't we just get on with the walk? I want to get back and paint the wheels on my cart."

"Oh blow you and your silly cart," said Laura impatiently, undoing the elastic band on her ponytail and shaking out her hair. "Don't you want to find out who trampled all over our sunflowers? There could be important evidence here. Now, just stand where you are, both of you, and hold on tight to Izzie – I don't want her running all over the place."

She scooped her hair up, twisted the elastic band back on and then stood for a long time, studying the ground where the sunflowers still lay in the mud.

"I thought so," she said at last.

"What is it?" Emily asked, catching the note of excitement in Laura's voice.

"Well, look at the earth where the sunflowers are – there are lots of footprints, aren't there?"

Harry and Emily nodded, wondering where all this was leading.

"If you think about it," Laura went on, "all those footprints must have got there *after* the rain last night, mustn't they? I mean, before that the ground was too hard for anyone to leave footprints, wasn't it?"

"That's true, I suppose," agreed Harry grudgingly. "So what?"

"Well, think about it," said Laura. "You and I were both wearing sandals weren't we, when we came rushing down here after breakfast? And Emily had her flip-flops on. And if you look, you can see our footmarks, can't you? Look, there, there and there."

They peered over to where she was pointing at the jumble of footmarks by the sunflowers. If you looked carefully you could just make out which was which. And then they noticed another set of footprints, larger ones.

"Those bigger ones must be Uncle Wilf's old trainers," said Harry.

"Well done, Sherlock Holmes," said Laura, rather sarcastically, Emily thought.

"But whose are those other ones then – quite small, aren't they? None of us was wearing shoes like that, were we?"

"They're trainers too, aren't they?" Emily said.

"Exactly!" said Laura triumphantly. "And come over here. There's a really clear footprint here at the edge of the plot. Look at it carefully and tell me what you think? Do we know anyone who has trainers like that?"

Emily bent down to look and right away she recognised the pattern she'd seen on Lip-Up Stinky's trainers that time he'd boasted about them at the market. She straightened up and she and Harry looked at each other. "Lip-Up Stinky," they both said together.

"Well, that's what I think too," said Laura.

Harry whistled. "So it was Lip-Up Stinky who cut off our sunflowers and trampled them into the mud," he said in a low voice. "Well, that certainly fits. He always wins the

Sunflower Competition. I guess he wasn't going to let anybody get in his way."

"What a mean thing to do," Emily shouted, feeling really angry.

"Shhhh," said Laura. "We don't want everyone else to hear. Let's stand over there."

They moved up the slope, out of earshot of people on the allotment. Laura had it all worked out. Lip-Up Stinky wouldn't have come down to the allotment in the middle of the night, while the storm was raging; he wouldn't have been brave enough. No, he'd have waited till the storm was over and it was just getting light. Then he'd have come creeping down, before anyone else was around, and he'd have cut the sunflower stalks and gone home again. What a stinker! His name certainly suited him. Laura said she thought he was probably woken up in the night by the storm, and realised that everyone would think that the wind had blown down the sunflowers. But of course, he hadn't realised he'd left his footprints in the mud!

Harry looked at his watch. There was only an hour to go before the judging, but none of them felt like going to it. There was no way anyone would think their sunflowers were the tallest and most beautiful. They wandered home along the lane, feeling sad but angry too.

"Not going? Of course we're going," said Uncle Wilf when they told him and Gertie and Bert about the footprint and that they were almost certain that it had been Lip-Up Stinky who'd ruined their chances of winning. Uncle Wilf's eyes were flashing.

"The little devil! Now, we're not going to accuse him of anything because we haven't got proper proof, but that little stinker's not going to have the satisfaction of winning and we're going to make him feel pretty uncomfortable!"

The sun had almost dried up the puddles as they walked back down the lane again for the fourth time that day. Gertie was wearing her best yellow dress, which made her look like a sunflower, Emily thought, although not as thin. Bert and Uncle Wilf had tidied themselves up too.

When they arrived at the allotment loads of grown-ups and children were walking around, admiring each other's flowers and chattering away. Emily should have been excited, but instead she just felt sad. People came wandering over to their patch of ground and when they saw the sunflowers lying face-down in the mud, some of them looked shocked and walked away, others were sympathetic and asked what had happened. Uncle Wilf said that they must have blown down in the wind. They said, "What a pity," and "Never mind" and "Better luck next time" - things like that.

But why was Uncle Wilf lying? Emily was cross with him – he knew quite well that it wasn't the wind that had blown them down.

"Shhhh, Emily," he said gently and put an arm round her shoulder. "Just wait, lassie."

In a little while, a lady in a flowery dress came walking down from the top end of the allotment where the main road was. She had a nice, smiley face and waved to everyone. She was carrying a very long ruler with big numbers on it and there was a man with her, carrying a loud speaker and a book with a yellow cover. The man said good afternoon to everyone through the loudspeaker and then welcomed Mrs Wiseman, who had come to judge the competition for the Tallest and Most Beautiful Sunflower, and everyone clapped. Emily thought that Mrs Wiseman was a really good name for a judge.

They all crowded round to watch as each sunflower was measured in turn and the height recorded in the yellow book. It took a long time to get round to Gertie's allotment because, as well as measuring each sunflower and telling everyone through the loudspeaker how tall the sunflower was (and some had more than one), Mrs Wiseman stopped and talked to people as well. Emily wanted to go home, but Bert and Uncle Wilf went up to the road and came back, carrying ice-creams, which was nice because Emily was feeling hot as well as sad.

At last, Mrs Wiseman got to Coddie Rowe's plot. Lip-Up Stinky was standing by his sunflowers looking very confident and pleased with himself, as if he'd been the one who'd planted them and watered them and looked after them, when everyone knew it wasn't him at all, but his father. Mrs Wiseman measured each one and the man told everyone through the loudspeaker what the measurements were and then wrote them down in the yellow book.

Then, at last, they came to Gertie's plot. Mrs Wiseman looked shocked when she saw their sunflowers and asked who'd grown them. Uncle Bert pushed the three children forward. Emily felt like crying, but she bit her lip hard, determined that she wouldn't because she could see Lip-Up Stinky looking over at them with a horrible smirk on his face.

"Well, what's happened here then?" asked Mrs Wiseman.

"It looks very much as though they were blown down in the storm last night, doesn't it?" said Uncle Wilf. His ears were very pink.

"That's a terrible thing to have happened," said Mrs Wiseman. She waited for a moment or two, looking puzzled, and then stepped forward and turned the sunflowers over, one by one, so that their battered faces could be plainly seen. "They were indeed very fine specimens, but no-one could call them beautiful now, could they?" she said, turning to the crowd of people who had been following her.

"They were also wonderfully tall," she said and bent down again and examined the stalk of each one carefully. "This is very strange," she said. "Give me the measuring stick please, Tony."

The man handed it to her and with great patience she tried to measure the stalks, but they were so mangled and twisted that she had to give up.

"I'm so sorry," she said, "it looks as though I'm not going to be able to get a correct reading for these. It must be very disappointing for you. But don't give up – try again next year and good luck." She smiled at them uncertainly.

Emily looked over at Lip-Up Stinky. He was hiding his mouth behind his hand, trying to smother a laugh.

"Er, just a moment, Mrs Wiseman," said Uncle Wilf, stepping forward. "I wonder if you'd mind looking at these photographs, which I took just a couple of days ago."

He handed an envelope to her and went on, "As you can see, Emily and Laura are each standing next to their sunflower – makes a charming picture, doesn't it? When they grew them, they took particular care to plant them very near to the shed, so they would be protected from the wind, yet still get the maximum sun. It is extraordinary then, isn't it, that the wind still managed to knock them over?"

Uncle Wilf was speaking in a loud voice so that all the people who were gathered round could easily hear what he was saying. They started murmuring to each other.

"It is strange too, isn't it, that no other sunflower on any other allotment appears to have been seriously affected by the wind?" The murmuring grew louder and Emily saw that

Lip-Up Stinky was looking around nervously and his face had gone red. Coddie Rowe was looking at him angrily.

"Now I happen to know that the shed is just over 2½ metres tall," Uncle Wilf went on, "and you'll see from the photograph that the sunflowers are a good deal higher than that — probably another metre higher, which by my calculation would make them between 3½ and 4 metres tall. Do you agree? And I think you'll also agree that not only are the sunflowers very tall, they're also extremely beautiful."

Mrs Wiseman looked at the photographs, then at the shed, then at the photographs again and then at the sunflowers lying on the ground. Tony, the man with the loudspeaker, was peering over her shoulder and nodding his head.

"The world record for the tallest sunflower is 6 metres," Uncle Wilf went on, "but unfortunately, Emily and Laura were rather late planting theirs this year or I'm sure they could have come somewhere near that."

Mrs Wiseman looked confused and she and Tony went into a huddle and the photographs were passed from person to person through the crowd. After they'd talked about it for what seemed a very long time and Tony had measured the shed with the measuring stick and then measured Emily and Laura, he announced through the loudspeaker that Emily and Laura were the joint winners! They couldn't believe it! They hugged each other and jumped up and down.

The crowd gave a huge cheer and behind her Emily could hear Gertie and Bert cheering louder than anyone. Finally, Tony announced the names of the people who'd come in second and third place — Lip-Up Stinky's name wasn't even mentioned.

When she looked over to where he'd been standing, he'd disappeared. And so had Coddie Rowe. Well, she wasn't really surprised about that!

Chapter 24

The Reward

Mrs Wiseman presented Laura and Emily with a certificate for winning the competition. It had "The Tallest and Most Beautiful Sunflower Competition," printed along the top and underneath Mrs Wiseman had written their names and "Joint First Prize". She shook them each by the hand and congratulated them. The certificate had a picture of a sunflower's smiling face in the corner. Emily couldn't believe it! One minute she was feeling sad and disappointed and the next, she and Laura were the winners.

She showed the certificate to Tolly when they got home, but she wasn't interested, so Emily propped it up on the mantelpiece. She knew Tolly was missing her egg, which made her feel sad all over again and angry too. She kept thinking about it, about the storm and about the shed window being open. She pictured Lip-Up Stinky skulking down to the allotment before it was properly light and wondered if indeed he'd been the one who'd taken the egg.

Next day, she and Laura were helping Harry paint the wheels of his cart. He didn't seem to mind that Hanky-Panky hadn't won a prize in the competition. The cart was yellow because he'd used some paint left over from when Bert had painted the back door. He would have liked the cart to have black wheels – that would look classy, he said – but they had to paint them green, because that was the colour Bert had used on the water butt and there was a bit left.

"Now I've got to think of a name for it," he said, standing up and admiring his work. The cart looked excellent now it

174

was finished and Emily hoped Harry would take her for another ride.

"Those two colours remind me of the sunflowers," said Laura, sitting back on her heels. "Why don't we call it 'The Sunflower Express'?"

"Or what about 'The Wheely-Bin Express'?" Emily suggested.

Harry didn't like either of those, besides he wanted to be the one to choose the name. But he couldn't think of one. "I'll come up with something later," he said.

Harry and Laura seemed to have forgotten about the egg being stolen; well perhaps not forgotten, but they said there wasn't a lot of point thinking about it because there wasn't anything they could do. But Emily wanted them to think about it.

"It could have been Lip-Up Stinky, you know," she said. "Who stole the egg. He could have done it after he'd cut down the sunflowers."

They all had green paint on their hands and Harry had it on his T-shirt too and his face.

"We could look and see if there are any footprints under the window," Laura suggested.

"I'm not going all the way down there again now," said Harry. "Anyway, it's nearly supper time. We'll look tomorrow."

"That's not a bad idea though, is it?" said Laura, playing the detective again. "Somebody might have left footprints there."

When they did go down the next day there'd been another shower of rain in the night and if there'd been any footprints under the shed window, they'd been washed away.

"You know, if you think about it, there were quite a lot of people who knew about Tolly being kept in the shed and that she'd laid an egg," said Laura. It could have been any of them."

Emily remembered that, when the three of them and Uncle Wilf had been in the shed looking for Tolly and the egg, she'd been able to hear people outside on the allotments, talking to each other. It had been quite clear. Suppose Lip-Up Stinky or Coddie had been standing near the shed window on other occasions when they'd been down there feeding Tolly? They might easily have heard them talking about the strange egg.

"Well, I suppose they might have known about it," said Laura. "But then there's the Porcupine and Professor Watkins who knew about it too, and Tom and his mum, remember? They were there that evening after we came back from the vet and they could all have told other people, so who knows how many people knew. Anyone could have taken it."

"But it was such a mean thing to do," Emily protested. "I can't imagine that any of those people would do it."

"I know what," Harry said excitedly. "Why don't we put a notice up, offering a reward?"

"For bringing back the egg?" Emily said.

"Wow! That's not bad, Harry," said Laura generously.

"Well, it might work," Harry said, smiling modestly. Emily could see he was well chuffed to have thought of the idea. "I mean whoever took the egg might get bored just looking at it," he said. "And it would have got cold without Tolly sitting on it, so it's never going to hatch now, is it?"

"They might have kept it warm with a hot water bottle or something," said Laura, "you never know."

They all agreed that offering a reward was worth a try. Laura got out her pad of paper and her pack of felt tips.

"What shall we say?" she said, tearing off a sheet of paper. "I know – 'REWARD FOR THE RETURN OF VALUABLE PARROT'S EGG' and then our phone number." She pulled out a red pen and began to write.

"Let's write lots of notices and stick them up all over the place," said Harry, taking the pad from Laura and tearing out another sheet of paper. "We'll write them in all sorts of different colours to attract attention. I'll do an orange one. There you are," he said pushing the pad towards Emily. "You do some too, go on."

"I'm not sure how to spell valuable," said Laura before she'd got very far. "Hang on a moment and I'll ask Mum." She disappeared into the kitchen.

Emily looked at Harry's piece of paper to see how to spell reward, but he didn't seem too sure either.

Laura came back, followed by Gertie, drying her hands on her apron. "What's going on then?" she asked. She didn't seem in a very good mood and Laura told them later it was because she hadn't won the Devon house competition. They told her what they were planning to do and she sat down at the table with them. The first thing she said was, "And what's the reward you're going to give? If someone does bring the egg back." They had to admit they hadn't thought about that.

"Well, there's no point putting up the notice till you've decided what the reward's going to be, is there?" she said. "I mean, is the reward going to be money, or is it going to be something else?"

"Like what?" said Harry.

"Well, I don't know," said Gertie. "What have you got?"

They sat there gloomily, chewing the ends of their felt-tip pens.

"If I was you," Gertie went on, "I'd leave out the word 'valuable' for a start. If somebody thinks it's a valuable egg, they're not going to give it back unless they're offered something pretty valuable in return, are they?"

"So what do you think we should do then?" asked Laura.

Gertie said they should see how much money they had between them and then decide how much of it they wanted to give as the reward. She also said she thought they were wasting their time and they'd be better off finishing their school projects.

But they weren't going to be discouraged. Harry and Laura ran upstairs and a moment later came down, carrying their money-boxes. They tipped the money out onto the table and counted how much they'd got. Emily didn't have any, which made her feel very left out. Harry had £5.63p and Laura had £9.28p. They didn't want to give all their money for the reward, so they decided they'd each give £4.

"That's £8," said Laura. "Do you think that's enough? Haven't you got any money at all, Emily?"

Emily squirmed uncomfortably. Mum did give her pocket money at home, not very much, but she hadn't got any with her.

Gertie said they didn't have to write how much the reward was on their notice. If someone rang up, then they'd tell them. She also said it would be better if they worded it differently. It should say: 'Reward for information leading to the return of a parrot's egg stolen on 2nd September.' She didn't think that the person who'd stolen the egg would ring up, but somebody who knew about it might.

They wrote out six notices and Gertie gave them some 'Blu-Tack' so they could go and stick them up. They decided to put one on the oak tree at the end of the close, so that whoever was walking past on the main road would see it. They put one up in the newsagent's, one in Blood Sucker Leach's shop and one in the pet shop. That left two remaining. One should definitely be stuck on the allotment shed and they put the last one on the front gate.

Emily felt miserable that she hadn't got any money to add to the reward. She thought about it and thought about it and then she had an idea. When Gertie was on her own she asked her, "Gertie, what does curio mean?"

Gertie was sewing some name-tapes on to a pair of new school trousers she'd bought for Harry.

"Talk about your sunflowers growing," she said, "I'm sure Harry's grown at least two inches during the summer holidays and I've had to buy him so many new things; none of last term's clothes fit him now." She sighed. "Laura's grown too, but not quite so fast." She looked up at Emily. "You don't seem to have got any taller though, do you, Em?" She smiled and rumpled Emily's hair. "Neat and sweet that's you, isn't it, love?"

Thinking about the summer holidays coming to an end brought Emily back down to earth with a bump. She knew there were only a few more days till they went back to school, and she had a sinking feeling in the bottom of her tummy. Of course she wanted to see Mum again, but she hated the thought of leaving No. 14 Willow Close and going to live in an upstairs flat with no garden. And I wouldn't have Tolly to look after any more, she thought. But before that, she had something important to do.

"Gertie," she said again, "do you know what curio means?"

"What's that, luvvie?" Gertie said, biting off a thread with her teeth.

179

"Curio," Emily repeated. "Do you know what it means?"

"Curio? Umm, curio. Let's think now. Well, I think it means something unusual or curious. Yes, I'm sure that's what it means. I'd call Uncle Wilf a curio. Yes, he's a fine example of a curio." She laughed. "Why do you want to know, love?"

Emily didn't tell Gertie why she wanted to know, but she had to tell someone so she told Laura.

"But you can't sell your appendix!" she cried. "You love your appendix."

"Well, I know I do," Emily said. "But I love Tolly more and I want to add something to the reward money. "Do you think Blood Sucker Leach would buy my appendix from me, to sell in his shop? I mean, do you think it's a curio?"

"We could ask him. But are you really sure, Em? I mean it is very special, and you've only got one."

Naturally, Emily didn't *want* to sell her appendix, and she wasn't sure that Blood Sucker Leach would want to buy it anyway. She just thought if they had a bigger reward to give, they might have a better chance of getting the egg back. And, if someone had been keeping it warm with a hot water bottle, Tolly might still be able to hatch it and then she'd be happy again.

She decided not to tell Harry. He'd probably laugh and he'd want to hold the jar and it might break. She got Laura to go with her to Blood Sucker Leach's shop, with the appendix in one of Gertie's shopping bags.

There it was, written over the top of the shop: "B. S. Leach, Antiques and Curios."

Blood Sucker had charged them 25p to put up their notice, but they couldn't see it in the window. Trevor and Jo at the newsagent's hadn't charged them anything.

Emily found her hands were shaking and she was worried she might drop the appendix, but Laura seemed very sure of herself.

"Come on," she said. The bell over the door jingled as they went inside.

Chapter 25

The Appendix

When they got inside they spotted their notice on the wall, near the cash desk. Emily recognised it as one she'd written in blue felt tip and felt a bit stupid when Laura pointed out that she'd spelt parrot with only one R.

The interior of the shop went back a long way and the only light, apart from that coming through the window, was from a single chandelier hanging from the ceiling. Emily could smell the same smell as before, sort of musty but with something else mixed in. It made her nose tickle. There was no sign of Blood Sucker, but she remembered that he was very good at appearing from nowhere. Last time, he'd given them a fright by emerging suddenly from behind a screen.

They held hands and walked slowly towards the back of the shop, past the skeleton and the skull with the candle burning inside it, Emily clutching tightly to the handles of the shopping bag. They looked behind the screen, but there was no-one there. She hadn't noticed before but there were clocks everywhere, some on the walls with pendulums swinging to and fro, some inside glass cases, some on shelves and several grandfather clocks, all busily ticking away. She felt as though they were watching her. Blood Sucker didn't seem to be in the shop and then they saw a door in the back wall which was partly open.

"Perhaps he's in there," Laura whispered. "Excuse me," she called out. There was no reply.

"Maybe that's where he keeps his stolen goods," Emily whispered. "Mum's box might be in there."

"Shall we have a look?" said Laura.

Emily didn't really want to – she'd rather have gone home - but Laura was holding tightly to her hand and, with a quick glance behind, she opened the door wider and pulled Emily inside.

They found themselves in a small room crowded with loads more junk – chairs, tables, chests, lamps and stacks of books. Near a pile of boxes was a glass cabinet full of beautiful butterflies, each one labelled in tiny writing, and next to the cabinet a little black chest containing lots of drawers, rather like a doll's chest of drawers.

Laura pulled one open to peep inside. And what did they find? An egg! It was white with little brown speckles on it. She pulled open another drawer and found another egg, like a blackbird's or a thrush's. Emily had seen pictures of birds' eggs at school. They squatted down and pulled all the drawers open, one by one, and each had an egg inside – different colours and different sizes.

"Wow," Laura breathed and looked at Emily who knew immediately what she was thinking: it could have been Blood Sucker Leach who'd stolen Tolly's egg, to add to his collection! They shut the drawers. Emily was desperate to go, but Laura still wanted to open some of the boxes to see what was inside.

Suddenly, there was a whirring sound, which nearly made them jump out of their skins and Emily almost dropped the shopping bag containing the precious appendix.

A cuckoo had flown out of a clock on the wall above their heads shouting 'Cuckoo' very loudly. Then, behind them, they heard all the clocks in the shop starting to chime the hour, some fast and shrill, some with deeper voices and they didn't all do it at exactly the same moment. When one stopped, another started and the noise seemed to go on and on and on.

"Laura, please let's go," Emily said urgently, pulling her towards the door.

Then, as the last chime faded away there was total silence. Even the clocks seemed to be listening.

As they crept back into the shop, Emily and Laura heard the jingle of the doorbell. It was Blood Sucker Leach returning. He was carrying a newspaper and, stepping behind the counter, he spread it out in front of him and started to read. It was obvious – he had no idea they were there. Emily was terrified. How were they going to get out without him seeing them? They crept forward, then stopped quickly as he turned a page, before creeping forward again. It was like playing Grandmother's Footsteps and they soon realised there was no way they could get past him and out of the door without being seen.

They'd nearly reached the counter when he turned round and started to fiddle with some things on a shelf behind. Emily felt Laura squeeze her hand and knew that she wanted to make a dash for it, but oh dear, at that exact moment she felt an enormous sneeze coming on. Mum had taught her a trick to stop you sneezing and it was really good if you did it in time. You pressed the side of your finger hard underneath your nose and the sneeze would go away, but Laura was holding one of her hands tightly and she was clutching the shopping bag with the other.

"Atishooooo!"

Blood Sucker jumped about a metre into the air and turned round with a look of panic on his long pale face. As soon as he recognised them, the look of fear turned to one of anger.

"What are you two doing creeping about in here?" he demanded furiously.

Laura recovered herself quickly. "We came in to show you something, but you weren't here, so we were just looking around," she replied. Emily was full of admiration at how calm she sounded. "Show him, Emily."

Emily's hands were so shaky she was scared she'd drop the jar as she pulled it out to place it on the counter. Blood Sucker picked it up and peered at it, then put a magnifying glass, which hung on a string round his neck, into his eye and stared at it some more, screwing up his face.

"I think it's a c-c-c-curio," Emily stammered, "and I thought you might like to buy it and put it in your shop."

He turned the jar on one side, so that the appendix moved around in the liquid.

"Ugh," he said. "In heaven's name what is it? Some kind of worm that you've dug up?" He turned the jar the other way and gave it a little shake. "Ugh, it's moving – it's quite disgusting."

"Do please be careful with it," Emily said. "It's very precious and you're not supposed to shake it about."

"But what is it?" Blood Sucker persisted and Emily could tell he really wanted to know.

"It's curious and unusual," she replied helpfully, "and so we think it's probably a curio, don't we Laura?"

She was relieved when, at last, Blood Sucker put the jar down on the counter. He shuddered and wiped his hands down his trousers.

"All right, all right, it is curious and unusual, I'll grant you that, but WHAT is it?"

Emily took a deep breath, looked him boldly in the eye and announced proudly, "It's my appendix."

"Good heavens!" he said, picking up the jar again and fixing his magnifying glass back into his eye. "Well, well, well." He let the magnifying glass drop and put the jar down on the counter. "So, it's an appendix, is it? And it's yours?"

"Yes," Emily said. She thought that maybe he didn't believe her. "Do you want to see my scar?" She started to hitch up her skirt.

"No, no," said Blood Sucker hurriedly, "that won't be necessary." He clasped his long white fingers together.

"It is a curio," isn't it?" said Laura, taking charge.

"Well, I suppose you could call it that."

"And this is a shop that sells antiques and curios, isn't it?"

"True, but I'm not sure that anyone would actually want to buy it."

"Course they would," said Laura. "Think how proud they'd be having it standing on their mantelpiece. All their friends would want to look at it and give it a shake. And they could have a game guessing what it was."

"Mmmmm," said Blood Sucker uncertainly.

"'Course if you don't want it, I'm sure we can sell it to someone else," said Laura, picking up the jar and turning to go.

"No, no, just a moment," said Blood Sucker, reaching forward and taking it from her. Poor Emily was worried that one of them was going to drop it.

"Look, I'll buy it from you and put it over there on the shelf near the skeleton and the skull and if no-one buys it by the end of the month, you can have it back. What do you say?"

He said he'd give them £10 for the appendix and they agreed that if he hadn't sold it by the end of September, they'd give him the ten pounds back and he'd return the appendix.

"We have a deal then," he said, holding out his hand and giving Emily a watery smile.

His long fingers were limp and chilly. A bit like shaking hands with a corpse, she thought. She was glad to get out of the shop and wipe her hand on her shorts. She was thrilled though that she'd got £10 to add on to the reward. That meant they'd got… £18 all together.

"What happens if he doesn't sell it," Emily said, "and someone claims the reward?"

"We'll think about that another time," said Laura firmly.

Gertie had asked them to get some more food for the cats, so they called in at the pet shop before going home. Trevor was looking bright and chirpy as usual and had a different T-shirt on, which said 'Grrrr, Feed Me' with a picture of a fierce dog underneath.

"Found that egg of yours yet?" he asked, putting the tins of cat food into the shopping bag.

"No," Emily said, "and Tolly's very sad."

"Don't worry, somebody's bound to ring soon, you'll see. Here, you give Tolly one of these." He handed Emily a long cluster of special parrot food, which she knew Tolly loved. "There, that's sure to cheer her up, poor old thing."

When they got back Harry was sitting on the wall outside the front garden, swinging his legs. He wanted to know where they'd been.

"We went to get some more food for the cats," said Laura. "And we went in to Blood Sucker's shop because we couldn't see our notice in the window. But then we found it inside."

They told him that they'd looked in the room at the back of the shop and that they'd seen his collection of eggs.

"Wow!" said Harry, clearly impressed. "So you think it was Blood Sucker who took the egg then? Because he collects birds' eggs?"

"Well, yes, we do," said Laura.

"But how did he know about it?"

The Porcupine was coming out of her front gate and started walking up the hill towards them. She didn't look like a porcupine any more. The short, black prickles had grown and now there were shiny black curls all over her head and her grumpy expression had gone. It was amazing how having some hair had changed the whole look of her.

"'Ow's that parrit of yours?" she asked as she reached them. "Can I see 'im?"

"She's not feeling at all well," Emily said. "Her feathers are falling out and she looks sad. She's missing her egg."

"Well, can I see 'im anyway? she persisted, walking up the path with them. "Is yer Uncle Wilf in?"

They weren't sure whether he was there or not, but Gertie was sitting at the kitchen table, sewing on yet more name tapes. "Put the kettle on, Laura," she said as they all came trooping in. "You've both been a very long time. Where have you been?"

Just then Uncle Wilf came through the door, so luckily they didn't have to answer.

"I think we're going to have to take Tolly back to the vet," he said in a worried voice. "She's looking very poorly. Oh, hello," he said, seeing the Porcupine. "My word, don't you look a picture!" He beamed at her and she smiled and blushed.

They followed Uncle Wilf into the sitting room and Emily was very upset when she saw Tolly. She was sitting on the floor of her cage again, not as she usually did on her perch, and her head was hanging limply. She looked a pathetic sight, with several bare patches where her feathers were missing.

"Oh please can we go to the vet straight away?" she said anxiously. "She looks as if she's going to die!"

"Just a moment," said the Porcupine quietly. "Before we do anything, will you all please sit down and listen. There's something important I've got to tell you."

Chapter 26

Mrs Skeet's Revelation

They all did as Mrs Skeet asked and looked at her expectantly.

"Now this is very 'ard for me," she said, after a long pause, "but I've thought about it a great deal and there's no way out. I've got to get this orf me chest." She sat down heavily on one of the chairs.

What on earth did she mean? Wasn't she pleased with her hair? It looked fine - shiny and black and curly, just as she'd ordered. It couldn't be that. So what was it that was so important? She didn't speak for a moment, just sat there, looking at the floor and twisting the sash of her dress round and round between her fingers. At last she raised her eyes.

"My, but this is 'ard," she said again, shifting her weight around in the chair. They waited patiently and then, just as she looked as if she was about to say something, Gertie interrupted by coming through from the kitchen, carrying a pile of clothes over one arm.

"I'd just like you to try these trousers on again, Harry," she said, putting the clothes down over the back of one of the chairs. "They should be about the right..."

"Shhhhh," everyone said and Gertie looked up in surprise.

"What's going on?"

The Porcupine seemed to gain courage from seeing Gertie, and taking an enormous breath and gripping the arms of the chair, the words came out in a rush.

"I know who's got yer egg!"

This was astonishing news. How could she possibly know?

"Who is it then?" said Laura, twisting her ponytail round and round very fast.

Another long pause as the Porcupine crossed and uncrossed her large feet. "I don't think I'd 'av told you if it 'adn't been for this," she said at last, running her hand through her shining curls. "You see, 'aving 'air again... well, it's changed me life and I'll never be able to thank you enough for what you've done for me." She looked across at Uncle Wilf and there were tears in her eyes. "And then I'm very fond of that parrit of yours and I don't like to see 'im lookin' so miserable."

She stopped again and looked down at the floor. Get on with it, Emily thought, why doesn't she just get on with it? The Porcupine sniffed, then blew her nose with a loud, trumpeting sound. Everyone waited, but she just didn't seem able to bring herself to go any further. Emily felt she was going to burst.

"I'll go and make us all a nice cup of tea," said Gertie, going to the door. "Come and give me a hand, Laura."

"Oh Mum, not now!" Laura groaned, but Gertie insisted and a few moments later they came back with mugs of tea and a big plate of chocolate buns.

"Just take your time, dear lady," said Uncle Wilf, passing the Porcupine the chocolate buns. "You'll feel a lot better after one of these."

She sipped her tea with a loud slurping sound and then bit thankfully into her bun. It seemed a huge waste of time to be drinking tea and eating buns when they were just about to find out what had happened to Tolly's egg. Emily just hoped the Porcupine wouldn't suddenly change her mind. The buns were delicious though, with icing on top and extra bits of crunchy chocolate inside. Emily had two. They all licked their fingers and then sat looking expectantly at the Porcupine. She couldn't put it off any longer, could she?

"I don't like grassing on me own family," she said at last, brushing the crumbs from her lap. Emily wondered what 'grassing' meant. "But 'e's 'ad it coming to him, that's all I can say."

"Go on, dear lady," Uncle Wilf prompted gently.

The Porcupine's mouth turned down at the corners and it looked as though she was going to burst into tears, but taking a shuddering breath, she managed to blurt out, "It's me nephew what's got yer egg!"

Her nephew? Well, who on earth was that? They didn't even know she had a nephew.

"Yes, I'm afraid so," she went on and sniffed again, "and I remember 'e used to be such a lovely little boy, nice manners and that."

Was she talking about Lip-Up Stinky? Emily couldn't believe that he'd ever been a lovely little boy with nice manners. She was sure he'd always been a little stinker.

Gertie went over to the Porcupine and put an arm round her shoulder. "Mrs Skeet," she asked kindly, "who is your nephew?"

The Porcupine looked up at her in surprise. "I thought you knew," she said. "I was sure I told you – 'e's me brother's boy."

"Is Coddie Rowe your brother then?" asked Laura. It was obvious everyone was thinking the same thing.

"Coddie Rowe?" asked the Porcupine and now it was her turn to look astonished. "Oh, you mean Colin Rowe, 'im wot looks like a fish?" She snorted and drew herself up indignantly. "'Course he's not me brother! No, I'm talking about Leonard who lives down in Southampton."

Leonard? Southampton? Emily was totally confused – they didn't know anyone who lived in Southampton, did they? What was she on about? Why didn't she get to the point? She glanced over at Tolly at the bottom of her cage, and felt she couldn't stand it any longer. She ran over to the Porcupine and knelt down in front of her.

"Please, Mrs Skeet," she pleaded, "who is your nephew? Do we know him? What's his name?"

"'Course you know 'im, you all know 'im."

"Well, who is he then?" shouted Harry.

"Shhh, Harry," said Uncle Wilf. He turned to the Porcupine and spoke to her kindly. "Can you tell us his name, dear lady?"

The Porcupine ran both her hands through her hair again, as if to make sure it was still there, then sucking in a deep breath, she said, "Me nephew's Trevor Barnes up at the pet shop."

Everyone gasped. Emily couldn't believe her ears and by the look of it, nor could anyone else. They all started talking at once, hurling questions at the Porcupine like rubber balls: had Trevor climbed into the shed through the window on the night of the storm? He'd known that Tolly was going to lay an egg, because they'd mentioned it to him, but nobody had ever said what an unusual egg it had turned out to be. So who had told him? And where was it now? Had it hatched?

The Porcupine put her hands over her ears and rocked back and forth in her chair.

"Oooooo," she wailed.

Uncle Wilf stood up, and bellowed, "Be quiet, all of you. Can't you see she's very upset?" He had a very loud voice for such a little man.

The questions tailed off.

"Now if you'll just be patient for a little while longer," he said, "I think I'll be able to get to the bottom of this."

With Uncle Wilf's gentle questioning, the story slowly unfolded. The Porcupine's brother, Leonard, had had a parrot and his son, Trevor, had grown up with an interest in animals and birds, especially strange and unusual ones from foreign lands. The Porcupine had told him about Tolly's extraordinary egg one day, when she'd been in the pet shop getting some birdseed for her budgie, and never thought any more about it. But when the egg was stolen she was suspicious and decided to challenge him. He said he didn't know anything about it, but he'd always been a bad liar and she knew he wasn't telling the truth. It wasn't the first time that he'd done something dishonest, she said.

The disappointing thing was that she didn't seem to have any idea what he'd done with the egg, whether it was in the shop or if he'd sold it. What were they to do? They'd tried telling the police before and they weren't interested. But they had to get the egg back and time was short.

The Porcupine seemed to have told them all she knew and so, with promises that they wouldn't tell the police about Trevor, Gertie took her back home with the rest of the chocolate buns.

Once they'd gone, everyone started chattering at once.

"Let's go up there and make him give it to us," said Harry.

"No," said Uncle Wilf. "We need to think about this carefully." He started to pace up and down with his hands behind his back, looking at the floor. "From what I've heard about Trevor, I think he'd want to keep the egg himself. I don't think he'd sell it. He's fascinated by exotic animals and birds and I think he's keeping it warm somewhere, waiting for the day when it's ready to hatch. But we've got to think of a clever way of getting it back and there's no time to waste."

"Do you think he's got it in his shop?" Emily asked.

"He's not going to just hand it over to us," said Laura. "We've got to think of a way of getting him out of the shop, so that we can go in and search for it."

"You're absolutely right," agreed Uncle Wilf and I've got a plan of how we're going to do it. Everyone's got their part to play and the timing of it is crucial."

The next day they put the plan into action.

It was Friday morning and Uncle Wilf went into Jo's newsagent's and bought a copy of the local paper, which had just arrived, and stayed chatting to Jo. While he was there, the three children went into Trevor's shop. At first there was no sign of him, and then he suddenly appeared through a door at the back.

"Hello again," he said, grinning cheerfully. He was carrying several trays of dog food, which he dumped on the counter and then started stacking them on the shelves.

"Back again? How's that parrot of yours? Did she enjoy her treat?"

"We'd like some biscuits for Izzie please. Oh and we'd better have some of those tins of dog food too," said Laura. She was such a good actress, Emily thought. She knew she wouldn't have been able to act so calmly. "Three will be enough for now," said Laura. She put the tins and the carton of biscuits into Gertie's shopping bag, handed over the money and they followed her to the door.

Turning back she said casually, "Oh, by the way, thanks for asking about Tolly – she really enjoyed her treat. I think she's feeling better today. You see, she seems to know that we'll soon have her egg back."

Trevor stopped what he was doing, and for a fraction of a second the grin slipped from his face. Then he recovered himself and smiled. "Someone rung you, have they?"

"No, it's not that," said Laura. "No, we reported it to the police and they say they've got an idea who stole the egg. There's an article about their investigations in the local paper this morning. Haven't you read it?"

Trevor's face had turned chalky white. "In the G-G-Gazette?" he stuttered.

"That's right," said Laura. "It's very exciting, isn't it? We'll soon have the egg back. Bye for now." She opened the door and they all trooped out of the shop.

The next part of the plan was that they should wait around the corner and see what happened. Sure enough, after only a few seconds, they saw Trevor come out and hurry along to the newsagent's. The next part of the plan depended on luck. They were banking on him not having locked the door of the shop – after all, he was only nipping out to get a copy of the local paper. They waited till he disappeared inside Jo's shop, and then the three of them bolted from their hiding place and tried the door.

He hadn't locked it!

They knew they had only a very short time to search the place. Uncle Wilf had said he could keep Trevor in the newsagent's for ten minutes, but probably no longer.

They'd all agreed that the most likely place for him to have hidden the egg, if it was in the shop, was in the storeroom behind, where he kept all his extra supplies. The door was unlocked so, while Harry kept guard looking out into the street, Laura and Emily slipped into the storeroom.

It was chock-a-block with all sorts of stuff, not neatly stored on shelves, but stacked in great heaps on the floor – trays of pet food, piles of cartons and sacks of sawdust, cages for rabbits and guinea pigs and lots of big cardboard boxes and packing cases.

Laura and Emily stood there, wondering where on earth to begin. They hadn't a moment to lose. And then they listened. And they listened. And they heard a familiar humming sound. It was coming from behind an enormous packing case right at the back of the storeroom.

They picked their way through the piles of stuff and crept over to it. The packing case was too tall to look over, so they craned their necks round the side of it and then immediately shrank back. They stared at each other in horror. For a moment neither dared to move. Then Laura, clutching Emily's hand tightly, peered round the edge again.

"I don't believe it!" she whispered. Emily pulled her out of the way, so she could have another look.

On the other side of the packing case was a massive glass tank. And inside the tank was a huge snake. Luckily, it was asleep and hadn't seen them. Laura pushed her way in beside Emily.

The snake must have been eight metres long, a rich, chestnut and tan colour with large scales on its head and a black zigzag pattern all along its body. It was coiled round a vast number of eggs – there must have been fifty at least – and amongst them was one that was different. It was bigger than the others, a deep glowing amber colour, and it was giving off a gentle hum! No doubt about it, it was Tolly's egg!

Laura put her finger to her lips and pointed to a printed label on the side of the tank. It said 'Danger - Reticulated Python'. There was a lamp in the roof of the tank to keep the eggs at the right temperature. They noticed that there was a sliding door at the back, which was probably where Trevor pushed the python's food through. Emily wondered what it ate.

Suddenly they heard Harry's voice behind them and it made them both jump.

"What are you doing?" he called. "Do hurry up, he'll be back in a minute."

The python stirred and wound itself more protectively round its huge clutch of eggs. Laura gripped Emily's arm and they tiptoed as quickly and quietly as they could out of the storeroom. Emily was shaking as they joined Harry by the door, and then the three of them darted out and hid once again round the side of the shop. A few seconds later, Trevor appeared from the newsagent's, carrying a newspaper, and disappeared into his shop.

Uncle Wilf's plan had only half worked. They'd found Tolly's egg, but they hadn't managed to rescue it. What was the point of knowing where it was if they couldn't get at it? They'd never have such a good chance again. They were so disappointed and Harry was furious too because he hadn't even seen the python.

They ran round the back of the shops to the other end and found Uncle Wilf waiting for them, still in the newsagent's.

"Well?" he said. "Any luck?"

They didn't want to talk about it in front of Jo, so they pulled Uncle Wilf out into the street.

"So where is it then?" he asked, "Didn't you get it?"

Laura and Emily told him about the python and how it was lying coiled round Tolly's egg with lots of others and that there was no way they were going to be able to get hold of it. Uncle Wilf looked disappointed and then he chuckled.

"He's a crafty one that nephew of Mrs Skeet's, isn't he? So, if you're going to get that egg back, you're going to have to be even craftier, aren't you? And you can't leave it much longer or the egg'll hatch, and the chances are that the python will eat whatever comes out of it."

"Oh no!" Emily cried in horror.

"Oh, yes," said Uncle Wilf, "I'm afraid so."

"So, what are we going to do now?" asked Harry.

"I think we're going to have to forget the whole idea," said Laura firmly.

Chapter 27

Another Idea

It was all a huge disappointment. They'd hoped to come back with the egg and give it to poor Tolly. What were they going to do now? Uncle Wilf had said they were going to have to be even craftier than Trevor if they were to get hold of it. What did he mean? Did he have another plan? When they arrived home it was lunch time and they all agreed that it was probably better if they didn't tell Gertie about the python.

After lunch, Harry and Laura went outside to play with the cart. They seemed to have given up all idea of rescuing the egg, but Emily certainly hadn't and she went to talk to Uncle Wilf about it. He'd be bound to have another plan, she thought, but she was in for another disappointment.

"I'm sorry," he said, "but tomorrow's Saturday and I've promised Bert I'll help out on the stall. It's up to you now."

"But Uncle Wilf, please," Emily pleaded. "How are we going to do it?" She looked at Tolly, lying on the bottom of her cage. Even more of her feathers seemed to have fallen out. Emily was desperate. Didn't Uncle Wilf care about Tolly anymore?

"If you want something enough, little Emily," he said gently, "there's very often a way you can get it. But I'm not sure that you'll succeed this time — it's too dangerous. Better to forget about it. And you're not to worry about Tolly. I'll take her back to the vet and get her a tonic — that'll put her right."

But Emily didn't want to forget about the egg. She told Laura what Uncle Wilf had said. Laura was the clever one.

Surely she could think of a way to get the egg back. But both she and Harry seemed to be scared off by the thought of the reticulated python.

"Get real, Em," Harry snorted. "There's no way we're going to be able to get Trevor out of his shop again. And even if we could, how do you imagine you're going to get that egg out of the tank, with that hulking great python guarding it?"

"Uncle Wilf's right. The only thing we can do is to take Tolly to the vet again," said Laura. "He's sure to be able to give her some medicine to make her feel better. And maybe Uncle Wilf can make her feathers grow back by giving her the same treatment as he gave the Porcupine. But he'd have to change it a bit." She giggled, "We don't want Tolly growing hair instead of feathers!"

Emily didn't think it was funny at all. She was sure that Mr Barker wouldn't be able to come up with anything that would help Tolly. The only thing that would make her better would be to have her egg back again.

That night she lay in bed, unable to sleep. Laura and Harry had given up, but she thought about what Uncle Wilf had said: 'If you want something enough, there's very often a way you can get it.' He hadn't said there's *always* a way you can get it though. She certainly wanted it badly, so she decided to think about it really hard.

Gertie had promised Mrs Skeet that they wouldn't tell the police about Trevor, so that was out. She thought about going and pleading with Trevor to give her the egg, but somehow she didn't think he would. She'd tell him how unhappy Tolly was, but he already knew that and he didn't seem to care.

Maybe she could sneak into the shop when someone else went in and hide behind the shelves until he'd gone home. But then how was she going to get the egg out of the tank? She was terrified of the python. Harry had said pythons eat animals whole. She felt herself breaking out in a sweat. She thought and thought, but every idea she came up with seemed more ridiculous than the last. She wished they hadn't promised the Porcupine that they wouldn't tell the police.

She tossed and turned and the thoughts raced round and round in her head. She was worried that Tolly was going to die. She heard the clock downstairs striking two and began to think about all those clocks in Blood Sucker's shop. There must have been thirty or more of them. She wondered if he'd sold her appendix yet. Anyway, they didn't need the reward money now that they knew where the egg was. She hoped he hadn't sold it and she'd be able to ask for it back. She remembered how scared he'd looked when she and Laura had come creeping up on him from the back of the shop. In spite of everything it made her giggle.

And then she sat bolt upright in bed. Suddenly, a great idea came into her head. She thought and thought about it, and the more she thought about it, the better it became. She wanted to tell someone, but she knew how Laura hated to be woken. It would have to wait till morning. Perhaps they would think it a mad idea, but she needed them all if the plan was going to work. It needed the four of them.

Chapter 28
Plan B

By the time they came down for breakfast Bert and Uncle Wilf had already left for the market. Emily thought about her plan, which had seemed so brilliant in the middle of the night. Now, it seemed crazy and there was no guarantee that it would work. She wanted to tell Laura and Harry about it, but she was worried they'd laugh at her. But the plan depended on them – she couldn't do it by herself. When she took the cover off Tolly's cage she was looking just the same, although she did take a few pecks at a piece of apple, which Emily held out for her. Emily looked at her sadly and knew she just had to do something.

After breakfast, Gertie wanted to know if they'd finished their holiday projects – writing about something they'd grown. She reminded them that they only had three more days till they were back at school. Oh no, Emily thought, today's my only chance to carry out my plan – after that it'll be too late. She wished they could leave the projects till Sunday, but Gertie insisted that they went upstairs to their rooms straight away and got on with them. She said they weren't to come down until they'd finished.

"I don't want to be disturbed," she said, getting an enormous bowl out of the kitchen cupboard. "I'm going to make the Christmas pudding and I need to concentrate. Last year, I forgot to put the brandy in!"

Upstairs, Emily knew she wouldn't be able to concentrate on her project and told Laura and Harry that she'd got a new idea for rescuing the egg. They both groaned. She could tell they'd given up hope and were getting bored by the whole idea, but she made them sit down on Laura's bed and listen to what she had to say.

"There are four of us in this plan," she explained, "and each of us has a very important part to play. And we've got to do it today, because tomorrow's Sunday and the shop will be shut and Monday will be too late – Tolly's egg will have hatched by then, and the python will eat the chick, I'm sure of it.

"Ugh," said Laura. "That horrible python!"

"We can't do it today, silly," said Harry. "Even if we get our projects finished, you know Uncle Wilf's not here."

"I know that," Emily said.

"Well, you said there were four of us," said Laura, "you, me and Harry… who's the fourth person? Mum won't want to do it."

Emily swallowed. This was the first difficult part – getting them to listen to what she was going to say next.

"The fourth person is really the most important," she stammered. "The whole thing depends on him. And the fourth person is… Tobias… the pirate!"

"What?" Harry gave a shriek of laughter and rolled around on the bed with his feet in the air.

"What are you like, Emily?" Laura joined in the laughter.

Emily waited patiently for them to stop. She'd figured it would be like this, but she was determined to tell them the plan… because she knew there was a small chance it could work, if only they'd listen and take her seriously.

A lot of giggling and hooting with laughter went on, but bit by bit, they calmed down and she was able to explain her idea. By the time she got to the end she could tell they wanted to have a go.

Of course, the whole thing depended on whether or not Trevor was one of those people who could see the pirate. So far, the Porcupine and Emily were the only ones who'd been able to see him – and Izzie too, of course. But what if the Pink family were the exceptions and that most people could see him? The only way to find out was to try. Emily had never been in charge of anything before, but she'd thought up this plan and realised it was up to her to make sure the others did as she told them. The first thing, of course, was to find Tobias and ask him to help them. And they're going to have to come with me, up to the attic, Emily thought. She was far too scared to go on her own. She knew they wouldn't be able to see him, or hear him, but at least they'd be there with her.

Gertie was downstairs and they didn't think she'd disturb them. She had shut the kitchen door firmly behind her and they could hear her clattering around. Emily felt a bit guilty going up into Uncle Wilf's room when he wasn't there, but they had to do it.

So, here goes, she thought. She was first up the ladder, followed by Harry and then by Laura. The sun was streaming in through the windows and it felt quite warm so Emily knew that, for the moment, Tobias was nowhere around. She wondered how she'd get him to appear.

Suppose he was busy doing something else? Suppose he refused to help?

The three of them sat on Uncle Wilf's bed and waited. Emily's heart was thudding. She could tell Laura was nervous too. She kept giggling and squirming around on the bed, but Harry pretended not to be bothered. He picked up a book that was lying nearby and turned the pages.

Nothing happened. After a while Harry sighed, then Laura sighed and started wriggling round even more and Emily could tell they were getting fed up.

"How long is this going to take?" whispered Laura. "We're supposed to be doing our projects."

Emily reminded herself that Harry and Laura had never seen Tobias and deep down didn't really believe he existed.

"Tobias," she called softly. "Tobias, are you there?"

Gradually, the room got colder, although the sun was still shining through the windows. Harry put down the book and Laura slipped her arm through Emily's and moved closer. Laura had shorts on and Emily could see the goose bumps on her legs. They waited a few more minutes. It got even colder and they could all smell the salty sea air. Emily felt Harry on the other side of Laura shifting closer and suddenly the rocking chair creaked and began to move gently to and fro. Harry and Laura both gasped and Laura gripped Emily's arm so tightly it hurt.

"Oh my goodness," she whispered.

A thin mist began to swirl around the chair. Slowly it became denser and gradually a shape began to form and there at last was Tobias, just as she'd seen him before, with his big hat shading the top of his face. She knew he was looking at her. His legs were stretched out in front of him and his cutlass swung from the belt hanging on the back of the chair.

"Well, Emily, we meet again," he said in his out-of-focus voice.

Emily tried to swallow, but her mouth was dry.

"Is he there?" whispered Harry.

Emily nodded. She didn't seem to be able to speak.

"I'll tell him, if you like," whispered Harry. "Do you want me to?" Emily nodded again.

She was surprised at how well Harry did it. He was much calmer than she was, but then of course, he couldn't see

206

Tobias, or hear him. He told Tobias about Tolly and how she'd laid an egg and how surprised they'd all been because they'd thought she was a boy. Tobias rocked back and forth in the chair and gave a low chuckle.

Harry told him how the egg had grown and changed colour and about the humming sound it made and that someone had stolen it one night from the shed. Tobias stopped rocking and his hand moved towards his cutlass, paused, then dropped back on to his knee. The rocking continued again.

Harry went on. He told Tobias that they knew it was Trevor from the pet shop who'd taken the egg, and that it was being guarded by an enormous python. Again Tobias gave a deep chuckle. At this point Emily's courage came back and she managed to tell him about her plan and that they needed his help. She explained that it had to be today, because the egg was on the point of hatching and they didn't want the python to eat the baby chick.

"Please will you help us, Tobias?" she pleaded. "Do you think you could do it?"

He didn't answer straight away, just went on rocking and laughing gently to himself.

"Tobias?" Emily said again, thinking maybe he hadn't heard her. Would he be able to do it, she wondered? Maybe it wasn't possible for him to move out of the house – perhaps he needed to ask Uncle Wilf first or something. This was worrying – the plan wouldn't work without him.

Just then they heard Gertie's voice calling.

"Laura, come down a minute, luvvie, I need you to get me something."

"Oh drat," said Laura, getting up unsteadily from the bed. "I'd better go and see what Mum wants." Keeping well away from the rocking chair, she disappeared down the ladder. "Back in a minute – wait for me," she called from below.

She returned after a few moments. "Mum needs us to get a tin of black treacle for the Christmas pudding. She thought there was one in the cupboard, but we used it all up for the Porcupine's hair, remember?"

Emily couldn't believe their luck. This was a marvellous chance for them all to go up to the shops and carry out her plan. Now that they were actually about to do something she felt excited and not so frightened any more. But of course they needed Tobias. Plucking up all her courage, she got up from the bed and walked over to the rocking chair, managing a watery smile, though she could feel her knees shaking.

"Please will you help us to get the egg back, Tobias?"

He stood up suddenly, making her step back in fright.

"I'll be glad to help thee, little maid," he said, buckling his cutlass belt around his waist.

What a relief. Perhaps everything was going to be all right after all.

"Get a shopping bag, Laura," she said and was surprised at how calm she sounded, "and put one of your sweaters in it. We're going to need to keep the egg warm till we get it back. And Harry – we'll need your cart because we'll get home much quicker. If we run, we might drop it."

Harry beamed. "You're right. It'll get us back in half the time. I'll bring it round and meet you by the gate."

They both disappeared down the ladder, and for a moment Emily was left alone with the pirate. She looked up at him.

"Thank you," she said. "Tolly's going to be so pleased to get her egg back. Can you meet us down by the gate too?

208

Straight away?" He didn't answer, but the different bits of his body began to melt away and then gradually disappeared all together.

Laura was waiting for her downstairs by the front door and she had the shopping bag over her arm. "Harry's getting the cart," she said quietly, "let's go."

"You might as well take Izzie with you," Gertie called from the kitchen, "she hasn't had her walk today."

"You didn't tell her, did you?" Emily asked, suddenly worried.

"'Course not," said Laura. "She'd have a fit!"

As they were going out of the front door, Emily remembered to take a walking stick from the umbrella stand and they joined Harry by the gate. They only had to wait a few moments and then Emily saw a mist rising up out of the ground and Tobias took shape again. She could see him quite clearly in the bright sunlight and couldn't understand how it was that neither Harry nor Laura knew that he was there. Izzie did though. All her hackles went up and she started to bark furiously. Harry quickly put her on the lead.

"He's here, isn't he?" he whispered.

"He certainly is," Emily said with a big smile on her face.

"Laura, you take Izzie," he said, handing her the lead, "and Emily you get in the back of the cart and I'll give you a ride to the bottom."

They waited for Laura and Izzie and Tobias to catch them up and then turned right, into the road, and began walking up the hill towards the shops. Tobias was following a little way behind and Izzie kept barking at him and jumping around. They'd almost reached the top of the hill when Laura stopped.

"Shut up, Izzie," she said crossly, jerking the lead, "and stop pulling all the time."

Izzie took no notice. "Look, I don't think it's a good idea for the pirate to walk along by the shops," she said. "If some people are able to see him then it's going to make them panic and run around and we'll probably get arrested or something."

She was right – they didn't want to draw attention to themselves. Emily turned to Tobias.

"Could you just disappear for a moment," she asked him politely, "and then meet up with us at the pet shop? It's just over there," she pointed.

Tobias swept his hat off his head and bowed. "I shall await thy call," he said.

It was Saturday morning and there were loads of people around doing their shopping.

"I'd better get the treacle first," Laura said and Emily could tell she was putting off going in to see Trevor. "We'll probably forget otherwise."

"OK," Emily said, "but be as quick as you can. See you at the pet shop."

Laura tied Izzie, who was still barking, to a post outside Jo's shop, and Harry and Emily walked along the pavement, Harry pulling his cart proudly behind him. They passed the butcher's shop and the greengrocer's and the junk shop, then stopped outside the pet shop and looked through the window.

Chapter 29

Tobias to the Rescue

Trevor was behind the counter, serving a customer, as the three of them traipsed in. There were a couple of other customers waiting their turn, so the children went over to the rotating bookstand behind the shelves and pretended to look at the books.

"Let's wait till everyone's gone," Emily whispered.

It seemed ages before the last person left, closing the door behind him and Emily felt it was safe to call Tobias. As instructed, Laura and Harry went round to the counter to distract Trevor and Emily stayed, hidden behind the tall shelves.

"Tobias," she called softly and waited. Almost at once, the air around her started to vibrate and she felt it getting colder. After only a few moments, the familiar watery mist began to appear and then, as before, it took shape. She couldn't help stepping back a few paces as Tobias appeared just in front of her: she was still scared of him. Trevor's voice came from the other side of the shelves, talking to Harry and Laura.

"Well, I couldn't see any sign of that report in the newspaper that you were telling me about. Your Uncle Wilf and I searched the paper from cover to cover and we couldn't find it." He laughed. "Wishful thinking on your part, eh? How is that parrot of yours, by the way? Feeling better, is she? Now then, what can I get you today?"

Horrible man, Emily thought. How could he be so mean? She looked at Tobias and nodded her head at him. "Now!" she whispered.

Harry had explained to the pirate what they wanted him to do and Emily was hoping against hope that her plan would work: Trevor would be terrified by Tobias and run out of the shop, so that they could get into the back room and rescue the egg. She expected Tobias to walk round the shelves to the counter, but instead he passed right through them. So she quickly ran round to the other side - and there he was, standing next to Harry and Laura, although it was obvious they had no idea he was there.

With a blood-curdling scream, he drew the cutlass from his belt and brandished it in the air, then leapt forward and gripped Trevor by the throat. Emily was absolutely terrified! But, as she had dreaded might be the case, there was absolutely no reaction from Trevor — except that he began rubbing his hands together and blowing on them.

"My, it's got cold in here, hasn't it?" he said. "Feels like winter's suddenly come and it's only the beginning of September."

Emily's plan had depended on Trevor being able to see the ghost... and he couldn't. Tobias didn't seem to want to stop though — he was really enjoying himself and ran up and down and through the rows of shelves, yelling at the top of his voice, waving his arms and his cutlass, but Trevor remained completely unmoved. It was quite obvious he couldn't see the ghost.

"Tobias! Tobias!" she called out, cowering back against a stack of dog beds and putting her hands over her ears, but the pirate was having a great time and she had to shout really loudly before he was able to hear her.

"Tobias! You'd better stop now! Please, Tobias! Just stop!"

"What are you on about, little 'un?" said Trevor, staring at her in astonishment. "Who's Tobias? He looked at Harry and Laura. "She feeling all right, is she?"

Emily had to bite her lip to stop herself bursting into tears. It hadn't worked. Her wonderful plan hadn't worked!

"You horrible man," she yelled. "We know you've got Tolly's egg. You've got to give it back to us – it doesn't belong to you!"

Trevor's usual friendly smile disappeared and an ugly expression came over his face, turning it blotchy red.

"Oh, so you know, do you?" he snarled. "I had a feeling you did. There's no way you can prove I've got anything belonging to you. So, unless there's something in here you want to buy, you'd better clear out of my shop!"

Emily couldn't wait to go. Her face was burning and she ran outside, determined not to cry. She was seething, but there didn't seem to be anything she could do.

The twins joined her a few seconds later, both of them looking glum.

"Didn't Tobias do what we told him?" Harry asked. "What happened?"

"Yes, he was terrifying," Emily told them, "but Trevor's like you – he couldn't see Tobias. Oh, I'm so angry!"

Laura put her arm round Emily. "We've done everything we can, Em," she said comfortingly. "We're just going to have to forget about it."

"But we can't just give up now – there must be something we can do!" Emily insisted.

Laura tried to change the subject. "Look, let's just pop in to Blood Sucker's and see if he's sold your appendix. If he hasn't, we'll ask if we can have it back - there's no point in selling it now."

213

Emily didn't feel in the mood to do anything, but Laura had told Harry about the appendix and he wanted to see it, so Emily followed them reluctantly into the junk shop. There was no sign of Blood Sucker, but they could hear voices coming from the room at the back - the door was ajar and the light was on. They tiptoed towards the skull with the candle inside it and there, on the shelf next to it, was Emily's appendix.

"Isn't it amazing?" whispered Laura. "Just think – that used to be inside Emily!"

"Wow," Harry breathed, looking very impressed and, in spite of her disappointment, Emily felt a glow of pride. The voices continued from the open door and they felt it best to speak quietly.

"I bet he's got another delivery of stolen goods," whispered Laura. "Do you want to wait till he comes out, Emily, or shall we come back another time?"

She was just going to answer when she felt the now familiar swirling of cold, damp air and, more quickly this time, Tobias appeared, sitting in one of the old armchairs. She had to admit to herself that, for a moment, she'd forgotten all about him.

"Tobias is here, isn't he?" whispered Harry and began rubbing his arms.

Emily nodded and pointed to the chair.

"Are you sure?" said Laura.

Before she could reply, Tobias got up and moved slowly over to the skeleton, hanging from its stand. He examined it closely for a second or two, then walked round so that he was standing directly behind it. As Emily watched, the most extraordinary thing happened. He stepped forward so that the skeleton was hanging inside him – and she gasped as she saw that it fitted him exactly. The skull fitted inside his

214

head and its long, bony spine was the right length for him too, as were the leg and arm bones. She could see the watery shape of him around it, so it was like looking at an X-ray.

"Come and unhook the bones, little maid," he called in a soft voice. Emily couldn't move. "Come!" he called again, "Do not be afeared – we'll beat that scoundrel yet!"

While Harry and Laura watched, Emily picked up a stool that was standing nearby and carried it over to the skeleton. Her hands were shaking as she climbed onto it and tried to lift the end of the chain supporting the skeleton off the hook that attached it to the stand. But the bones were heavy and she couldn't lift them.

"What on earth are you doing?" whispered Harry, as he and Laura stood with their mouths open.

"Just help me," Emily panted, "you'll both have to help me – it's far too heavy!"

Harry picked up a chair and he and Laura climbed onto it and the three of them managed to lift the skeleton off the stand.

"Oh wow," breathed Harry, "it weighs a ton – what do we do now?"

"Let go, just let go now," commanded Tobias.

"Tobias says to let it go," Emily repeated, expecting the skeleton to crash to the floor.

They climbed down, staring in amazement. It looked even more extraordinary to Harry and Laura because, of course, they couldn't see Tobias, but somehow or other, he was supporting the bones of the skeleton so that it appeared to be standing up! It was terrifying to see – the three of them just stood there, unable to move or speak. As they watched, Tobias took a step forward and, as he moved, the skeleton moved with him. He raised his arm, and the skeleton raised its bony arm. He turned his head towards them and the skull turned on its bony neck and looked at them with its great hollow eye sockets. He took a few steps forward towards them... and Laura screamed!

The door to the room at the back of the shop flew open and Blood Sucker came marching out, followed by a scruffy-looking man with stringy hair. At first, they didn't notice anything strange because Tobias was keeping very still.

"What's going on?" demanded Blood Sucker, seeing the children standing there, looking as though they'd seen a ghost!

Slowly, Tobias turned himself round and started to walk towards Blood Sucker and his companion. Emily couldn't tell if they were able to see him or if they could only see the skeleton, but either way, the two men stood paralysed with fear, their eyes and mouths wide open and their faces as white as the skeleton's bones. The bones made a rattling noise as they moved across the floor, and suddenly Tobias raised both his arms and let out a shriek that made Emily's blood run cold. The two men screamed in terror and ran backwards, tripping over each other as they tried to get away. They tumbled into the little storeroom and slammed the door after them.

Tobias turned and the skull was grinning down at them. "The key is in the lock," he told Emily. "These are wicked men." Emily realised what he was telling her to do and managed to run forward quickly and turn the key.

"Now," said Tobias, who was obviously enjoying himself hugely, "let us tackle yon scoundrel who had the gall to steal Tolly's egg." And his deep, hollow laugh echoed round the shop.

Emily had to take several deep breaths to calm herself down. "It's all right," she told Harry and Laura. "It's going to be all right. We're going to get Tolly's egg."

She gripped the handle of the walking stick she'd been holding all the time and opened the door of the shop.

Outside people were still milling around, going in and out of the shops and stopping to chat to each other.

"Just wait a second," she told the others, "and I'll look through the window of Trevor's shop to see if there's anyone there." Luckily it was empty, apart from Trevor who was behind the counter, reading the paper and eating a doughnut. She ran back.

"Come on," she beckoned, "we're just going to have to chance it."

What they needed to do was to drive Trevor out of his shop and make sure he stayed out long enough for them to rescue the egg, but they didn't want him to run into the storeroom, so the three of them had decided that they would stand in front of the door to make sure that he couldn't escape that way.

"Are we ready then?" asked Harry. "Is Tobias going to follow us in?" Emily nodded. "Right then," said Harry, taking charge. "One, two, three, GO!"

They walked quickly out of the junk shop, with Tobias supporting the skeleton following slowly behind. Harry flung open the door of the pet shop, setting off the loud buzzer, and they burst in. Running down between the rows of shelves, they stood in a line in front of the storeroom. Trevor appeared around the end of the row of shelves with a surprised and angry look on his face.

"Not you lot again!" he spluttered as bits of doughnut and jam flew out of his mouth. "I thought I told you to stay out of here!"

Behind him came a rattling sound as Tobias and the skeleton moved slowly towards them. It was a terrifying sight and Laura let out a piercing scream, pointing a trembling hand and wailing, "Look, he's coming to get us."

Trevor swung round; by now the skeleton was only two metres away. It stopped and stretched out its bony arms. The children watched in delight as the blood drained from Trevor's face, showing up the bright red of the plum jam smeared around his pale lips. He dropped the doughnut and backed away, almost squashing the children against the door. Emily clutched the walking stick and prodded him hard in the ribs. Giving a howl of pain, he sprang forward, dodging past the skeleton, and raced out of the door.

The children waited for a moment in silence and then all three of them and Tobias too burst out laughing.

"It worked! It worked!" Emily shouted in triumph. "Oh, Tobias, you were absolutely brilliant! Thank you so much!"

Tobias's voice came from the skeleton's grinning mouth, "I shall keep a guard on the door, my friends. No-one shall enter! But time is short, you must rescue the egg. Go!"

Chapter 30

The Python

Harry opened the door of the storeroom and they stepped inside. There were no windows and the only light came through the doorway from the shop, but Laura soon found a switch on the wall. The bare bulb hanging from the ceiling gave a dim light. Harry and Emily tiptoed behind Laura, picking their way between the stores until they got to where the enormous packing case stood. There wasn't enough room for all three of them at the same time, but Laura had got there first and Harry, dying to see the python, pressed impatiently against her as she peeped around the side. At once she leapt backwards, treading on his toes and he howled, crashing back into Emily.

"You idiot," he shouted "what on earth did you do that for?"

"Shhhh!" she said excitedly, putting her finger to her lips. "You'll never guess what's happened!"

Harry pushed her out of the way impatiently and peered round the side of the packing case. He stood looking for what seemed like ages and Emily, who couldn't wait any longer, tugged at his sleeve. At last he moved out of the way so she could take a look. What she saw took her breath away. The huge python was awake, which wasn't surprising after all the noise they'd been making, and she was slithering around between her eggs, her forked tongue flicking in and out.

But it wasn't that which had made Laura jump backwards – it was the sight of all the baby pythons beginning to hatch! It was fascinating. The eggs made a tiny cracking sound as the little pythons pushed their way out and dozens of them were already moving around, glad to be out of their eggs at last.

"Oh!" she breathed, but then she saw Tolly's egg, lying to one side. It seemed to have grown even bigger and its amber shell was glowing and giving off the familiar humming sound. She felt Harry pulling at her arm and tore herself away, stepping carefully back.

"What on earth are we going to do?" he whispered, rubbing his foot.

"Let's go home!" said Laura fearfully. She'd already turned and was heading for the door.

"Wait!" Emily said. She couldn't believe Laura was going to give up so easily, not now that they'd got this far. Although she was absolutely terrified at the thought of what they had to do, she found herself saying calmly, "We decided we were going to rescue Tolly's egg and that's what we've got to do."

"No way!" said Laura. "It's far too dangerous. Come on, let's go!"

"Wait!" Emily pleaded. "Please don't go! Listen - I'm sure I can do it, but I need your help."

Harry wasn't looking at all keen on the idea either. "We were counting on Ma python being asleep," he said. "But now she's going to be even more dangerous with all her family starting to hatch."

"I know, but we've come this far. Please let's just try," Emily pleaded. "Why should we let that horrible Trevor have Tolly's egg?"

"So, how are we going to do it?" asked Harry. Laura was standing by the door – but at least she was still there.

"We need to distract her," Emily said. "Listen, if you both stand up this end of the tank and tap on the glass she won't see what I'm doing. I'll go round to the back and push the walking stick through the sliding door and hook Tolly's egg out."

It sounded simple. Laura stood in silence, twirling her pony tail round and round.

"Come on Laura," said Emily, "give me the bag so that I can put the egg into it."

Reluctantly, she came back and gave Emily the shopping bag. "I don't want to do this," she said through gritted teeth.

"I know, I know," Emily said and she didn't feel at all brave either.

She led the way, and one by one they squeezed round the side of the packing case again. As soon as she saw them, the python raised her huge head and hissed, showing her fangs. For a second they froze. Then, holding hands, Harry and Laura squatted down and stared at her through the glass as Emily made her way, as quietly as she could, round to the back of the tank to the sliding door, hoping the python hadn't seen her.

Tolly's egg was lying about a metre away from the door, but there were several python eggs next to it, some of them just hatching out, and their mother's scaly tail lay, coiled around them. Emily's hands shook as she quietly slid the door open and knelt down. How was she going to get Tolly's egg out without touching the python's tail? She realised she couldn't.

She slid the door shut again and stood up so that Harry and Laura could see her. She couldn't speak in case the python turned round and spotted her, so she waved her arms, trying to make them understand that they'd got to get her to move out of the way. They saw her and nodded and Harry began to tap on the glass. Laura was looking absolutely petrified and Emily was worried that she might run away, but then she started tapping too.

She bent down again and slid the door open. The python's tail still lay in a protective coil around the eggs. Harry began to knock more loudly on the glass and the huge snake, really angry now, uncurled her long tail and slithered towards them, leaving Tolly's egg and several of the others unguarded. Quickly, Emily pushed the hooked end of the stick through the doorway and managed to knock a couple of the python's eggs out of the way, but the stick wasn't quite long enough to reach Tolly's egg.

She wondered what to do, then worked out that if she lay on the floor and stretched the whole of her arm and shoulder inside the tank, she'd just about be able to reach the egg. But the enormous snake suddenly gave a great flick of her tail and sent Tolly's egg rolling across the floor of the tank, well out of her reach. Emily couldn't believe it. There was no way she could get it now! Well... not unless she actually crawled inside the tank.

She stood up and looked across at Harry and Laura again. She didn't dare make a sound, but she could feel herself breathing very fast. At the moment the python didn't seem to know she was there and somehow she had to get the others to do what she wanted without speaking. She waved her arms wildly at them and then pointed at the snake, trying to make them realise that they had to do more than just knock on the glass. They had to make her really angry, so that she moved right up to their end of the tank. They looked at her blankly and then suddenly, they understood what she was going to do.

"You're mad!" shouted Harry. "If she sees you, she'll... she'll kill you!"

"For goodness sake, Emily," yelled Laura. "It's far too dangerous!"

But now, Emily was determined to get the egg whatever she had to do. She pointed at herself and then pointed at the tank and nodded her head. Then she pointed at them and silently clapped her hands together and made a fierce face and whirled her arms round.

They could see she wasn't going to change her mind and understood what they had to do. Harry got up and disappeared round the side of the packing case. Emily thought for one dreadful moment that he'd decided to go home, but he came back, carrying a couple of metal dog bowls which he gave to Laura. A moment later, he returned with two more and he and Laura started jumping up and down in front of the tank, shouting as loudly as they could, and banging the bowls together like cymbals.

The furious python slithered towards them, uncurling her tail and leaving her family unprotected. Emily crouched down and slid the door open again, pushing several of the little pythons out of the way with the stick, then lay down and put her head into the tank.

The opening was small – certainly neither Harry nor Laura would ever have fitted through! Suppose I get stuck half way, she thought. Her heart was thumping so hard she was sure that the python would hear it, and she forced herself to keep still for a moment. She then wriggled her shoulders through the opening followed by the rest of her body. Harry and Laura were making a fantastic din and the tank was shuddering as they banged on it. She hoped they wouldn't break the glass!

Feeling the lamp hot on her back, she inched her way forward towards Tolly's egg. The end of the python's tail lay alongside her, the bold black pattern on its scales only inches from her head! She reached out and with the tips of her fingers managed to touch the precious egg. Another tiny wriggle and she was able to flick it gently towards her. It was too big for her to pick up with one hand, so she rolled it carefully along with her as she wriggled her body backwards.

She felt the opening behind her and then her legs were out. Next came the difficult bit as she squeezed her shoulders through the tight doorway again, then at last her head. She was free!

Reaching back inside the tank, she lifted the egg out with both hands – it was warm and heavy and throbbing. With great care, she wrapped it in Laura's jumper and put it into the shopping bag before sliding the door shut. For a moment she just sat there, feeling sick and shaking all over.

The twins cheered loudly which revived her and picking up the bag, she carried it round to the front of the tank. The python opened her enormous mouth and hissed loudly – it was a terrifying sight.

"Well done, Emily!" they both cried and Laura hugged her.

"I never thought you'd do it, Em – you were amazing!" she said.

Carrying the shopping bag as if it had the crown jewels inside it, Emily led the way out of the storeroom and into the pet shop, where Tobias had been keeping guard by the door all this time in his skeleton disguise. Now all they had to do was to get the egg home to Tolly, as quickly and safely as they could, before it got cold.

"We've got it!" Emily shouted triumphantly and Tobias laughed his deep, echoing chuckle, making the bones of the skeleton shake and rattle together.

"I have no need of this now," he said and suddenly, the skeleton collapsed with a clatter onto the floor beside him.

"Do be very careful," said Emily, as she handed the shopping bag with the precious egg inside it to Harry. The cart was there, waiting for them where Harry had tied it to a drainpipe. He put the bag into the passenger seat of the cart, then untied the rope.

"You've got to get back as quickly as you can so the egg doesn't get cold!" she reminded him.

"I know, I know," said Harry. "Don't fuss! I'll pull the cart along to the top of the hill and then whizz down to the bottom. You two'll have to run behind. Don't forget Izzie!"

He ran ahead and they followed (Emily was relieved to see that Tobias had disappeared again) along the little parade of shops till they reached Jo's newsagent's, where Izzie was waiting patiently, still tied to the post. Poor Izzie – Emily had no idea how long they'd been. Laura untied her lead and Izzie began to bark. Emily soon realised why – Tobias had reappeared and climbed into the back of the cart, nursing the shopping bag between his long legs. Emily started to laugh – it was such a funny sight, but of course, the others couldn't see it.

Harry pulled the cart to the point where the road started to slope down, then leapt in and away they went, hurtling down the hill. Emily could hear Tobias yelling with delight and saw his long pigtail streaming out behind him. She and Laura and Izzie raced after them – all the way down the hill they ran, and Emily couldn't stop laughing till they got to the close.

Harry had stopped the cart and was already walking up the hill to their house, pulling it behind him. He had no idea that Tobias was sitting in the back, because of course, he weighed nothing!

Emily and Laura were out of breath by the time they caught up with him and suddenly, they saw Gertie with her apron on marching towards them down the hill, looking very angry.

"Where on earth have you been?" she demanded.

Chapter 31
Christmas Pudding

There was a wonderful spicy smell of Christmas pudding when they all trooped through the back door. Actually, it wasn't all of them – Tobias had disappeared again.

Gertie was mad at them for being out so long and keeping her waiting for the treacle. When they looked at the clock they realised they'd missed lunch – it was almost half past four. But she stopped scolding them and stared in disbelief when Emily opened the shopping bag and showed her the egg. Thank goodness, it was still warm! Of course, she wanted to know where they'd been and everything that had been going on, but there wasn't time to explain – they could do that later. What was important now was to give Tolly her egg and hope that she'd be able to hatch it.

They needed to make a nest and Gertie took her laundry basket out of the kitchen cupboard, put an old fleece of Harry's inside and Emily placed the egg carefully in the middle of it. Poor Tolly was a pitiful sight when Emily took her out of her cage and put her beside the gently humming egg. Everyone waited, expecting her to do something, but she didn't seem able to move. Please, oh please, don't let it be too late, Emily thought.

Just then, they heard the front door opening and Bert and Uncle Wilf came into the kitchen, followed by the Porcupine. They were chattering away, but stopped abruptly when they saw what was happening and joined the others round the table, holding their breath and staring in amazement at the egg. But Tolly just sat there miserably with one wing stretched out, propping herself up.

"Come on, old girl," said Uncle Wilf softly and tickled her gently on top of her head. "That chick of yours has come a very, very long way, hasn't he? You need to keep him warm now so he can hatch himself out."

Tolly cocked her head and looked up at him with her golden eye. Then, with a huge effort, she shook herself, fluffed out her remaining feathers and clambered onto the egg. Everyone felt like cheering, but they didn't want to do anything to upset her.

Uncle Wilf lifted the laundry basket with great care and took it through into the sitting room.

"Let's give her a bit of peace and quiet," he said, coming back and closing the door quietly behind him.

A few moments later they were all sitting round the kitchen table, sipping tea and eating home-made jam tarts. Bit by bit, they recounted what had happened – how they'd locked Mr Leach into the room at the back of his shop and how Tobias had made the skeleton walk into the pet shop and scare Trevor away, so that they could get into the storeroom where the python was guarding the egg.

Gertie was horrified when she heard that Emily had actually climbed inside the tank among the newly hatched pythons.

"Great heavens!" she cried, fanning herself with the newspaper. "You shouldn't have done that, Emily. It could very well have killed you! You know that, don't you? My goodness, whatever is your mum going to say?"

"She was absolutely brilliant," said Harry. "The python was gigantic and it had horrible fangs and teeth!"

"You'd never get me to do that in a million years," said Laura, "I just wanted to come home!"

"You're a brave little lassie, you are," said Uncle Wilf.

Emily felt herself blushing. Nobody had ever called her brave before.

They left Tolly in peace and quiet for the rest of the day and Emily made sure that she had plenty to eat and drink. She wondered how long it would take for the chick to hatch and what it would be like.

Gertie finished the Christmas pudding and asked them all to give it a stir and make a wish before she put it in the saucepan to boil.

"I always like to get the pudding made early," she told Emily. "There's so much to do once term starts. Maybe you and Mum would like to come and have Christmas Day with us this year. What do you think?"

"Oh yes, please, Gertie, can we?" Emily said breathlessly. She couldn't wait to ask Mum.

When the pudding was bubbling away merrily, Bert phoned the police and told them that Mr Leach and another man were locked in the room at the back of his shop and that there was an enormous python in a cage in Trevor's storeroom. They guessed it would be quite a while before Trevor dared to go back there!

But where was Tobias? Emily wondered if he'd gone up to the attic again. He'd really enjoyed his time of freedom and they'd never have been able to rescue the egg without him. She realised she didn't feel so frightened of him anymore.

They were going to go outside and play, but Gertie insisted they go upstairs first and finish their projects. It didn't take long and then they raced outside to have a few goes on the cart. Harry even let Emily sit in the front and steer it down to the bottom of the close all by herself.

"I've decided what I'm going to call it," he said proudly as they pulled the cart back up the hill. "I'm going to paint a black zigzaggy pattern along the sides and call it 'The Python'. What do you think?" It was a brilliant name and Harry had thought of it all by himself.

Emily's mum rang after tea. She sounded fine and accepted Gertie's invitation to have Christmas with them. She said she was moving back to the flat at the end of the week, and would be at the school gates to meet Emily when she came out of school on Wednesday. Emily was glad Mum was well again, but her heart sank when she thought about leaving No. 14 Willow Close and going back to live in the flat. She'd miss everyone so much, especially Tolly, and she wouldn't be able to look after the baby parrot. Of course, she'd see Harry and Laura and Gertie again at school, but it wouldn't be the same. She remembered how homesick she'd felt when she'd first come to live with the Pinks, but it had been the best time she'd ever had.

She took a last look at Tolly before going up to bed. The parrot had settled herself over the egg and seemed happier – not nearly so droopy – and she ate a piece of fruit, which Emily held out to her.

"Sleep well, Tolly," she whispered.

It wasn't quite six o'clock when she woke the next morning. Everyone else was asleep, but she was dying to see if the chick had hatched so she crept downstairs in her pyjamas and went to look in the laundry basket.

For a moment or two she wondered if she was dreaming. She was so surprised by what she saw that she just stood there. Then she rubbed her eyes, blinked several times and stared some more before turning round and racing up the stairs to tell Laura.

Chapter 32

Raphus

Tolly's baby had hatched in the night and it was the strangest thing Emily had ever seen. She'd been expecting a fluffy yellow chick like the cute little ones on Easter cards, but this was far bigger – a clumsy, comical creature with stubbly grey down. It had the beginnings of red tail feathers like Tolly's, but what really drew your attention was its large, hooked beak. Tolly, however, was absolutely thrilled with her new offspring. She walked round and round it, making soft cooing noises and grooming its scruffy down with her beak, now and again nibbling it affectionately on the back of its head. Emily noticed the broken amber shell in a corner of the basket and wished so much she'd been there to see it hatch.

As soon as Laura saw it, she woke everyone up and made them come downstairs straight away. They stood in bewilderment round the laundry basket in their night clothes, Gertie's red corkscrew curls sticking up round her head and Uncle Wilf's bushy hair standing on end. Both looked as if they'd had a terrible shock! Emily couldn't help giggling.

"Well, whatever next!" cried Gertie, her eyes almost popping out of her head.

"Well, blithering heck fire!" exclaimed Uncle Wilf, running a hand through his hair, making it wilder than ever.

Even Bert had been made to come downstairs, yawning and rubbing his eyes. He was a bit cross because he liked a good lie-in on a Sunday morning, but he soon got over it when he saw what was in the laundry basket with Tolly.

"Well, I can't believe what I'm seeing. Are you sure you didn't pick up the wrong egg, Emily? Maybe that rascal Trevor had one belonging to some other creature that he was hatching in the python's tank."

"No, no," she insisted. "It was definitely Tolly's – it's always made that funny humming noise, remember? Even before Trevor stole it from the shed."

"Well, I've never seen anything like it in all my life," said Bert, scratching his head. "I mean – just look at the size of its beak. It's going to have the same tail as Tolly I grant you, but the rest of it's just plain extraordinary. Sort of half parrot and half something else. Can't make it out at all, can you, Uncle Wilf?

But Uncle Wilf was just as puzzled.

"Tell you what," said Bert. "Why don't you get that Professor Whats'isname to come over again and have a look at it, Gert? He calls himself a zoologist, doesn't he? He's bound to know what it is."

"That's not a bad idea," said Gertie. "I'll give him a ring soon as soon as we've had breakfast."

Professor Watkins arrived in the afternoon, carrying a big book under his arm which he put on the table.

"My goodness me, whatever have we here?" he said bending over the laundry basket.

Tolly was looking extremely pleased with herself. Her chest, which was almost bare because she'd lost so many feathers, was puffed out with pride as she gazed fondly at her chick, making little clicking noises and prodding it with her beak.

The professor chuckled. "Well, we've got a very proud mum here, that's for sure. A Congo African Grey, of course, that's the easy bit. A fine example in fact, although she seems to have been through some sort of trauma, judging by her loss of feathers." He puckered his forehead. "But... are you absolutely sure this is her chick?"

"Oh yes," Emily said. "Someone stole the egg, but we got it back yesterday and it hatched in the night."

"Is that so?" said the professor, stroking his beard. "Well, this is extraordinary, quite extraordinary." He straightened up and, taking a magnifying glass from his pocket, examined the broken eggshell, turning it this way and that, before putting it down and blowing out his cheeks. "Well, I have to confess I'm extremely puzzled. This is no ordinary African Grey chick."

He put on a pair of glasses and crossing to the table turned the pages of the big book. "Yes, here we are – Psittacus Erithacus or, as we know it, the African Grey, and here," he said, pointing, "is a photograph of a newly hatched chick." Everyone clustered round to look. The picture was nothing like the strange creature in the laundry basket.

"This really is most interesting," he went on, whipping off his glasses. "Quite exceptional – a sort of throw-back it seems. You see, your parrot's chick reminds me very much of a bird that became extinct many hundreds of years ago – the dodo. It lived on the island of Mauritius, off the coast of Africa, but the last one died over three hundred years ago." He put his glasses on again and turned the pages of the book. "I may have a drawing of one somewhere – ah, yes, here we are, look – 'Dodo, flightless bird from Mauritius, became extinct by 1681'."

"What's extinct mean?" asked Laura.

In his excitement, the professor's glasses had steamed up and he polished them on his handkerchief. "Extinct means there aren't any dodos anymore," he said and his voice was shaking slightly. "Not a single one anywhere in the world! They couldn't fly, you see, and so they were easily caught – and in the end they just died out. You must have heard the expression 'dead as a dodo', haven't you? Well, now you know what it means – dead and gone forever."

He tapped the illustration in the book with his finger. "Here we have a drawing of an adult dodo, not a young one, but you see the similarity – the large, curved beak, the dumpy shape. And yet your youngster here has red tail feathers, like his mother, an African Grey, whereas the dodo's tail feathers were white – look, there. Bizarre, completely bizarre. I'm afraid I'm quite unable to explain it."

"You mean you think Tolly's chick is half African Grey parrot and half dodo?" asked Laura.

The professor laughed. "I know, I know - it sounds impossible, but yes, that's exactly what it looks like. This really is exciting – a most unusual case. I don't suppose your parrot has ever been to Mauritius, has she – the island where the dodos lived all those years ago?"

There was a stunned silence, then Uncle Wilf cleared his throat.

"Er, well, she did go on a little trip recently – to that part of the world, we think. Someone… a friend… took her on a little holiday."

"Well, well, well. This gets more and more extraordinary," said the professor.

"What do you think we ought to do?" asked Gertie. "I mean, how do we look after it?"

"My dear Mrs Pink, you look after it as if it were the crown jewels!" cried the professor. "I shall get my colleague, Doctor Zoot, to come and have a look at it without delay – he specialises in tropical birds. I would say that you have something here, which is utterly unique – and therefore priceless. No wonder the egg was stolen!"

The next day Doctor Zoot arrived, not on his own, but with three other parrot specialists and they were all just as excited as Professor Watkins had been. They measured Tolly's chick and listened to its heart with a special machine. They were very interested in its small wings and said it would never be able to fly. They took dozens of photographs and wrote things down in notebooks and rang people up on their mobile phones.

Gertie made lots of cups of tea for the professors, but they were far too excited to drink them. In the end, they all agreed that the chick was half parrot and half dodo, but they couldn't explain how such a thing had come about. They said that the Latin name for dodo was *Raphus Cucullatus*. Despite being extremely clever, no-one seemed to be able to tell if the chick was a girl or a boy.

Emily wondered what on earth they were going to call such a strange creature – it had to have a name. Uncle Wilf said she should be the one to choose, so she decided they'd call it Raphus.

The Porcupine came to have a look and then Emily asked Gertie if Tobias could come down from the attic and see it too. Gertie wasn't keen, but said it would be all right if he didn't stay too long or they'd all catch colds.

Tobias told Emily that he had indeed been to Mauritius with Tolly and to another island where there were dodos. They'd travelled more than three hundred years back in time, to the days when he was a living pirate and Tolly had disappeared into the jungle on her own for a few days. That must have been when she'd met a handsome boy dodo and they'd decided to have a family! Emily told the others what Tobias had said and they were flabbergasted.

The following day was the last of the holidays and suddenly, No. 14 Willow Close had become famous. Even before they came downstairs for breakfast the phone started ringing. Dozens of cars blocked Willow Close and hordes of television and newspaper reporters came ringing the doorbell. They wanted photos of Tolly on her own, photos of the chick on its own, then both of them together, and then photos of everyone living at No. 14. Emily had to hold the chick and talk into a microphone and describe how she'd rescued the egg from the python's tank. And they were all on the telly that evening!

Eventually, they had to come down to earth because it was school the next day. As promised, Emily's mum was waiting for her at the school gates. Emily hadn't seen her for weeks and they gave each other a big hug before walking along to the crossing where Gertie was holding up the traffic with her lollipop.

Emily was happy to see Mum again, of course, but she was also so sad to be saying goodbye to Gertie and Laura and Harry. She didn't know whether to laugh or cry. In the end she did a bit of both, but Gertie said she could come back to Willow Close any time she wanted, which made her feel a bit better.

The flat seemed even smaller and more cramped than she remembered and the first night she and Marigold cried themselves to sleep. She didn't tell Mum she was sad – it wasn't her fault that they had to live in the flat. She realised that now. When she'd got ill Mum had been forced to give up her job, so money was short. That's why the house had to be sold. She did tell her though all about the things she'd done, and Mum said once again that they could go to Willow Close for Christmas, if Emily really wanted to.

She went back there lots of times after school and took Izzie for walks and played with Firefly and Josephina. Bert had bought a much bigger cage for Tolly and Raphus, and Tolly grew all her feathers back. One day when Emily was there her voice came back too, and she'd learnt some new words - now she liked to shout, "Put the kettle on, put the kettle on!"

Sometimes, Emily climbed into the attic to see Tobias, but he wasn't always there – she supposed he liked to go off on his trips from time to time. Once, when she was feeling really brave, she asked him if she and the twins and Uncle Wilf could go with him one day, but Tobias didn't answer.

Uncle Wilf told Emily that Tobias seemed happier these days because he was allowed to come downstairs and listen to the story on Sunday evenings. Bert was reading *Robinson Crusoe*, which Tobias was really enjoying. As long as everyone knew when he was coming and could wrap up nice and warm, Gertie didn't seem to mind too much. They always invited the Porcupine too, so that if necessary, she could communicate between Tobias and Uncle Wilf.

In the weeks between the start of term and Christmas, Tolly and Raphus became world famous. There were Tolly and Raphus T-shirts, Tolly and Raphus cuddly toys and even battery-operated ones in the shops just in time for Christmas. It seemed that people just couldn't get enough of them.

When Emily and her mother went to No. 14 for Christmas Day, there was an exciting-looking parcel beside her place at the table. It was wrapped in Christmas paper with a label tied to it, saying 'Fragile – open with care'. Whatever could it be, Emily wondered? Everyone watched while she untied the string and tore off the paper, and laughed to see the expression on her face when she discovered what was inside. She was so pleased because she'd thought she'd never see her appendix again after

Blood Sucker's shop had been shut down, but Bert had rescued it for her.

Then Bert had something very interesting to tell them. He said Gertie was sick and tired of people queuing up outside the house all day long, ringing the front door bell and asking to see Tolly and Raphus. Plus, they were worried that someone might steal the birds when there was nobody in the house. He went on to say that a very rich man had called and said it would be a much better idea if people paid to see the birds – as they would do if they were in a zoo.

They should be in a proper aviary, he told them, with palm trees and tropical plants and flowers like in Mauritius, so they'd feel at home. Maybe there could even be a few other parrots there too for company. In that way, people could see them in their natural surroundings.

Uncle Wilf had told him that Tolly would be unhappy to be stuck in a zoo away from everyone, but the rich man explained that wasn't at all what he meant. No, he was offering to move them all to a stately home in Devon, which his family had owned for centuries. He'd been restoring it for the last ten years, with the idea of opening it to the public, but he needed someone to look after it for him, as he was abroad a great deal. He asked Gertie and Bert and Uncle Wilf if they would be interested in becoming caretakers. He went on to say that in no time at all, the crowds would come flocking to see Tolly and Raphus in their beautiful temperature-controlled aviary. His plan was that Bert and Uncle Wilf would be in charge of the visitors and grounds and that Gertie would run the tearoom.

He was delighted to be introduced to Tobias (whom he could hear as well as see) and insisted that the pirate should go with them – he could have the entire east wing of the house to himself. He intended to leave that part as a ruin, so there'd be plenty of room for Tobias to roam around. People would pay extra to go into the haunted part of the house.

It was too good an offer to turn down, so the Pinks had decided there and then that they'd move to Devon in the spring. Emily and her mum listened as Bert told them the exciting news. It seemed amazing. What a change in their lives – it would be wonderful for them.

But Emily was very quiet as she tried to eat her Christmas lunch. Suddenly, her appetite had gone. And when Gertie brought in the Christmas pudding with the brandy flaming on it, she knew she wouldn't be able to eat any of it. She remembered how they'd all stirred it and made a wish the day they'd rescued Tolly's egg. Well, so much for wishes, Emily thought sadly; hers certainly hadn't come true. She'd wished what she always wished for – a dog of her own – but it was never going to come true.

"The thing is," said Gertie, handing round the cream, "this Devon idea is all very well, but with all those hordes of people coming to the stately home, I'm going to have a job coping in the tea room on my own. I'll need someone to help me, someone I get on with really well."

"And Bert's going to be rushed off his feet, selling tickets and coping with the visitors, while I'll have my hands full looking after the gardens," said Uncle Wilf, shaking his head. "I don't see how we're going to have time to look after Tolly and Raphus and the other parrots in the aviary. We'll need another person who has a way with birds and animals. I suppose we'll just have to advertise for a couple of people."

There was silence. Even Harry and Laura didn't speak: everyone was looking down at their plates. Emily glanced at Uncle Wilf and noticed that his ears had turned pink and suddenly, he looked up at Emily and his eyes were greener and more sparkly than she'd ever seen them and a little smile was creeping around his lips.

"We've got a bit of a problem, haven't we?" he said very quietly and then he winked at her.

Emily stared at him, then looked at Mum, who was smiling at her too and then everyone looked up and they were all smiling and laughing... and at last she understood.

The stately home was enormous and they wanted her and Mum to move there with them. To Devon - that wonderful place by the sea where Gertie and Uncle Wilf came from. Emily pinched herself to make sure she wasn't dreaming, but no, she wasn't. This *really* was going to happen! She and Mum would be able to move out of their horrible little third-floor flat. Her eyes shone as she realised something else. It meant that she wouldn't have to say goodbye to the Pinks and Uncle Wilf and Izzie and Firefly and Josephina. And, of course, Tolly and Raphus. She thought her heart might burst with happiness.

Then something even more wonderful popped into her head, causing a surge of excitement to bubble up inside her. Could she dare to believe it? Maybe... just maybe, she would finally be able to have her longed-for puppy. And this time, she wouldn't have to give him back.

This time, she would be able to keep him.